Heavy breathing e

After a long m

understand. I do. But I would ask you to reconsider. There are thousands of unsolved murders and deaths. Cold cases. Some have elements that can't be explained by any normal method." He paused, letting the information sink in. "It's my job to see if I can get answers—closure for these families. I've experienced the paranormal. You just witnessed part of it. I almost became a victim because of a…whatever the hell it was."

Crock moved closer to her, resting one hand on the counter. "If you have psychometric abilities, then I'm asking you to consider—consider—helping me, in whatever capacity you are willing to." He glanced at Laz. "Both of you. You're a team, right?"

Tess tried to say something, but the lump in her throat was thick. She glanced at Laz, who seemed to be waiting for her decision, although his protest was written all over his face.

All her life, she'd run from the shadows. Laz could only share so much, but he had tried his damnedest to protect her from the unknown. She had wanted to prove she was stronger, both to her brother and to herself.

It was past time to woman up.

Praise for And They Danced

"Beautifully written story. The characters captured my heart, and the setting enhanced the story wonderfully. One of the best stories of any genre I've read in a long time."

~ *Granbury Writers' Bloc Short Story Contest, August 2020, 1st place.*

And They Danced

by

Tiffany Seitz

This is a work of fiction. Names, characters, places, and incidents are either the product of the author's imagination or are used fictitiously, and any resemblance to actual persons living or dead, business establishments, events, or locales, is entirely coincidental.

And They Danced

Contact Information: info@thewildrosepress.com

Cover Art by *Diana Carlile*

The Wild Rose Press, Inc.
PO Box 708
Adams Basin, NY 14410-0708
Visit us at www.thewildrosepress.com

Publishing History
First Edition, 2023
Trade Paperback ISBN 978-1-5092-4673-1
Digital ISBN 978-1-5092-4674-8

Published in the United States of America

Dedication

To Richard
"More Than Words"--Extreme

To the Myrtles
"My Wish"--Rascal Flatts

To FAWN
"A Little Help from My Friends"--Beatles

To the Breakfast Club
"Good Friend and a Glass of Wine"--LeAnn Rimes

Prologue

Dan shuffled across the threshold, stumbling over the worn entry mat emblazoned with the hotel logo. Hoping no one noticed his weakness, he set his ancient suitcase on the floor by the reception desk. The usual warmth and friendliness met his muttered greeting.

"Hello, Dr. Green. It's good to see you again." Mary had worked at the hotel for many years. She was an attractive woman, almost as pretty as his Esme.

Almost.

From the moment he met Esme, Dan's heart had sought no other. Her bright hazel eyes and chocolate brown hair had matched the warmth of her servant's heart.

"Evening, Miss Mary. Is my room ready?"

"Yes, sir, as always. Let's get you checked in." Efficient as always, she completed her task with a smile and a flirty wink. "Is there anything else I can get for you?"

"No, I can't think of anything."

His heart paused at the sight of her dimmed smile. "I have some bad news for you, Dr. Green. The Smith's Crown Hotel might close after Christmas. The hotel was sold last month, and we expect it to be torn down to make room for a shopping center."

His breath held. "I see. That's terrible."

Mary's eye watered. "It is, isn't it? All the effort to

save this bit of history failed. The previous owners got tired of dealing with complaints about ghosts and guests leaving in the middle of the night. Carl and I tried to raise the money to buy it, but my mom's health problems put a stop to that."

He offered her a weak smile. She didn't need to know—yet. "I guess all things must end. But there is always a new beginning for those that work hard and keep the faith."

With those words, he declined to use the elevator and headed up the stairs to the second floor. He paused at the landing to catch his breath. The rest gave him a moment to consider Mary's concern. He decided nothing had changed and continued to lug his tired body up the steps. At the top, he stopped again; his heart was willing, but his old legs refused to take another step. A grumble rose from his chest. There had been a time when he and Esme danced the night away.

He missed those days.

Sheer will and determination forced his stubborn, aching knees to move down the hallway. He was gasping for air by the time he reached the ancient door labeled with a tarnished brass *27*.

He took a moment to recover before finger-combing his fine, silver hair and straightening his robin's egg-blue tie. Esme loved the pale shade of blue, saying it matched his eyes. He never wanted to give her less than his best.

The door creaked as it opened. He didn't blame the door; he creaked, too.

Fifty-two years.

Fifty-two times he had visited this same room. The years faded as he stepped across the threshold. The room had changed, but his memory had not.

In place of the standard queen-sized bed and white linens, he remembered the four-poster bed with a reddish-wood stain standing in the center of the room and a matching nightstand on one side. Esme had called it a cherry bedroom set dating from the late 1800s. She'd fallen in love with the bright, handmade quilt covering the mattress. He hadn't known what kind of wood it was, nor cared whose grandmother had made the blanket. All he knew was that he would make love to his beautiful bride in that very bed. Nothing else had mattered.

The antique bedroom suite and the handmade blanket were long gone, but his vision of the room would never change.

"Esme-Belle! I'm here," he called out as he turned to pull the curtains from the bright afternoon sun.

It was early, so he took the time to hang up his suit jacket and moved to unpack the white, Samsonite case Esme had bought for their honeymoon. The faded, pink satin inner lining was little more than shredded ribbons, and one hinge broke away from the plastic as he opened the case.

He stared at the damage in dismay. With a heavy sigh, he forced himself to put his few belongings away and prepared for the evening. After a quick wash and shave, he combed his hair, splashed his face with a little aftershave, and donned his newest pajamas. He placed a glass of water and a small amber bottle on the bedside table. After taking a dose, he pulled out the book of poetry which Esme had loved.

He propped himself on the bed and selected one of her favorite verses to read. His eyes grew heavy as his exertions caught up with him.

The room was dark when he woke, but he knew she was there, lying next to him.

"I thought I might find you here," she teased.

He smiled back, relieved that she had come. "Happy anniversary, Esme-Belle."

She giggled. The sound brightened his soul. "And happy Halloween, Danny Boy."

"I can't believe you talked me into getting married on a holiday. Especially Halloween!" No matter how many times they had this conversation, he never regretted it. He would have married her no matter when or where.

Her laughter filled his lonely heart as they read and talked the night away until light leaked through the closed shades to reveal the first sign of sunrise. He sat up to take the medicines which would take away his suffering. With a sigh, he laid back. Her hand covered his, and he savored the coolness of her touch.

"Is it time, my love?"

He reached a trembling hand to stroke her fading features. "Yes, it is, dearest. Happy anniversary."

"Happy All Saints, Danny Boy."

Her face dimmed as the light from the window brightened. His eyes closed against the glare and the vision of her smiling eyes led him into the dream-like state he longed for.

It seemed no more than a few minutes had passed when he felt a tap on his shoulder. He rose from the bed, pleased to feel lighter and more fit than he had in over thirty years. He glanced at the still form lying alone on the bed. He would not miss it.

"Come, Danny Boy."

He smiled at her familiar tone. Turning to face her, he held out a hand. When Esme took it, he pulled her into his embrace.

And—for the first time in twenty-two years—they danced.

Chapter One

A file landed on his desk with a *thud* accompanied by a gruff greeting, "Here's a welcome-back present. How's the leg?"

Crock Ward glanced up at his boss. He'd barely logged into his computer before being ambushed. After six weeks of medical leave had almost driven him insane, he was glad to be back at work. He had a few restrictions, and he'd have to pass the physical testing required by the Department of Public Safety before returning to full duty as a Texas Ranger. But he was at his desk in Company B's office, and he wasn't going to complain.

"It's fine. The only time it bothers me is when I'm tired." Shoving the laptop away, he brushed off any concerns his captain might have. The last thing he wanted to do was admit any weakness to his supervisor.

He stretched his left leg out from the confines of the desk, ignoring the twinges of burning discomfort. His khaki pants concealed the healing bullet wound that was responsible for the time off work. His doctor and physical therapist had warned him that the leg—while strong enough to work—would take time to rebuild strength and to feel normal.

Captain BJ Childs was a large, dark-skinned man. He claimed the worn leather seat next to the desk, stretching tan-clad legs out before him with ankles crossed. It was difficult to determine which was more highly polished: the bald head or the black boots, but the custom-made, size fifteens definitely created a tripping hazard. "So a bit of good, old-fashioned work shouldn't be a problem."

Crock paid more attention to the captain's sausage-sized fingers as they drummed the top of the desk. He'd done nothing to piss off his boss—yet—so he didn't rise to the bait. But the moment to ease back into duty was apparently over. He picked up the folder and flipped it open. "What's this?"

The captain's face revealed a toothy, white grin as he pointed to the paperwork. "This is what we Rangers like to refer to as 'light duty.'" He hooked his fingers into air quotes.

Crock snorted. "I thought light duty consisted of answering phones or some such bullshit."

Childs smirked. "Yeah, well, can't say there won't be a lot of phones involved on this one. But it should be right up your alley, given your injury."

"Which we won't mention." The official report was that Crock's gun went off while in pursuit of a suspected child abductor, all of which was true. The suspect had reportedly hidden away in a derelict mansion. Crock had cleared the second floor when an unexplained shove sent him plunging down the stairs. There was also no explanation for his gun mysteriously going off.

Crock eyed the coffee in his captain's hand. Same old black goo—some things never changed. He'd forgotten to make his custom brew before leaving the house, but he wasn't so desperate as to brave the office swill. Hopefully, this case would get him on the road and *anywhere* in the vicinity of a decent coffee shop.

He flipped through the file to scan the contents. “What’s the short version?”

“Original case involved the 1995 death of one Esme Green, wife of Dr. Daniel Green. No children. One niece and one nephew. Dr. Green was a professor at Texas Christian University until his apparent heart attack about two years ago.”

“Apparent?”

“Well, he did die in the same hotel room where his wife was found. Manner of death was considered natural since he was in his eighties. According to the family, there was a question about his mental state. Apparently, he had a habit of buying her diamonds instead of helping his brother’s kids, and for that they thought he was crazy.” Childs took a sip from his mug and grimaced. “Man, that’s strong! Anyway, the good Dr. Green had a strong alibi for his wife’s death—he was teaching a class. According to his statement, it was their anniversary, and the hotel was where they had spent their honeymoon—something they did every year to celebrate. The clerk watched the couple go their separate ways the morning of 31 October.”

Crock mentally corrected to October 31st. The captain took a lot of harassment around the office for his military lingo.

“The wife returned on or about thirteen hundred hours,” *—or one in the afternoon,* Crock calculated— “carrying a shopping bag. Dr. Green returned at seventeen hundred hours” *—five o’clock—* "with a couple of takeout bags for a romantic dinner, wine, and a wrapped gift. The clerk helped him up to the room where they discovered the body together. There was no evidence of a struggle, but she was on the bed, ready for the viewing. The coroner ruled it suspicious."

"Cause of death?"

"She had a good-sized fracture on her skull and there was bruising on her upper body and throat. No weapon was found." Childs took another sip of his coffee before going on, "The good professor was inconsolable, but he continued the annual pilgrimage until two years ago when he arrived at fifteen hundred hours to stay in the same room on Halloween night. The manager usually ate breakfast with him at oh-seven hundred hours, but when he didn't come down by oh-eight hundred hours, she went to check on him. According to the report, he was laid out on the bed like his wife was, dressed and ready for his funeral."

"So, his death is in question, too?" Crock's brain gave up calculating the military time. He'd figure it out later. His interest had peaked, but he wasn't sure why this case was 'right up his alley'.

"There were no other suspicious circumstances. The coroner didn't look further. There have been some issues with the will that have cropped up. Somehow, during probate, an addendum to the will and a stack of suspicious notes surfaced, citing Dr. Green's plan and—get this—leaving all the diamonds and cash to the grieving niece and nephew."

Crock lifted an eyebrow. "With no other family, wouldn't they get the jewels as part of the estate?"

"Not if all said jewels got buried with the wife in 1995."

"Ah." Crock nearly snorted at the audacity of the family. *Yeah, let's dig up Auntie and grab all her bling. Idiots.*

"We've got a handwriting analyst looking into it, but that'll take a minute. In the meantime—" Childs sat up, taking another slurp of coffee, "—check it out. You'll need to contact the estate's attorney. There might be a later will floating around. The attorney said he can't locate it, so it was either never filed or never written. He's concerned about some assets that aren't mentioned in the one that's being probated." The captain rose from his seat and stretched his big frame. "By the way, that hotel is rumored to be haunted. Maybe you can run your little experiment."

"Yeah? That'd be a bitch if it worked." Crock snorted. He'd mentioned the idea of a paranormal investigation to his boss while under a butt-load of pain meds. He wasn't even sure if he'd believed in ghosts, but he'd felt something weird in the mansion, and that something had shoved him down the stairs. Apparently, his experience was now the office joke. Still, he tucked the idea in the back of his head. Thinking outside the box made him a damn good Ranger.

"Whatever. Do what you need to do to close the case." With that, the captain stalked away, turning back to add, "But if you wind up shooting yourself again, I don't want to know about it."

Of all the things Crock expected to be doing when he returned to work, working a cold case wasn't on the top of his list, but one he'd gladly take. The other option of spending his days answering the phone was high on his list of things to do in Hell. He'd be shooting everyone in the ass by lunchtime.

Lamenting his lack of caffeine, Crock read through the case file. Pulling his laptop closer, he opened the search engine and went to work.

Chapter Two

"Oh, *hell* no!"

Tess Corona threw her head back and groaned. It wasn't the type of response she expected from her niece, Domatila Theresa Corona. Until she remembered that Tila was a Class A brat, aged three-going-on-thirty.

"Tila," she begged, mentally counting to ten, "you can't go to school naked."

"I can so!"

Tess silently counted, alternating English, Spanish, German, and rudimentary Arabic. It was a practice she'd perfected over the past four months. On days like this, Tess wished she could go back to the serenity of a third world country filled with IEDs and fanatics trying to kill anyone who grew up listening to rock-and-roll while eating apple pie and watching baseball.

Reacclimating to civilian life was hard enough. No one issued orders. No being nice to someone even though she'd rather kick their ass into next week. It was all harder than she had expected. Being an aunt—*that was a whole 'nother ball of yarn entirely.*

"Miss Karlyn will be waiting for you, Miss T. You need to get dressed."

Tess couldn't believe she was trying to reason with a pre-preschooler over clothing—or the lack thereof. She had to keep reminding herself that Tila was only three. Surely between a psychology degree and training in negotiations, she ought to be able to manipulate a child into clothes.

"No!"

Apparently not.

"Argh!"

The Corona family had expanded in her absence. The pictures of her dark-haired niece had not done the child justice, but Tess had fallen in love with the adorable little girl with her brother's lop-sided dimples. Brimming with excitement to finally meet Tila, Tess returned to Texas soil with visions of doing girly things with her niece: painting her nails, braiding her hair, teaching her to shoot guns and to throw a baseball hard enough to make the boys cry. To her mother's dismay, Tess had been more of a tomboy, but now she was ready to release her inner child and feminine side.

Those fantasies had disappeared as fast as reality set in.

Laz, her brother—in all his scholarly wisdom and worship of history—had decided to honor the family by naming his firstborn child after his grandmother and sister. Tess didn't think he intended to give her their combined attitudes.

The idiot.

Desperation meant Tess was no longer above begging. "At least put on your panties!"

"No!" screamed the naked heathen.

Tess struggled to keep her temper under control. She reminded herself of what else she could be doing with her life—like hunting the far corners of the earth in search of whichever doofus of the moment who had decided to screw with the United States. Traveling the world—both officially and personally—had given her a vastly different perspective than she had grown up with. She had changed, and she wasn't sure if it was for the better.

But it had been time to come home. For good. Tess thought she'd had enough to deal with: a butt-load of secrets, unemployment, a broken heart, a bum knee, and a case of non-military-induced PTSD. Army life hadn't been a walk in the park, but at least she'd known what to expect. She had left plenty behind. The good was good, but the bad was—well, awful and sufficient reason for her to leave the military.

The doorbell saved her from saying or doing anything she might regret.

Thank God!

"Put your clothes on!" Tess shot back as she headed for the stairs, yelling, "Coming!"

At eight in the morning, they weren't expecting company. The little hellion's daddy had escaped the house early for finals. Most of his students had stopped by last week with pleas for help and sundry bribes. Tess couldn't count out his student stalkers, as she referred to the handful of so-called dedicated interns and barely legal co-eds who sought more than just tutoring.

Tess wasn't really biased. Even she had to admit that her twin brother was hot—a hot mess. For all his brains, he attracted a steady stream of horny, college-aged fashion dolls looking to score with the good-looking, archeology professor because they thought he was some swashbuckling globetrotter who could give them adventure and amazing sex. And an A.

He's not.

Well, Tess couldn't—and wouldn't—speak to the sex part, but she highly doubted her intellectual brother would give out grades based on a good time. And the adventure part? Her advice to the ill-advised: join the military. That was enough excitement to last a lifetime or three. The most adventure Laz got up to was getting into an argument with Gram over whose turn it was to fill the fridge with beer.

Nope, her brother was nothing but a cute dumbass, prone to making mistakes of the female variety when Tess wasn't around to keep him on the straight and narrow. Hence…Tila.

The doorbell rang again as Tess raced down the worn stairs of their home, automatically skipping the fifth step that creaked loud enough to disturb the dead. "Just a second!"

She hoped she could get to the door before Gram. Sounds from the back of the house was her first clue that her grandmother was a little busy. Creative curses in English, Spanish, and whichever indigenous language Gram chose flew from the kitchen to burn her ears. Gram was a fantastic cook, but from the multi-lingual cursing and the gawd-awful stench, whatever witch's brew she was creating instead of breakfast wasn't turning out too well. Tess made a mental note to stop by the donut shop on the way to daycare. There was nothing like dropping a sugared-up devil child on unsuspecting childcare workers.

She grabbed the door handle and yanked it open. Her jaw promptly hit the floor. On the other side of the screen door was the sexiest man she had ever laid her full-of-shit peepers on. And she'd laid eyes on one or two. That was one reason she went into the military. Sweaty men. Physical training. Uniforms. Mix those prime assets with big guns and things that go *boom*—

sold American!

It didn't take Tess long to realize that sweaty men stink, PT sucked, and things that went *boom* made her eardrums rupture. The uniform was the only thing that remained sexy in her book, but the problem with uniforms was that other women felt the same way and didn't give a fuck if the uniform was already spoken for. That left the guns and explosives. Earplugs made the *boom* tolerable.

Before her was no uniform, but he was built and there was a gun strapped to one lean hip.

Mr. Sexy stood on the front porch step like a gift from the gods. Tess was a respectable five-nine, but this guy made her look up. An educated guess put him at six-three. His light brown hair was close cut. A pale blue, button-down shirt, dark blue tie, buff pants, polished boots, and a cream-colored cowboy hat completed the man of her dreams.

Piercing green eyes looked her over. Tess couldn't tell if he liked what he saw, but she sure as hell hoped so. "Morning, ma'am." *Hot damn!* The voice matched the body. "I'm looking for Lazaro Corona."

"Uh." Her eyes wouldn't stop checking out the man on the front step, and her mouth wouldn't work for shit. Tess swished what little spit she had in her mouth to moisten her tongue while trying to think of something to say that was reasonably intelligent.

A wave of self-consciousness hit as Tess realized what she was wearing. It was probably the least-attractive outfit any woman could possess—running shorts and an old, paint-splotched, Army T-shirt. No bra. She didn't need to be dressed up to spend the day job-hunting online, and, if she got an interview, she could be dressed to impress in less than an hour. She sure as hell didn't realize she was going to meet *Mr. Right Now*.

Great. Just freaking great.

"Ma'am?"

Even better. Señor Gorgeous thinks I'm a loon. He wouldn't be wrong.

"Uh. Yeah. Laz. Uhm, that's my brother. I mean," Tess stuttered, attempting to smooth her shirt and hair while not exposing the sweat-stains on her armpits. "He's not here at the moment."

"Pardon me for just stopping by. I'm Sergeant Crock Ward with the Texas Rangers."

Awesome. Mr. Sexy had a name and a Texas drawl and...what?

A white business card found its way into her hand. Sure enough, under a Texas Rangers seal, the name D. Crockett Ward, Sergeant was printed in plain black lettering. A badge flashed in the corner of her eye. Tess looked up to see a silver circle surrounding the cut-out of a five-point star in his hand. Etched around the circle were the blackened letters: TEXAS RANGERS.

Her eyes roamed to the rest of the package on the front porch. Besides the prerequisite gun, hat, and boots typical of the iconic Rangers, a tooled belt held the trade requirements of a law enforcement—taser, spare magazines, badge, radio—held together by a hefty, silver belt buckle bearing the State of Texas official seal. Before her was the real shebang, not some glorified Hollywood mock-up of a Texas legend.

It was all she could do to keep from squealing like some idiotic tween-age girl.

Get your shit together, Tess.

Señor Gorgeous, aka Sergeant D. Crockett Ward with the Texas Rangers, kept going as if she wasn't drooling, "Do you know when he might be back? I have a couple of questions to ask him."

"Is he in some kind of trouble?" Laz was the boring Corona. What could he have done to get the attention of the Rangers? Too many dull lectures on early Texas law enforcement? Misquoted Stephen F. Austin—the Father of Texas and its infamous Rangers? Laz was determined to live a sedate life despite the crazy which surrounded the family. Yeah, he had his little hobby, but Laz understood the need to keep up the appearance of normal. Tess was the one who didn't know what normal was.

But hey, what were evil twin sisters for? If this Ranger had some dirt on one nowhere-close-to-perfect, bone-headed brother, she would use the knowledge to the best of her ability.

"No trouble, ma'am. I understand he's an expert on certain…subjects. I have some questions he might be able to answer."

Tess glanced up with a flirty smile but was quickly derailed when her finger was yanked from its socket.

"Aunt Tessie!"

Flirting immediately became the last thing on her mind. Standing next to her, in front of the world's sexiest Texas Ranger, stood a naked three-year-old.

Tess prayed for a sinkhole.

"Get your clothes on!" Tess wondered what she could be charged with: indecent exposure of a three-year-old? Neglect? She risked a glance at the object of her lust, only to see one eyebrow arched and a gleaming green eye.

"No!" the hell-spawn shrieked.

Since swatting her niece's little ass in front of a lawman was probably frowned upon, Tess reached over to the nearby rocking chair and plucked a crocheted afghan from the wooden back. With as much finesse as she could manage, Tess dropped the wrap over Tila's head, concealing all evidence.

Ignoring the smothered squeals and growls, Tess turned back to Sergeant Señor Gorgeous Ward with as much dignity as she could muster. "I'm not sure when Laz will be home. It's finals week."

"That's all right. I'll try to catch him at the school, but if you would, please give him my card. He can call me at his convenience. I'd appreciate it."

Tess glanced at the lean, tanned fingers holding out another official-looking card, one with writing on the back. "I will."

With a nod, the Ranger stepped off the porch and headed toward a shiny, burgundy truck parked at the curb. The sexy truck matched its sexy owner.

Tess wiped the drool from her lip before moving to close the door. Something clanked against the heavy wood door. A hand-painted sign swung from a nail underneath the peephole.

WE DON'T CALL 911.

Tess wondered if CPR was helpful when someone died of embarrassment.

Chapter Three

After two frustrating weeks back on the job—in and out of court for old cases while investigating his newest assignment—Crock had finally found something to laugh about, and it was epic. Somehow, he kept a straight face until he reached the end of the street. Adjusting his mirrored aviators against the sun's glare, he realized it'd been too damn long since he'd had that much fun, and all he'd done was knock on a stranger's door. A face full of meth fumes or gunfire was more typical in his line of work.

Sweet Jesus! The look on her face!

Kids were awesome.

The woman wasn't too bad either. Corona's sister, she'd said. He'd been leery about the last name. For some reason, a warning bell sounded in his brain, but he had no idea why. That didn't stop him from looking at the package in front of him. Long, almost black hair, dark brown eyes, and a killer body. He wasn't sure what she was doing with her shirt, but that just made the meeting more memorable.

For the first time in several years, Crock was interested. As soon as the thought crossed his mind, he sent it packing. First, she was kin to a potential consultant, therefore work-related and off-limits. Next…well, there was no *next*, but that didn't mean he needed to chase a woman right now.

His research over the past couple of weeks hadn't given him anything new. Just the same old, unanswered questions. Unfortunately, the initial investigation report was riddled with holes. He had spent much of his time verifying the available details, then attempting to fill in the mysterious gaps. To complicate matters, the Johnson County evidence room couldn't locate the evidence box. Captain Childs had gotten on the phone with the Sheriff's office as soon as he heard about the missing box.

Visiting with Dr. Green's family had been a psychological pain in the ass. They'd been arrogant, snippy, and cagey, answering all his questions in an almost rehearsed manner. His bullshit meter had pinged into the red zone.

On the other hand, the staff of the hotel where the couple died tried to be helpful. None had worked at the hotel when Mrs. Green died, and the manager—Mary Dunham—was the only employee remaining from the time of Dr. Green's death. She hadn't been in the office at the time Crock stopped by, but he hoped to talk with her soon. Off-hand comments from the staff suggested paranormal activity in the hotel, specifically that room. That, paired with an odd twinge in his injury, had led him on his current quest.

Crock refused to consider that his leg might be some God-awful ghost indicator. *Normal* people's injuries only predicted the weather. He didn't want some cosmic reminder of life-after-death or whatever was going on in the universe. He had enough shit going on in this life to deal with without some other dimension getting involved.

The investigation had a few similarities with the

previous incidents. The major difference was that Dr. Green had died twenty-two years and a day after his wife was found dead; not to mention he was in the same room, in the same pose, and in the same manner as she had been. While many of the previous hotel deaths were considered murder-suicides or murder with suicidal intent, the professor had apparently died of natural causes.

His mind returned to the Coronas. If the sign on the door was any indication, the 1920s Craftsman-style home held some hell-raisers. Except for a cool last name, his research on Lazaro Corona, PhD had revealed no earth-shattering information. Aside from his expertise in paranormal investigations, the man was a respectable professor of Texas history, anthropology, and archeology. The only other things Dr. Corona seemed outwardly passionate about were Rangers baseball and the TCU Horned Frogs.

The Aggie in him found the whole idea of a purple, horned toad as a mascot hilarious. The scientific and animal nut in him liked the Texas Horned Lizard. Not to mention, he liked all things Texas.

Crock's family roots were steeped in the history of his home state, although he could have skipped out on the name—*thanks, Dad.* Anything related to Texas was right up his alley. He had a feeling he was going to enjoy working with Dr. Corona.

And—hopefully—the sister.

****

Crock checked the campus map to get his bearings. His information said he would find Dr. Corona in either of the liberal arts buildings on the west side of University Drive. Rumor had it that there was a frog fountain in the vicinity.

What in the hell did a frog fountain look like?

Curiosity killed the investigator, and it was a gorgeous day, so Crock directed his steps toward the famous fountain. He figured it wouldn't take long, and it might put him in the right place to hunt for one history professor.

He rounded the side of a building to find what he was looking for: one fountain. No frogs. Just four giant, metal lily pads rising from a circular stone fountain. Water spilled from the pads to the pool below. Around the edge were eight smaller waterspouts. The wind kicked up a light spray as he approached. Crock ducked his head, letting his hat block the drops from his sunglasses.

Students lounged around the fountain. Several were grouped together, talking animatedly, while others lazed on the green space. If he remembered correctly, the second week of May was finals week, so either students were studying for an exam or were relaxing afterward.

It had been a *long* time since he'd enjoyed the well-earned relief of finishing a semester of intense deadlines and exams. Back then, the only consequence was having to retake a failed class, which he fortunately never had to do. Now, there were no deadlines. But the longer it took to close a case, the longer questions went unanswered, the longer the public remained at risk from embezzlers, kidnappers, or murderers. He'd learned the hard way—there were no breaks. He barely remembered what a vacation was like. The last time he'd been off was thanks to the medically induced nightmare responsible for the current work assignment, one bum leg, and too many unanswered questions.

That's what you get for putting a bullet in your own damned leg, dumbass.

It was time to move on. It was time to work.

Crock ignored the co-eds who turned to track him. Unfortunately for him, they seemed to be on the hunt. One ambitious blonde, clad in short-shorts and a tank top, broke away from her pack to block his path and could be mistaken for an over-eager puppy. "Hey!"

He thought about ignoring her, but his momma and her quilting-group cronies would take turns smacking him upside the head. Instead, he gave a quick nod as he stepped around the girl. "Hello."

She didn't take the hint and followed. "I haven't seen you around here. Maybe I can help you find your way around."

Sweet Jesus, he hoped she didn't mistake him for a student. That ship had sailed a good fifteen years ago. "I'm good. Thanks."

His shadow followed. "I'm Mallory. What's your name?"

She had a thick southern accent—possibly Georgia or Alabama if he had to guess. Crock wondered what she would do if he flashed his badge—or his weapon. He'd kept his jacket on to minimize curiosity or alarm on campus. Kids her age were usually scared off by law enforcement. "Ward."

"Ward? That's an old-fashioned name. Is it short for something?"

Crock kept his face in the usual concrete mask. "Not that I know of."

"Okay, Ward. Would you like to get a latte? I know a great place…."

He stopped. The puppy-shadow plowed into him. It was time to channel her enthusiasm into something productive. "Maybe you *can* help me, Mallory."

She grinned and nodded, her blonde ponytail bounced up and down, giving him permission to proceed. "I'm looking for Dr. Lazaro Corona. Do you know where I might find him?"

Her pink lips stretched into a delighted grin as she bounced excitedly from one foot to the other. She really did remind him of a puppy. He hoped she wouldn't pee on his new boots. "Do *you* study anthropology, too? That is so cool! Dr. Laz is *awesome*!"

Crock didn't doubt the good professor's coolness factor with a name that was a college-cooler staple. "Do you know where his office is?"

One thing he had nearly forgotten was how diligent young co-eds were in their pursuit of male flesh. They were almost as bad as young men—or men of any age, for that matter. If he had hoped to get directions and leave the puppy to play with her litter, he was sadly disappointed.

"Follow me."

Well, shit.

He was stuck. If Corona's office was in the depths of Hell, Crock had no choice but to follow Mallory. He just hoped Hell wasn't via the local student hang-out.

Resigned to his fate, he dutifully followed his self-appointed tour guide into the nearest liberal arts building. More students congregated quietly, but Mallory moved confidently down halls and up a flight of stairs, chattering the entire way. He tuned out most of her inane dissertation but gathered that the history and anthropology professor was young, single, and hot.

Apparently, an attraction to her teacher didn't stop Mallory from eyeballing *him*.

I should have stapled my freaking badge to my forehead.

Finally, Mallory opened a door and turned her exuberance onto a small, middle-aged woman seated behind a tidy desk. An engraved nameplate read *Claudette Hudgens, Administration*. Her graying, blonde hair was tucked neatly into a bun, and red glasses perched precariously at the end of her slim nose.

"Hi, Mrs. Hudgens," his guide said.

The secretary peered over the rim of her glasses, giving the student an assessing appraisal. "Good afternoon, Mallory. How can I help you? It's too soon for grades to be posted."

Crock stepped forward, drawing the woman's attention. Her lips pursed and her spine straightened with recognition as she rose to greet him. While Mallory hadn't recognized him as law enforcement, Mrs. Hudgens obviously did. "Afternoon, ma'am. My name is Sergeant Crock Ward with the Texas Rangers." Habit made his badge and card appear in his hand.

Out of the corner of his eye, Mallory's eyes bulged, and her mouth gaped like a fish. If he hadn't been trained to not show emotion, the reaction would have made him laugh. Instead, he would have to wait until later, maybe over a beer with his neighbor.

"Oh, cool!" The puppy got excited again. "Are you a *real* Texas Ranger? What position do you play?"

"He's not a baseball player, Mallory," Mrs. Hudgens admonished. The woman was nothing but professional. She took the offered badge and studied it, followed by the business card. She pulled a sticky pad to her and jotted down his credentials. *Smart woman.* "How may I help you, Sergeant Ward?"

"I'm looking for Lazaro Corona. I understand he's an instructor here."

The older woman's expression remained guarded as she turned to the confused, gawking student. "Did you have other business here, Mallory?"

"Uhm, no. I'll just…uhm…Is Dr. Laz in trouble?" Mallory seemed to be a smart puppy after all.

But Mrs. Hudgens was smarter. "Dr. Corona's business is not yours. You may go."

The girl lost some of her enthusiasm. Tail tucked, she turned to go. At the door, she stopped. "If you're not a Texas Ranger, then what kind of ranger are you?"

"A *Texas* Ranger," Crock replied with the straightest face he could muster. He'd had *a lot* of practice messing with people's minds. It was a perk of the badge.

The administrative assistant put the kibosh on any further questions from the girl. "That will be all, Mallory. Thank you for bringing Sergeant Ward to me."

After the disgruntled blonde obeyed, the older woman turned back to business. "*Is* Laz in trouble?"

"No, ma'am," Crock said. "I believe he might have information to help me understand a case I'm working on. Do you know where I might find him?"

Satisfied with his answer, Mrs. Hudgens shuffled through a planner on her desk. Her finger located the date and ran down to find a name. "He's one of our adjunct faculty. He has probably finished his last class by now, though. If he's still here, he'll be in two-twenty-three or in his office—room B-thirteen. Do you need directions?"

A bustling group of students burst through the door. A sharp glance from the assistant gained their attention and their silence.

"No, thank you, ma'am. I'll find it." Crock decided he liked the woman. She was efficient and demanded respect from the otherwise unruly students. Probably from the staff, too.

She'd be a perfect fit for Company B.

Chapter Four

Tess turned onto her street with a sigh of relief. The drive down the tree-lined lane helped to soothe her pounding head. She hoped there'd be a cold beer and tacos waiting for her. Or better yet—no drama.

Her day had only gotten worse. A job prospect called while she was getting Tila ready. With a hard-to-get interview scheduled for the afternoon, Tess had rushed to finish getting herself and her niece out the door. Tila had finally consented to wear a sundress—with shorts underneath, thank God—but only with her fuzzy winter boots. The boots lasted until they were in the car due to complaints of being too *pinchy*. Once they arrived at daycare, sans boots, Tess learned that footwear was a requirement of the establishment—oh, and by the way, Tila's favorite teacher was no longer with the school. She apparently wasn't a 'fit.'

Whatever the hell that meant.

Tila had pitched a god-awful screaming fit—which also violated the rules. After arguing with the director, Tess had wanted to throw a tantrum of her own. Several hours were wasted calming the child down, arguing with the dragon-bitch-director of the daycare, tracking down the distraught teacher, messaging Laz, and learning an assortment of details about the child-care industry which she'd preferred not to know. To top it all off, her morning headaches had instigated a state investigation into the day care's operations and licensing.

All of which made her late for the interview.

Which proceeded to be a disaster.

Which meant she didn't get the job.

Again.

Discouragement brought home the reason she'd come back to Texas. For ten years, she had felt she was part of something important. She had a purpose. There were things she didn't like about the Army, but she didn't like everything about her family—like the fact that they were insane. But for the most part, she could focus on the good and ignore the bad. Some situations—and people—didn't deserve to have her waste time or energy on.

If she could get through the evening without committing any major felonies, the promise of a lavender-scented bath with a glass of wine would be her reward. She would start fresh in the morning, after a good night's sleep.

A sexy, shiny pickup in a gorgeous shade of burgundy sat in front of her house. It was pretty enough to make her drool. *He's baaack!*

Her day just got a little better.

Navigating her all-terrain convertible into the narrow driveway, she quickly shut off the engine and gathered her backpack. A quick check in the mirror gave her some hope. She had looked worse. Much worse.

She opened the door.

And hit the man who was reaching to open said door. "Oh! I'm sorry! I didn't see you," she gasped.

How had he moved so fast? Was I that slow?

"I'm all right." His eyes hid behind a pair of aviators, but his face showed no signs of pain. Texas Ranger Sergeant D. Crockett Ward might as well've been made of granite.

Or solid muscle.

Tess resisted the urge to lick her lips. "I…uhm, did you find Laz?"

"No, ma'am. I thought I'd try to catch him this evening."

Still no crack in his façade. "His car isn't here, but he shouldn't be too long. You can come in and wait if you'd like. We probably have some tea or lemonade."

"I can wait."

An uncomfortable silence spread between them. At least she was uncomfortable. He was too gorgeous to be uncomfortable. Hoisting her backpack-purse further onto her shoulder, Tess scooted to the back of the Jeep to unload her groceries. Tanned hands reached over to take several bags from hers.

"Oh, uhm, thanks." There was no ring on his fingers. Also, no tan line. Her day was definitely looking up.

Tess slipped the remaining sacks over her arms and cradled the bag with the eggs in her left hand. As she led the way up the steps, she fumbled with her keys. She wanted to impress this man. It'd been a while since she'd been interested in someone, and this specimen was not only drool-worthy, but considerate and polite. In all likelihood, he was…*normal*. Even her mother might approve—if the witch bothered to care.

Not that she wanted him to meet her *loco* family, but he had already seen Tila in her finest birthday suit. What else could go wrong?

Jinx.

Strategically placing her body to cover up the potentially offensive sign on the front door, she slipped the key into the ancient deadbolt. It was stuck. Again.

Juggling the eggs for a better grip, she tried to jimmy the lock. "Sorry to hold you up. These old houses can be a pain."

"No rush."

His calm attitude only made her more determined. It took a moment to get the bolt open, then another minute to kick the swollen door free of the frame. It finally opened with a spectacular shove that sent the eggs plummeting to the ground with a delightful *splat!*

"Ah, shi…shoot!" she caught herself before she said anything which could be held against her. Then… "What the fuck? Tila! Put your clothes on!"

There the little heathen stood, in all her three-year-old, naked glory. In the middle of the living room. Bouncing on the sofa. With *Baby Shark* blaring from the stereo speakers.

With Gram, who—*oh, dear God*—also happened to be butt-naked.

"I think I'll wait outside." The deep voice rumbled near her ear. Tess swore she heard laughter in his otherwise stoic voice. "Let me know when it's safe to come in."

Built-and-smart hides an asshole.

So much for getting the sexy Ranger's attention. This was situation FUBAR. It was never safe to enter the house. Never had been. Never would be.

Tess stood in the door, unable to tear her eyes from the disturbing scene. If she didn't have PTSD before, by-gawd she oughta have it now.

"Hi!" Laz's voice piped up behind her. "Hey, Tess, who's your friend?"

Tess turned to see her brother coming up the walkway, cursing herself for not hearing him drive up.

"You might not want to go in there just yet," Crock advised from the porch steps.

"Daddy!"

A dark-headed streak of nakedness sailed past her. Tess tried to grab the hellion back—what she thought she could grab onto was a mystery—but missed.

"Oomph!" Climbing onto the porch, Laz caught his daughter as she body-slammed into his chest. "Where are your clothes, Punkin? And why are we standing out here?" His attention swung from his daughter to the scene lying in wait.

If Tess needed a visual of eyes popping out of a man's head, then Laz delivered.

"Oh. Oh, crap!" Her twin shoved Tila into Tess's arms so fast Tess nearly dropped the squirming child on her bare ass. Laz was pedaling backward just as quickly. "Tila, put your clothes on. Uh, Gram? Oh, shit! I think I'll go talk to this nice man in the driveway."

Tess glared after the rapidly retreating backside belonging to her brother.

Jerk.

She heaved a sigh before shoving Tila inside.

I earn my mental illness. Every. Freaking. Day.

Chapter Five

Crock couldn't remember a day involving that much nudity since he and his team busted up a raucous party at Hippie Hollow. Visions of the grandmother and a little girl jumping on a couch in nothing but their birthday suits, combined with the frustration of a good-looking woman trying desperately not to lose her shit, brought tears to his eyes.

Now that he was heading home, he could let out all the laughter that he'd held back. How long had it been since he'd laughed that hard? Certainly not in the past few years, that's for damn sure. Lord help what the big rig in the next lane thought of a grown-assed man guffawing in the stop-and-go, game-day traffic on I-30.

Thinking about the game gave Crock an idea. The truck was so new that he hadn't programmed the radio settings yet. He fiddled with the radio until he found the baseball game he wished he was going to. A beer and a hot dog sounded great, right about now. Maybe he'd take Gemma Rae to one before it got too hot.

The phone rang just as they announced the score. With a sigh, Crock glanced at the dashboard display: *Captain*.

Oh, hell. "Crock here."

"Any luck?" Captain Childs's gruff, southern twang filled the cab.

"A bit. Might have found us a replacement for

Cheryl." Crock began with the most important detail—finding someone to replace their long-time receptionist and general keeper-of-chaos.

A grunt on the other end told him to keep going. "Claudette Hudgens. She herds college students like cattle and never breaks a sweat. Might be a challenge to lure her away from TCU though."

"College kids gotta be easier than cleaning up Ranger cow patties," the captain growled. It was all Crock could do to keep from snorting. His boss's aversion to cursing was weirdly hilarious. "I'll see what I can do. You said TCU? What'd you get up to over there?"

Crock quickly summarized his day. "Dr. Corona was—distracted, but it wasn't a total waste. I'm going to meet up with him tomorrow morning. If he's up for an investigation, we might be able to do it over the weekend."

It didn't surprise him that the professor wouldn't discuss the case in front of his family. What was interesting was the guy's nervousness at meeting with a Ranger. Instead of excitement to put his theories into action, Crock would have thought the guy had something to hide.

"Good. FYI, the family got riled up after you went to see them. The nephew wants the will probated yesterday, and he's being a right-righteous twit about it." Childs might never call someone an asshole, but he found creative ways to insult obnoxious idiots.

"Both he and his sister acted squirrelly. Their story didn't change. It was almost verbatim to each other's statement."

The latest details of the case ran through Crock's

brain. It was the family's own fault. There wouldn't have been issues with the probate if they hadn't presented those documents and the attorney for the estate hadn't suspected fraud.

Between the fraud and the unsolved murder, the overwhelmed small town of Joshua and the Johnson County investigators had invited the Rangers Cold Case Unit to step in. The strange circumstances surrounding both deaths placed the case squarely on Crock's desk.

"What's their hurry? Haven't they been sitting on this will for…what? A year or two?"

"The will stipulated no probate until the mystery surrounding the wife's death is solved. I don't know why Dan Green did that, but I guess twenty-two years is a long time to wait for answers. The family isn't happy with the estate's attorney and is fighting that stipulation. There's talk of lawsuits against the insurance company and the lawyers. And now the judge is on our hindquarter. He wants to clear his docket, so he can take a vacation."

Vacation? What's that? Hell, it doesn't look like I'll even get a weekend.

"Got it. I should have a preliminary report by Monday afternoon. Any word on the missing evidence box?"

"That's a negative. The evidence room in Johnson County is being a pain in my left butt cheek." A heavy sigh sounded in Crock's ear. "It'd be fantastic if you could get the case closed by Friday."

"Yes, sir. I'll get right on that."

The captain chuckled. "I'm sure you will. Get these people off my backside, and get me the contact info on that Ranger wrangler, will you?"

"Yes, sir."

****

A Latte Good was every bit the type of coffee shop Crock expected of the college crowd. Everywhere he looked there were people drinking yippee, frou-frou concoctions that contained more sugar than caffeine, busily typing away on their tablets or laptops, with earplugs blocking out the real world. Not his kind of place.

Walking in, Crock had spotted Laz Corona immediately. The professor gave every impression that his mind was elsewhere as he sat in the corner, sipping what appeared to be—shockingly—plain, black coffee. Without spending much time on the menu, Crock ordered his own large, black coffee and took it over to the table. "Dr. Corona?"

The historian started at his appearance but jumped up to shake his hand. "Sergeant Ward, thanks for meeting me here. Please, call me Laz. I'm sorry about yesterday. Gram and Tila…well, they're a little—"

"Nothing I haven't seen before." Crock pulled up a chair that might not have been meant for a full-grown man, positioned it with his back to the wall, and sat down to study his companion.

Corona looked younger than him by five or six years, young for a professor at TCU. He stood about six-foot with a medium build, dark brown hair and eyes. Either dodging sex-starved co-eds was physically demanding—which Crock could vouch for—or Dr. Corona was a gym regular to keep fit.

Laz cleared his throat. "What can I do for you?"

The question brought Crock out of his speculation. "You can call me Crock. I've got an investigation I think you might be in the best position to help."

"What kind of investigation?" Laz still looked rather tense, but curious.

Crock took his time answering. "It's a cold case that's come up for review thanks to some recent developments. You may or may not remember the death that happened in 1995 at a small hotel in Joshua. The name was Esme Green. The husband was Dr....."

"Daniel Green. He was one of my undergrad professors. He died—" Laz paused to think, "—about two years ago."

Crock nodded as he took a sip of his surprisingly good coffee. "That was about the time you joined the faculty, if I'm not mistaken."

Laz nodded. "Dr. Green was my mentor. He helped me get into grad school and critiqued my doctoral work. He wrote many references for me."

His voice faded, allowing Crock to fill in the final piece of information, "It was on his recommendation that you got your current position, correct?"

The prof seemed to find his coffee cup intensely interesting. "I didn't know there was an opening. TCU was my dream post. When the dean called me and told me to apply, I thought—" He stopped to take a steadying sip. "His death was kept quiet. I didn't know about it until my first faculty meeting."

"What can you tell me about his wife?"

Laz blew out a breath and visibly shook off the memory of his mentor. "Not much. I didn't get to know Dr. Green until several years after she died. I think she was a dancer or a model."

"Did he ever mention her?"

"Not often. He had pictures of her all over his

office. If you walked in unannounced, it wasn't unusual to find him staring at one of her photos. He sometimes talked to them."

Calmly nursing his beverage, Crock nodded. It wasn't new information. It was also not what he needed from Laz. "Your specialty is Texas history, correct?"

Laz appeared surprised. "Uhm, yeah. My degrees are in archaeology and anthropology, but my dissertation centered on indigenous folklore and practices of the peoples in Texas and surrounding influences."

Crock waited.

Laz looked like he could expound upon his life's work for the rest of the day but held himself in check. "But you aren't all that interested in my research, are you?" His enthusiasm deflated. "You need me for my sideline work."

Crock said nothing.

Laz exhaled roughly, running a hand through his short hair. "Ah, shit."

Crock's eyebrow lifted. "I thought you might be interested in an investigation. Especially when you knew one of those involved. Was I wrong?"

"No, actually, I've dreamed of working with law enforcement agencies for years. I even published on the possibilities." The other man sat back and closed his eyes. "It's an issue of timing, that's all."

"What's wrong with the timing?"

Laz shook his head and opened his eyes before leaning forward again. Taking a fortifying sip of caffeine, his gaze met Crock's. "What do you know about my family?"

"What should I know?"

The professor gave a hollow laugh. "Really? You want to let me give the scoop when I know you've probably done a thorough background check. I've tried to keep out of that bullet trap since I was in high school."

"But…?" Crock prompted.

"Look…part of my expertise includes ghost stories and legends. Yes, I lead paranormal investigations. And yes, my family is—" Laz struggled to find the right words, "—a special kind of bat-shit crazy. But I do not want them involved. Ever. *Especially* my sister."

Crock appreciated the other man's description of, and concern for, his family. The truth was he didn't know much about the Corona family, nor did he understand what the problem was. The more Laz insisted his family stay out of the investigation; the more curious Crock became. He made a mental note to do a little snooping.

Instead of asking questions Laz wouldn't want to answer, Crock shrugged. "It's my understanding that with the paranormal, like law enforcement, nothing is guaranteed."

Laz leveled him with a look. "The same goes with my family."

Chapter Six

A promise was a promise, and Tess had pinky promised Tila that she would check on her teacher, Karlyn Godfrey. After teaching her women's self-defense class, she took a batch of Gram's famous snickerdoodles, which were guaranteed to cure all ills. There was a lot more than gratitude waiting for her at the tiny studio apartment in Pantego.

Tess was accustomed to burly soldiers who expressed their feelings via fart jokes or belching the alphabet after too many beers. Her own frustrations and hurts were dealt with on a firing range or in a dojang where she could kick some ass. Female emotional purging was a concept she'd never fully grasped and wasn't sure she wanted to. Even in high school, where drama wasn't limited to the stage, she hadn't known how to deal with teenage angst. Of course, she'd had the typical, weird-family shit to deal with and really had no time for such things as the latest hairstyle and who was shagging whom.

For the past thirty minutes, Tess had witnessed a wider range of emotions from one person than ever before in her life. Not even her mother could achieve such a variety in a short period of time. The former preschool teacher vacillated between torrential sobbing and throwing furniture, ending with "That stupid bitch doesn't know a damn thing about childcare!"

And the emotion of the moment was a step-down from chucking sofa cushions around the room—thankfully. Tess had hoped for slightly less vehemence, but at least she could understand the cursing. Karlyn had an ugly cry-voice, and it was difficult to understand anything she said through the snot clogging her nose and throat.

"I agree." Tess tried to be supportive and still be the voice of reason, which was an amazing feat if she thought about it. Even Laz might be impressed with her restraint. "There were other parents making complaints, as well. The state board was interested in hearing from them."

Water welled up in Karlyn's eyes.

Oh, crap. "What now?" Tess had only experienced her mother's mood swings. Karlyn's were a little different and much less predictable. Innocent words seemed to set her off.

"That bitch stole it," Karlyn hissed.

Good. Clear and to the point. I can work with this.

"And…I-I d-didn't g-g-get to s-s-s-say g-g-g-g-goodb-b-bye!"

And we're back to the sob-screaming.

Tess didn't know how to respond, and it made her extremely uncomfortable. Instead, she replaced a cushion on the floral sofa so she'd have a place to sit and picked up a throw pillow which had seen better days so her hands would have something to strangle. Karlyn stepped, or rather tripped, over her to the armchair tucked in a corner of the tight living space.

"You might explain what exactly Jessica stole from you," Tess replied, fighting to keep the irritation out of her voice, "including the how and why."

"The school." Karlyn blew her nose which did little to clear the congestion. "Jessica changed everything."

Tess was confused. "Can't she do that?"

Karlyn snuffled, which ended with a snort. Tess handed her a tissue. Incoherent for a moment, the younger woman shoved some papers toward her. Unsure of how involved she wanted to be, Tess glanced at the top page, not intending to read much detail.

That didn't work.

The top page read *Last Will and Testament*. The name on the will blew all Tess's good intentions straight out the window.

Lanna Godfrey.

Laz's high school girlfriend.

Tess closed her eyes. She had never connected Godfrey Children's Day Care with the sweet girl whom Laz took to senior prom. Lanna had been a sophomore, but she looked much older dressed in her sky-blue, floor-length dress. The teen just out of braces was turned into someone who belonged on a red carpet in the six-inch platform heels, a belly peephole revealing an interesting piercing, and a slit that revealed never-never-land.

Tess was almost positive her goofy brother lost his virginity that night.

"Karlyn, how did you get in Lanna's will?"

"She was my half-sister," sobbed Karlyn.

It took a few minutes for Tess to catch up, but she discovered that Lanna had opened the daycare after college. After Laz went forth and multiplied, he put his faith and only child in the hands of a former girlfriend. Apparently neither party thought the arrangement strange, and Tila was happy.

According to Laz, all was normal until Thanksgiving when Lanna was killed in a car accident. The family hired a director to fill the vacancy. Over the past few months, the new director implemented stringent new rules and increased the tuition.

After Tess returned home, she'd taken over the childcare responsibilities. The changes began gradually but soon snowballed into massive upheavals. Strict attendance was enforced, and friendly staff disappeared from the welcome desk. Parents protested and—getting no response to their questions—took their children elsewhere. Despite the concerns, Tila still loved going to her school and loved her remaining playmates. Until she was thrown out for pitching a fit over no shoes and losing Miss Karlyn, her favorite teacher.

"So," Tess began, slowly understanding the information presented, "you inherited the daycare?"

Karlyn nodded, wiping her tears. "Half of it. My parents got the other portion. They retired a couple of years ago and didn't want to run the business, and I don't have enough experience yet, so we hired Jessica to manage the place."

Some of the information finally clicked into place. "Then Jessica fired you. She fired her own boss?"

More tears well-up in Karlyn's eyes. "I haven't completed all my certifications yet. I've been working on them, but some of the classes were full, and I didn't get them done in time for my," she raised her fingers to make the universal air quote sign, "'*performance review'*."

Tess sat back. Before she would form another question, Karlyn continued with a sniffle, "I told my parents, and we went in yesterday to question her. She waved these papers—" Karlyn picked up another packet of documents "—and told us to get off *her* property. We were no longer welcome."

Handing the distraught teacher another tissue, Tess glanced at the paperwork. Instead of *Godfrey Children's Day Care*, the business name had been changed to *The Wright Institute for Child Development*. She pulled the top document closer.

Her surroundings vanished.

The woman stood looking over the man's shoulder while he filled in the blanks on a legal document.

The woman pointed at the page. "That doesn't match."

"Sure, it does," he grumbled, knocking her hand away. Each hand sported a large silver ring on the middle finger.

"No, that squiggle isn't the same at all."

"Since when did you become a handwriting expert?"

Tess smothered a gasp as she snatched her hand away from the document, clearing the vision. Her heart raced. For one scary moment, she was afraid she might pass out or throw up. She had no idea what had just happened, but she sure as hell didn't like it.

She took a moment to calm down before glancing around. Karlyn continued to rant and didn't seem to notice Tess's temporary brain blip. At least, she hoped that was what it was.

Using a pencil eraser to avoid touching the pages, she flipped to the last page and checked the signatures. "This says you and your parents signed the business and the property over to Jessica Wright."

"But we didn't!" Karlyn shouted. "That bitch stole

Lanna's dream from us! Lanna wanted to share the daycare with me. We had plans. And that bitch took it!"

"Whoa. Take a deep breath." Tess thought quickly. The vision had disturbed her, but Karlyn's reaction seemed to confirm that the legal documents on the table were forgeries. She hated to think that greedy assholes stole Lanna and Karlyn's business. "The state is already investigating some of the complaints. I think they might need this information to help their case. If Jessica forged your signatures, it adds to the case against her."

Karlyn stared at her, gasps of air made her chest heave. A glimmer of hope rose in her eyes. "Do you think they'll take my word for it?"

God, I hope so.

"I'm sure they will be willing to listen." Tess tried to remain optimistic and calm. "You might want to get an attorney to help. Maybe they have a document examiner that can look over these papers."

And maybe one sexy Texas Ranger will have some suggestions.

Tess kept that thought to herself. She didn't know if a Ranger could help, but chances were that Sergeant D. Crockett Ward had bigger fish to catch. She didn't want to get Karlyn's hopes up. With her mind spinning with possibilities she asked, "Meanwhile, can you get those classes and certifications done?"

Karlyn nodded enthusiastically, saying, "I got into one class for the first summer session. Then there's one more that I hope to get into this fall."

"And is that it?"

"Then, there's my certification exam," Karlyn added. "I can take that while I'm finishing my degree in child development. It hasn't been a priority, but I guess it is now, right?"

"Right." Tess agreed firmly with that plan.

In the meantime, Karlyn would need all the help she could get.

****

Laz drove home with his gut hyped-up on caffeine, adrenaline, and fear. He'd had enough coffee to run about six marathons, and he was geeking out over an investigation.

Tonight. With a Texas Ranger, no less.

It was every paranormal investigator's dream—help find answers to unexplained events and bring peace to both the living and the dead. To solve the mysteries of the past through communication with those who lived through the events. Hell, he'd done dissertations on the subject. This cold case could be the opportunity of his lifetime.

After ten-plus years of paranormal investigating, Laz knew what preparations were necessary. He'd already called his team, and they were on board. A thorough history of the hotel and the surrounding area would give him an indication of what to expect as far as abnormal activity. Fortunately, he had studied Tarrant County and the surrounding region with a fine-toothed comb.

You'd never know if one of your ancestors committed murder at the corner of University and Rosedale unless you looked.

He'd looked. It wasn't at Rosedale at all. Great-Gramps got into a shoot-out at University and Seventh over a flat tire and an empty wallet.

After his meeting with Crock, he'd made a good start with Dr. Daniel Green's genealogy but would need to dig a little deeper into the man behind his mentor. Other than the deceased wife, Laz was fairly sure that Dr. Green had no living children. The respected, tenured professor had died at the age of eighty, leaving behind a legacy of work that only Laz seemed to appreciate.

The opportunity to discover what had happened was what kept him ghost-hunting. His mission was to uncover the mysteries behind the myths and legends, many of which were rooted in his family's history.

As an added bonus, Laz hoped to find answers for the family of the man who had done so much for him over the years. Dr. Green had fully supported and even seemed fascinated by Laz's investigations. From the referrals and references, to the forwards for his books, to his current position at TCU, Dan Green became a rock and much-needed father-figure to an otherwise lost young man.

The reason he had been lost—Tess. Well, his entire family was enough of an excuse, but especially his sister. As a twin, he'd known each time she was under threat and did his best to protect her. When their mother tried to separate them by dumping Tess on those "deranged Mexicans" as she referred to her ex-husband's family, Laz ran away no less than five times to join his sister. If it wasn't for Tess, his final attempt would have meant a one-way trip to join the dead. It also meant his mom finally gave up when Gram threatened to hex her into another dimension.

Laz was pretty sure Gram's actual curse didn't include another dimension and was mostly harmless. Mostly. He had no way of being certain.

A mooing cow sounded over the car's speakers,

indicating a call from his mother. *Think of the devil….* "Hi, Mom."

"Hello, darling. How's my boy?"

Tired of being treated like I'm six. "Good. What's up?"

"Am I disturbing you?"

Yes. "No, Mom, just heading to the library to do some research."

It was a little lie—he was going home to *his* library to check *his* resources because the TCU library didn't have much in the realm of paranormal studies. Interrupting his work was one of the few reasons which would get Clara Biery Corona Richardson off the phone quickly.

"Well, I won't keep you."

Well, crap. "Mom?"

"How is my little Domatila?"

"She's good. There's a situation at daycare, but Tess is handling it."

The heavy sigh from his mother pissed him off. Before he could respond, she spoke again. "Shall I pick up Domatila for a few days? It's been a while since I've kept her."

Laz held back a groan. His mother had won few awards for motherhood, but she tried to embrace being a grandmother. "We can work that out. I'll look at my schedule to see when I can bring her to you and call you later."

"All right." Again, his mother paused before asking, "Would you have Theresa call me?"

His gut clenched. "Uh…sure, but…why don't you call her? You've got her number."

"Maybe I will."

Laz wouldn't hold his breath. Mom hadn't made much of an effort to contact Tess in the four months she'd been home. He didn't know why he thought their relationship would have changed with Tess gone for the past twelve years. "Well, I've got to go, Mom. I'll call you later about my schedule."

"Love you, darling. Work hard."

As usual, his head gave a tiny throb of annoyance as the line went dead. He heaved a sigh of relief. His life was a screwed-up balance of crazy and crazier. The question was who won the prize: Mom or him. Or maybe Tess.

Something was wrong with his sister. Something big. She refused to talk about her time in the Army. 'It's classified' had become her standard response to any questions. Hell, he didn't even know what kind of job she'd held, or how a psychology degree had been of any help to the Army.

One thing he did know—his sister's fitness routine put his to shame. He was proud of his body, keeping toned through infrequent workouts at the gym and assisting the youth in Tai Kwon Do. It wasn't until he had picked up Tess at the airport that he had realized what a wimp he truly was. While the family had bombarded her, he'd performed his brotherly duty by grabbing her checked luggage. The duffle bag was a deceptively heavy canvas pack which held God knew what. That frigging bag was bulky and weighed something like seventy or eighty pounds! Nothing embarrassed him more than having his smaller sister take pity on his whining, grab the pack from his hands, and sling it over her shoulder like it weighed nothing. Zip. Nada.

It'd gotten his ass back into the gym on a regular basis and Tai Kwon Do training. There was no way he'd let Tess prove he was a useless weakling again. Ever.

His thoughts were interrupted a second time as a blaring siren filled the car. *"Warning! Warning! Your sister is calling! If you pick up now, you will be talking to your sister!"*

Laz snorted at the new ringtone he'd assigned to Tess, replacing *The Ghostbusters* theme he had used for years. She hadn't heard it yet. He didn't expect to live long if she ever did.

Suppressing his laughter, he hit the green button followed by the speaker to accept the call. "What's up?"

"My blood pressure."

That didn't sound good. His sister was notorious for being calm in a crisis. Laz tried to think what Tess had planned for the day. "You saw Karlyn, right? Was she okay?"

"If you consider violent mood swings and hysterical crying to be *okay*, then yes, she's doing dandy."

Laz winced. Thanks to their mother, highly emotional situations made Tess even more uncomfortable than him. "Yeah, well…she's a lot like Lanna."

He'd been young and—stupidly—thought he was in love. Trying to please his girlfriend had been time consuming, not to mention exhausting. While their relationship hadn't lasted into college, they had remained friends. When Tila was old enough to go to a daycare, he had gone straight to someone he trusted.

Lanna was thrilled to take care of his little girl and had asked few questions about the momma. It was a good decision—at the time.

Now, Lanna was gone, and the day care situation was a headache he had gladly handed over to Tess.

"Why didn't you tell me Karlyn was Lanna's sister?" Tess demanded.

Oh, shit! "Uhm…I didn't think about it?" *Lame—but true.*

He heard Tess mutter something about the location of his head in a deep, dark orifice which was physically impossible to achieve. It was time to pull into a parking lot so he could concentrate on the conversation. "So, what happened?"

In terse, military-esque terms, Tess gave him the details, then added, "She's getting screwed over, Laz."

"Sounds like it." He hated that Tila was so upset by not going to school and not having her favorite teacher there. He'd met the new director a few times. Lanna wouldn't have liked her. "What can we do to help?"

The hesitation on the other end of the line caused Laz's skin to crawl. "What happened, Tess?"

"I don't…I think…" Tess stopped, but he waited for her to continue. "I think the papers were forged."

Laz sat in disbelief for a moment before stuttering, "Wh…that's…what makes you think that?"

"I…uhm…Karlyn showed me the paperwork." Tess didn't sound right. "It—it felt wrong."

He was all for trusting his gut, and he knew Tess's instincts were usually correct. He also knew she was leaving out something important. Digging information out of his sister in person was hard; over the phone, it was next to impossible.

Swiping a hand over his face, he groaned. "Okay, that's helpful. What can we do about it?"

"I've called the state commission. There's already a case opened based on the complaints they've received this week. But the guy said it might take months to have any results." He heard Tess take a deep breath. Then she said, "Laz, I think Karlyn needs a lawyer."

"Agreed." After a few minutes of discussion, he concurred with Tess—the only person they knew who could offer advice was Crock Ward.

After disconnecting, Laz sat for a moment before starting his car. He didn't want to get involved with a fraud investigation. Ghosts and legends he understood, not forgeries and childcare. On the upside—if Tess was busy with the childcare dilemma, then she might not pay much attention to his latest ghost-hunting gig.

If he was able to prevent Gram and Tess from getting drawn into his dream investigation, that would be fantabulous. Knowing the pair, though, he might as well be a fairy princess in a tutu.

As he'd told Crock, the timing of this investigation sucked. Tess had been home for four months but still hadn't gotten settled. Her psychology degree didn't open many doors, and she was fighting to stay optimistic on the job front. He wasn't sure what she was looking for, but she wasn't finding it. Other than teaching a couple of self-defense classes and basic gun safety courses, his sister was drifting. Laz hated to say anything, but their mother was probably right—Tess needed to take advantage of her military benefits and go back to school.

She'd been a godsend, becoming the mother-figure that Tila desperately needed. The daycare nightmare pissed him off, but Tess brandished that sword quite well. All he needed to do was back her in the fight for justice for the teacher and a happy, safe place for his little girl.

Gram was a wild card on a good day. Her doctor seemed to think she had the beginnings of dementia, but the family knew better and used the diagnosis as an excuse. Gram knew exactly what she was doing and thoroughly enjoyed making people's lives crazy. Fortunately, she could be kept quiet by having her babysit Tila.

Dear God! Tila! What in the hell will I do if she takes after Gram and Tess?

The image of her naked butt bouncing on the sofa with her equally naked grandmother floated across his brain.

Ah, fuck! She already does.

Chapter Seven

Tess could tell when Laz was up to no good. The years in the military hadn't dimmed their twin telepathy—even across continents. Despite his best efforts, she was simply better at hiding her shit. Yet here he was, across the room, trying to pretend nothing was going on.

The dumbass had been acting weird all day. First, he'd disappeared when he was supposed to take Tila for their usual Friday morning donut date. When he returned, his daughter laid on a guilt trip which only resolved when he made open-faced hamburgers for lunch—burnt crusts and all. He claimed to have papers to grade—grades that he had reportedly turned in the day before—which got him out of cleaning the kitchen. He proceeded to disappear into his office all afternoon with an all-too-familiar backpack.

One she hadn't seen in over ten years.

As a teenager, ghosts had fascinated her brother. Witnessing her reactions to strange phenomenon led to amateur ghost hunting. His need to understand her abilities drove him to put together a group of nerds who then documented their findings. She'd been a willing part of that team until she left home. Even then, he'd continued paranormal investigating, trying to find the answers to her issues. Tess also knew Laz was driven by a lot of guilt.

Guilt he had no reason to have.

But if he thought she would let him wake the dead without her, he had another thing coming.

"What in the hell are you doing?"

Laz shot up from his pack and spun around. His bare foot connected with the foot of the desk which led to some inventive cursing.

Tess hoped Tila was occupied with Gram on the other side of the house. According to the daycare director, the little shit knew enough curse words and wasn't allowed back until she learned a few manners. After the way the daycare had treated her niece and her favorite teacher, that was fine with Tess. She still had to figure out what to do about Karlyn's situation. Laz fully supported Gram's plan to burn down the facility and hex the director with genital warts. Tess hoped neither would act on either threat.

On second thought, the warts wouldn't be traceable back to the Coronas.

But all approved retribution would have to wait until brother dearest spilled his guts.

"Don't do that!" Laz griped.

"Do what? Keep you from checking your equipment?"

"That and sneaking up behind me!"

"Should've turned on your twin-dar, eejit. I've been watching your hairy ass pack up for the past five minutes."

"My ass is *not* hairy! And you don't need to watch me do shit!"

Tess rolled her eyes. Her brother really was an idiot. "Yeah, I do. You're prepping for an investigation."

"So?"

"So, I'm going with you."

Normally, getting Laz to blow a fuse was quite entertaining. This time proved epic. His face turned an interesting shade of magenta, all the way to the ears. Several seconds of sputtering were punctuated with tiny balls of spit flying through the air.

That's really disgusting.

"The hell you are!"

"The hell I am!"

She shoved away from the door frame and moved into the office, stepping over a stack of books to mosey over to the desk. It wasn't a big space, but perfect for her nerd brother. Aside from the desk and a worktable, every wall was covered with bookcases. The small wall space over the light switch hosted a carved, Black Forest coo-coo clock as the sole reminder of their German ancestry. Around the room, hints of their Mestizo roots decorated what little space was available amongst the clutter, including pottery and a skull covered in a mosaic of turquoise-colored glass. Tess had no idea where the skull came from, but she had learned its name was Cedric. She was pretty sure it wasn't a family piece.

She hoped it wasn't a family member.

The books which Laz was studying covered the desk, while the ones he didn't have space for littered the floor in semi-organized piles. The only space not taken up with his obsession for Texas history was the child's drawing desk by the window.

It was cute to watch father and daughter working side-by-side between bouts of hellraising.

Tess glanced at the books he'd on the desk—*North*

Texas Landmarks, *Mysteries of Tarrant County*, *Texas Ghosts and Legends*. A small recorder sat on the corner of the desk. Her hand landed just right. "Is this what the Ranger wanted from you? I didn't think law enforcement bought into the paranormal."

"They don't usually, but this guy has his reasons." Laz turned back to the equipment spread out on the table. He inspected each piece for battery charge before packing it into its specialized compartment in his pack. "He's given me a job to do. Since it's an opportunity to test my theory, I didn't ask too many questions."

Tess speculated why a Texas Ranger might need to investigate paranormal activity and came up with exactly zero reasons. She wasn't buying it. Before she could respond, the doorbell rang.

"Ah, hell," she muttered, quickly pocketing her prize. "Gram, I've got it!" she shouted as she turned back toward the door, kicking the stack of books she'd managed to miss earlier.

Cursing as she hopped on one foot while holding her toe and the corner of Laz's desk, Tess glared back at her brother, who held up his hands in defense. "I didn't do it."

"Clean up your shit," she hissed. "And we aren't through discussing this little party of yours."

"Yeah, we are."

"No, we aren't." The doorbell rang again, giving Tess the last word. "Coming!"

She beat Gram to the door by microseconds. Denied the opportunity to maul a cute Ranger at the door, the old woman stormed away, cursing in Spanish, English, and probably Klingon—or maybe Romulan.

"Laz'll be out in a minute." Tess invited their guest

in but wished she could see the man's eyes. His mirrored aviators were firmly in place, shadowed by the cowboy hat. Tess wondered if the glasses helped block the images he had seen in her house. His face gave no indication of hearing Gram, although he couldn't *not* hear her.

"I heard shouting. Am I interrupting anything?"

"Nope. Nothing unusual." Tess plastered her biggest, friendliest smile on her face, trying for the *there's-nothing-to-see-here* look. "Can I get you something to drink? We've got water, lemonade, beer…."

"No, thank you."

Damn! I shouldn't have offered a beer. He might be on-duty.

She tried to look calm and casual. Then a horrifying memory surfaced. "I'm sorry about yesterday. Gram has dementia, and…well…."

What else could she say? The dementia line helped explain away the truth. Tess didn't know what a Ranger would do if he knew Gram controlled the demons of Hell and sometimes brought them out to play. It didn't matter. Some things could not be unseen, and seventy-odd-year-old naked boobs and ass bouncing around on a sofa were on the top of that list. If that hadn't been enough to send the man screaming for the hills, nothing would.

"Don't worry about it. I'm used to seeing some—interesting things in my line of work."

Crock removed his shades as he spoke, giving Tess a good, unhindered glimpse of hazel eyes. A light-green shirt brought out the swirling shades of green among the brown, amber, and hints of blue and gray. Although the rest of his face showed no hint of emotion, if she looked hard enough, she thought she could see amusement in the depths of his steady gaze. All evidence of the man's sense of humor disappeared as soon as she found it.

"Dammit, Tess!"

The shout would have startled her if she hadn't expected it. It was all she could do to contain her evilest grin.

"What the hell did you do with it?" Laz stormed into the room, his backpack in tow.

"I don't know what…"

"Bullshit! You took the EVP recorder off my desk."

Her best innocent look never worked on her brother, so Tess didn't try it. "You are *so* observant! Mom will be so proud."

She was prepared for his attack, although she was surprised that he would tackle her in front of a guest. One would think the Corona twins had outgrown public displays of juvenile behavior.

One would be incorrect.

"Ooph!" Her grunt erupted as her hip contacted the floor and Laz's elbow landed in her gut.

"Ow, fuck!" Laz yelled when she found his thumb and used it to twist the arm behind his back, between his shoulder blades. He retaliated by flipping over, but she landed on top.

Before she could shift herself to put a knee in Laz's back, a firm hand hooked the waistband of her jeans and hauled her back. Another hand yanked her brother's arm from her grip, and Laz disappeared from her sight.

“What the hell!” she shouted. *I was winning!* “Let me go!”

“Y’all are done,” Crock replied in a calm, no-bullshit tone.

Well, crap! She’d forgotten about the man she was trying to impress. *Good job, idiot.*

Realizing that it would be a massively *stupid* move to assault a peace officer, she stopped fighting her captor. Tess glanced around to find Laz restrained by the Ranger in an even more undignified position than her own. Her brother’s head was carefully, but firmly, tucked into Crock’s left armpit.

“Lepfgoome!” Laz tried to get loose but couldn’t move.

“Not until both of you act like adults.”

Tess wasn’t feeling very adultish. “He started it.”

It earned her a shake hard enough to rattle her teeth. “No, *you* started it. Hand it over.”

Reluctantly, she pulled the little recorder from her back pocket and tossed in onto the coffee table. Immediate freedom was her reward. Laz was released a moment later after promising to behave.

Attempting to regain some dignity, she smoothed out her hair and straightened her shirt. She glanced up to find her sulking brother checking the device for damage. Crock stood with arms folded, ready to stop any further altercations. Tess wasn’t certain, but she would swear it looked like he was biting his cheek to keep from laughing.

With a glare, Laz stuffed the recorder into his pack. Without a word, he hauled the bag and his ass out the front door. Crock eyed her with one lifted eyebrow, then silently followed her twin out of the house.

"Well, hell," she muttered. It felt good to let loose. She had needed to burn off some frustration.

"You can say that again."

Tess spun around to find Gram and Tila standing in the kitchen doorway. Gram held a mixing bowl, while her niece held two mixer blades, each covered in sticky, chocolate goo. The little girl's pink tongue licked along a metal tine. Salmonella had never been an issue in the Corona household, probably because they inoculated themselves by eating raw cookie dough and licking the mixing bowls at every opportunity. And in Gram's home, there was plenty of opportunity. From the looks of it, Gram was making a batch of her infamous pot brownies.

"If you'd kicked a little more, that sexy law man might have handcuffed you to a bed. Next time, don't give up so quick." Gram offered her expert advice.

"Humph." Tess grunted. There was something wrong about hearing her grandmother refer to sex play. She eyed the unlicked mixing blade in the little girl's hand. "Is that one for me?"

Tila considered her answer. "It's for winners. You didn't beat Daddy."

"I haven't lost to your daddy in years."

"Sure looked like it to me," the little smart-ass shot back.

"I'm not done with him yet," growled Tess.

Tila held out the prize. "You owe me ice cream if you lose."

"Deal."

Chapter Eight

"I'm sorry about what happened. The family drama. We don't usually lose control in front of others like that."

Crock glanced at the man seated in the truck next to him. It'd taken every ounce of willpower to not bust a gut when two grown-assed adults started beating on each other over a childish prank. If he hadn't sworn to keep peace, he might have wagered on the sister. "Don't worry about it. I've seen worse."

Laz huffed. "Yeah. I guess you've seen that type of domestic situation more than you'd care to admit. The Coronas are known for our own special kind of crazy, but we take care of each other." He hesitated. "But it still wasn't very professional."

No, it wasn't, but it was damned funny. "She can kick your ass if she wanted, can't she?"

"Yeah," Laz grunted, "she picked up a few tricks in the Army, I guess. Hell, she teaches a self-defense class. It's been a while since we had a knock-down-drag-out. I guess we were due. I'm just sorry you had to witness it."

"Like I said, I've seen worse." *A lot worse.* "At least your argument didn't end with bloodshed or a visit from the medical examiner. I've got a sister who drives me crazy, too."

"I bet she doesn't try to help you do your job."

"No." *Not when she doesn't understand my job.*

Laz sighed. "At least Tess didn't follow us."

Crock checked his rearview mirror. *Uh huh. There she is.*

He wasn't surprised to see the dark blue jeep lagging well behind them, and he didn't try hard to lose her. In fact, despite Laz's protests, his twin might be of some help. "Why don't you want her to come along?"

Laz's only response was a shrug before he turned away to study the passing scenery.

Since their morning meeting, Crock had done more research on the Coronas. Enough to know that this was one unusual family. He didn't find much about their parents, but he did learn that Lazaro Arthur Corona was a junior, and that name triggered something in Crock's memory—although he couldn't figure out why.

The twins began investigating cemeteries and easily accessible places as teenagers. By high school graduation, they'd investigated most of the haunted sites in and around Tarrant County and had amassed a reputation as paranormal experts.

One small, almost hidden, bit of information intrigued him. A small-town newspaper had done a piece on the duo and mentioned that Laz possessed the technical wizardry to take impressive videos and photos of apparitions. His sister, the audio expert, captured clear and intelligent conversations with the dead.

Crock found no further mention of Tess Corona until a license issued for a Texas Concealed Handgun License and an NRA Instructor Certification to teach gun safety turned up. Both would have been easy for her to obtain with her military background.

Her twin had continued both his education and the

investigations, creating a team with two of his buddies. A doctorate and two books on paranormal studies later, Laz was the only Texas history expert who suited Crock's needs.

But, if the sister was an asset, who was he to stop her from having input into the investigation? He didn't understand why Laz was against Tess's involvement but figured he would find out in due time. All he needed to do was keep an open mind and not shoot the siblings when they started arguing.

They didn't understand the blessing of what they had together. He wouldn't change his sister Gemma Rae for anything, but there were times when he wished he could take a breather from her.

Thank God Mom's doing better.

Laz checked his phone. "My team is on their way. They're about fifteen minutes out."

"Sounds good." Crock checked the mirror again. She had disappeared. He double-checked—no sign of the Jeep. That surprised him. He didn't expect Tess to give up so easily.

Disappointed, he steered the conversation back to his earlier line of interrogation. "You didn't answer my question. What's the deal with your sister? Y'all used to investigate together, right?"

The other man looked surprised—and a little nervous. "Uh, yeah. We did. She…ah…went into the Army…and, well…Tess's been out of the business for a long time. The equipment is new and I…you know."

Yeah, I do *know.*

Crock's bullshit meter pinged. The man was lying. Laz undoubtedly told some half-truths. He just didn't give the real reason Tess wasn't included in what appeared to have been the family business. Crock's gut told him that something had happened. Something that separated the twins for over ten years. And it intrigued him enough to figure it out.

Chapter Nine

Tess had a lot of experience following people around. In kindergarten, she got to hold a bright green rope with the other kids to go to the bathroom or the playground. In high school, she tracked her brother as he tried to sneak out of the house to meet up with the geeks he called friends. The Army became the ultimate test of her following capabilities. She had to pursue her fellow agents on assignments into known terrorist hot beds, never knowing if the dwelling she entered held a family eating dinner or a den of snipers waiting for Americans to make a fatal misstep. She'd always managed to keep up.

"Damn it!"

It was rare for her to lose her target, yet—somehow—she'd managed to do it this time. The gorgeous, red truck made it through a congested intersection, but the five cars she'd kept between them slowed to a crawl and missed the light. And the light lasted for an eternity.

She was cursing her luck when the phone rang. She knew who it was from the ringtone—the Munchkins happily sang *"Ding-Dong! The Witch is Dead"*—but glanced down anyway.

Shit.

"Hi, Mom." Tess hit the speaker button, trying—but failing—to be enthused by the interruption.

"You haven't called me."

"I talked to you the other day."

"That was three weeks ago, Theresa Marie."

Tess cringed. She hated it when her mother used her full name. "I'm sorry, Mom. How are you?"

When the cars finally moved, she glanced around. Nothing. She slapped her steering wheel in frustration, muttering curses under her breath.

"What was that?"

"Nothing. I just stubbed my toe."

"You should be more careful. If you'd studied dance like I wanted, you would have more grace."

"I was terrible at ballet."

"If you had tried, you would have done well."

Tess gritted her teeth to keep from resorting to a new level of bitchiness. She would never fit into her mother's definition of perfection. That had been proven multiple times by the age of eight.

Pulling into the parking lot of an empty office building, she idled the car and took a moment to regain control over her temper and her sanity. "I'm in a bit of a hurry, Mom. Did you need something?"

The irritation in her mother's voice was evident. "Do I *need* a reason to talk with my daughter?"

"No, Mom. I'm just on my way to meet Laz, and I'm almost there."

It was a little lie. But it would get her mother off the phone more quickly. Her twin was the favorite, and whatever Laz wanted, Laz would get. And right now, he wanted to lose his sister.

It's okay, Tess reminded herself, *Laz can't lose me. He can try, but he can't succeed.*

"All right, I'll let you go. I expect you to call me.

Give Lazaro my love."

With that, the line went dead. No love for the daughter who didn't live up to expectations. Tess blocked the hurt and focused on tracking her brother. She reached over to grab the gym sock she'd snatched from the dirty laundry. Her twin-dar didn't need a focus object to locate Laz within five miles, but she didn't have a clue where he was headed, so she would take the boost.

Pinching the rank sock between her fingertips, Tess tried not to inhale. She was thankful she hadn't accidentally grabbed a pair of his Jockeys. As it was, any passerby would think she was a lunatic for staring at a man's sock. "Where are you, asshole?"

Tess concentrated on her twin's location, asking the sock to show her the way. After what seemed like an eternity, but what was only a minute or two, the sense of fast, but steady, southward movement came to her. "They're on the highway," she muttered.

A glance at the clock told her the duo had a ten-minute head start. She could do this.

Carefully, she laid the sock where she could reach it if necessary and jammed the Jeep into gear. Within minutes, she was flying down I-35W, heading toward Burleson. Once she reached the Huguley Medical Center, she picked up the sock for additional guidance.

It wasn't necessary. A strong sense of Laz, like a whiff of his aftershave, made her move to the right lane and take the exit after the shopping and food mecca. She tried not to guess if the truck would stop in Joshua or go on to Cleburne. Her twin-dar could get screwed up if she made assumptions. The sock warmed indicating an upcoming turn. The sign read Main Street.

Downtown Joshua. It was one of many small towns in Texas which warranted little more than a dot on the map. Tess didn't know much more about it than that. Like most places in central and north Texas, it was safe to assume the town was founded in the mid-to-late 1800s as a farming community. The county seat was in Cleburne, so the Joshua downtown area was a strip of older buildings and homes and not much else.

She drove slowly, waiting to feel some indication of where she should go. She saw the pickup at the same time she felt the urge to stop. *Yes!* A lit-up sign identified the place as The Smith's Crown Hotel. Tess made an educated guess that whoever started the hotel was named Smith. The building was an old, three-story, boxy structure with no personality. Tess ignored the Texas Historical Commission plaque posted by the front door. As investigators, she and her brother paid no attention to the plaques until after the investigation was complete so their findings wouldn't be influenced.

She pulled into the parking lot and shut off the engine. Her pulse was racing. It'd been a long time since she'd done an investigation—well, a *paranormal* investigation. The last one had sent her into a tailspin. The experience had scared her away from her home and family for ten-plus years too long. Now, she was back—older, hopefully wiser, and ready to put that bullshit behind her. She just had to prove it. To Laz. To herself.

She tossed the dirty sock onto the floorboard—with a vow to fumigate her vehicle ASAP—and grabbed the EMF recorder she'd stolen from Laz's desk. He must have another one since he left the older model behind. It fit in her hand like an old friend.

Yeah, I can do this.

With grim determination, she hopped from the vehicle, locked it up, and headed inside. As expected, she found her target in the hotel lobby, talking with an older woman. Three sets of eyes turned to meet hers. Two were curious, but the set which matched hers was furious.

"Go home." Laz's growl broke the awkward silence.

"I'm not a damn puppy," Tess retorted. "You need help. I'm here to…."

"You're not going to do anything but turn your ass around and go home. What about Tila?"

Tess shook her head. "Gram has Tila, and they're making brownies and watching their shows." She had no idea what shows Gram would allow Tila to watch, but they were probably age inappropriate. "You've needed another set of hands since Trevor bailed on you two years ago."

Yes, she'd kept up with Corona Paranormal Investigations even though she was half a world away. Laz had done well on his own. He would do better with her covering his metaphorical and physical ass.

"I don't need…."

"Yes, you do."

The inscrutable man standing beside her brother stepped between them. "That's enough," Crock commanded.

Laz crossed his arms and glared at the pattern on the carpeted floor.

Crock sighed. "Laz, I know you and your sister were a team—and a damn good one as I understand it—before she went into the Army. If she has the expertise, then I don't have a problem with her involvement. Is there a reason you don't want her here?"

Laz closed his eyes, taking a deep breath. Tess knew there was a host of reasons why he didn't want her here. All of them intended to protect her. He needed to know she was stronger now. She could protect her own sanity this time. "Laz," she said, "I'm good. Let me do this."

Holding her breath, Tess watched her brother swallow hard against the tense muscles in his neck. He finally gave a small nod. An exhale escaped her as she launched herself to give him a hug. He grunted as he caught her.

Laz pushed her away but didn't release her. With eyes locked on hers, he said, "Don't do anything stupid."

Tess gave him a satisfied grin. "Then don't get into a stupid situation."

He snorted and rolled his eyes. A retort would have followed, but the front door opened again, and two men stumbled into the lobby.

"Tessie! Love! I haven't seen your sexy ass in ages!"

"Dude! You didn't say your sister was coming!"

Mike Stewart—or Mikey to those who put up with him—and Jonah Henley dropped their black equipment bags on a nearby bench and headed over to the small group. Tess suffered through affectionate, but brotherly hugs from the two nerd-geeks her brother had called friends since high school.

Mikey was the epitome of a technology nerd without being a gazillionaire. With a degree in electrical engineering and robotics, the guy was crazy smart, but Tess wasn't sure if the poor guy would know his left from his right at any given moment.

Jonah, on the other hand, was a quiet catastrophe waiting to happen. He was the cameraman-extraordinaire in life and on the investigations. He worked for a news station, driving a news truck around with a reporter. His specialties included anything involving a death wish, and he was frequently hauled out of the path of on-coming trains or tornados.

Laz shooed his partners away from her and made introductions. The guys were impressed by the presence of a Texas Ranger.

"Wow, you're like a badass and shit." Jonah didn't say much, accustomed to not talking while behind the camera, but when he did speak, it was highly intellectual and riveting conversation. Except in the presence of greatness. Then he turned into an overgrown twelve-year-old.

Crock didn't bat an eyelash. He simply nodded. "And shit."

"Can we *please* grow up?" Laz glared at his cameraman before returning to his all-business mode again, "This is Mary Dunham, the hotel manager. I'm sure she'd like to go home sometime this century."

Mrs. Dunham was a tiny woman with a big smile. "It's quite all right. I've got a couple of boys at home. I don't really want to see what they're up to right now, but I might need to borrow Sergeant Ward to help straighten them out."

"Any time, ma'am."

Tess suspected the Ranger enjoyed straightening out errant boys of all ages. If he could talk them into being responsible human beings at a younger age, then he might not have to throw them in jail later. She wondered if Crock could straighten out Gram and Tila; if so, it would be one more reason to like him.

At Crock's request, Mary told her story. She hadn't worked for the hotel at the time of Mrs. Green's murder, but she had gotten to know Dr. Green well. He had had a standing reservation for room twenty-seven every Halloween night, only to check out the next morning in good spirits.

The manager described the elderly man as sweet and endearing, but sad. Each year, Mary had a cup of black coffee and a cream cheese danish pastry ready for him at check-out. He would tell her stories of his wife while they sipped their drinks and enjoyed breakfast.

"It broke my heart to hear him talk about her. Esme was the love of his life," Mary lamented, wiping a tear from her eye. "About three years ago, I told him the hotel was struggling and might close. He was upset about it, but there wasn't much he could do."

Tess spoke up. "But the hotel is still open."

"Yes, we are." Mary gave a weak smile. "We had an anonymous benefactor who filed for historical status and grants. There were enough funds to get the hotel out of debt and to do some repairs. We were concerned when a new owner took over a few months before Dr. Green's last visit, but nothing has come of it. In fact," Mary added, "we've not heard from them at all."

Laz's eyes met Tess's, and she was forced to stifle a laugh. She recognized the look on her brother's face, having been the cause of his frustration and irritation on more than one occasion. First, he was working with a Ranger, an entity for which he had a not-so-secret fascination. Second, she'd shown up without his permission—because her following his orders was never going to happen. And third, he was getting more information than he liked to have about a case from the well-meaning manager.

A glance at Crock showed him making a notation in his pocket notebook. Further investigation would probably reveal the anonymous benefactor as a certain Dr. Daniel Green.

Tess wasn't surprised when Laz motioned to Mikey and Jonah, who grabbed their bags and headed for the elevator.

"Thanks, Mrs. Dunham. I think the guys and I will head upstairs and begin our set-up," Laz cut in before the manager could get going again. He turned to Tess. "Are you coming?"

Nope. I'm staying with the cute Ranger.

She gave him a nod. "Yeah, I'll be up in a minute."

He eyed her but didn't say anything. She knew why—once upon a time, she hadn't wanted to listen to the stories associated with the investigation either.

Not anymore. She didn't like surprises. Apparently, Crock felt the same way.

"We didn't get to speak when I came by last week, Mrs. Dunham. It's my understanding that Dr. Green died here, is that correct?" Crock prompted, steering the conversation back to his case.

"Yes," she said, "he didn't look well when he arrived—he was a little pale. I waited for him the next morning, but he didn't come down. I sent our housekeeper to check on him. She found him lying on the bed, but he was already gone."

Crock was quiet for a moment before asking, "Your staff mentioned having some...*disturbances*?"

Mary grinned at him. “Well, our housekeeper claims there is funny business on the second floor, and our maintenance man isn’t fond of the basement and the back stairwell. He says there are big spiders and snakes downstairs. Personally, I think he got ahold of some bad drugs while he was down there.”

Crock raised his eyebrow. “Do I need to have a word with him, as well?”

“Would you, please?” Mary gazed at him with hopeful eyes. “Charles is a good kid but could use a little incentive to do better.”

“Just point me in his direction.” Crock settled into his means-business stance, which Tess was learning wasn’t much different from his waiting-for-someone-to-do-something-stupid stance.

“Uhm…I guess I’ll go supervise the geeks while you’re making him crap himself?” Tess fought to keep her amusement under wraps. Just what Laz needed—the investigation of his career and a possible drug bust.

Laz is going to have kittens.

Poor Laz would have to get over himself.

Chapter Ten

On one hand, Laz was thrilled to have his sister at his back. She was good at what she did. But—and it was a huge *but*—he did not want a repeat of the last investigation they'd done together. The repercussions weren't worth it.

The memory of his fearless twin and her screaming still woke him at night, sweating buckets and in a full-blown panic. Unfortunately, his twin-dar had never distinguished the difference between the nightmare and any new threat Tess might be under while in the military. His creative mind had conjured too many gruesome scenarios.

Unlike many families who knew how and where their loved ones were serving, his sister had kept her family in the dark. He also knew she'd blocked much of their telepathy which had terrified him more than he liked to admit. He'd lived in constant fear of a knock on the door by a delegation of US Army officers reporting his sister's death.

He shoved the memories back, praying that this time would be different. This time, they weren't investigating the lair of a jacked-up serial killer. This was nothing more than a run-of-the-mill case of a husband and wife who'd died in the same hotel. Except the wife's death was suspicious. And the case was unsolved. But he'd known the husband. This shouldn't be a big deal. *Should it?*

As usual, he didn't tell his team much about their investigation to keep the findings unbiased. He followed his team to the second floor, then down the narrow hallway to the room where they would set up a command center. To his surprise, Tess and Crock arrived with Mary before the guys finished unloading their equipment. He dumped his backpack and followed the manager to room twenty-seven.

"Here you go." Mrs. Dunham opened the door. "We don't have many guests right now, so we were able to keep this floor and the third floor open, like you requested."

Laz was relieved. There had been a question whether they could even have an investigation. While not busy, the hotel did have a few rooms booked for the night, and the manager was reluctant to cancel the reservations. Having two floors free of wandering guests was the best they could hope for. The only contamination might be the night staff and the activity on the first floor.

"Thank you, ma'am. We'll holler if we need anything."

He glanced around, taking in the room's layout. It was a typical, small hotel set-up with a queen-sized bed and a nightstand on either side. A tiny writing desk and chair had been shoved into the corner next to the token window. A cramped bathroom and miniscule closet separated the sleeping area from the entry.

"Okay, while Mikey and Jonah work their magic, go check the rest of the rooms for potential contamination." Laz knew he could trust his friends to set up the cameras and the command center to capture the most evidence with the fewest blind spots and minimal interference. The windows needed to be covered to eliminate outside light anomalies. It was Laz's job to ensure there were no loose fixtures which might suddenly decide to jump off the wall or a lamp which might leap to its death from a side table.

The task gave him an opportunity to gauge the Crock's willingness to participate. And to check his sister's readiness for action. "Tess, can you…"

"I know what I'm doing, Laz." She headed toward the end of the hall, ready to check each room. "Don't fuss."

Well, okay then.

"Uhm…okay, Crock?" Laz turned his attention to the other man, who eyed him back.

"I don't need any fussing, either."

Thud!

Mikey poked his head into the hallway. "What was…oh, it's just you. Why are you banging your head on the wall? You'll scare off the ghosts."

Laz rested his forehead against the wall, pissed that he now had a headache. "Fish get scared by noise, Mikey. Or deer. Not ghosts."

"Huh? Fish get scared?" Mikey was already losing interest in the conversation. The great out-of-doors wasn't in his repertoire of small talk, especially when there was tech to set-up.

Laz pushed away from the wall in time to see his electronic technician vanish into the command center. He took a deep breath before turning to face the stoic Ranger. "Why don't we check the rooms down here?"

A nod was his only response. As he gave Crock a quick tutorial on what to check, Laz hoped the whole night wouldn't be the circus it was starting out as. He hadn't lost control of an investigation since—well, since Tess's last investigation.

"Tess!"

"What?"

Her voice came from near the stairwell. While Crock continued to check each room for security, Laz headed toward his sister. He found her in the small room that housed the vending and ice machines.

"Help me get these unplugged."

Laz breathed a sigh of relief. Trust Tess to think through any potential contaminant. The last thing they needed was an ice machine churning while trying to get a response from a spirit.

Together, they shoved the machines away from the wall. Since his arms were longer, he reached around to unplug the unit, finding and following the cord to the plug.

Zap!

"Son of a...shit, that hurt!" Laz yanked his hand back, shaking it, knowing that it did nothing to help the pain.

"Let me see." Tess grabbed his hand to check the injury. "What happened?"

He tried to draw away from her, but she held on with one hand and punched the button for some ice with the other. After placing a cube of ice on the reddened skin, she demanded again, "What'd you do?"

"Nothing!" he protested. "The cord must be frayed at the plug."

"Here, hold this." She shoved the ice into his hand, before peeking around the side of the machine. "Uh, Laz?"

"What?"

"The cord isn't frayed."

"What do you mean?"

Tess heaved an irritated sigh. "I mean, there's no exposed wire. In fact, the cord looks almost new."

"Is it grounded?"

She reached behind the unit.

"Wait!" He was too late.

Tess straightened, holding the plug in her hand. "Looks okay to me."

Laz took the cord offered to him. It was everything he could do to keep from yelling. His temper blew anyway. "What the hell, Tess! What if it'd shocked you, too? Or worse?"

She scoffed, lifting her foot. "I came prepared, jackass. See?"

He glanced down to find her thick, rubber-soled hiking boots. Then he looked at his own loafers with leather soles. "So…?"

Tess grabbed the plug from his hand and held it up. She was right—it looked brand new. "So…I think our hosts might be messing with us."

Their hosts. The ghosts.

Laz met his sister's dancing eyes with a glare. At least she was having fun. He had a job to do. A job which, if it went well, might cement his team a close partnership with the Texas Rangers. That and a much-needed book deal.

"Lighten up, Laz," Tess leaned close to whisper. "This is supposed to be fun. Not *work*."

Laz hated that she was right. They'd gotten into the business because it'd been cool. Something fun. He was trying to make it *work*, something they had agreed not to do. Ever. Because *work* was for *adults*.

Instead of admitting Tess was right, he smothered his laughter and said, "Come on, Tessie. Let's get this party started."

****

In late May, the Texas sun didn't set until around nine, leaving the evening hours to simmer with heat, humidity, and annoying mosquitos—all things Tess never expected to miss about Texas until she found herself in the parched depths of Hell with sand wedged in every crevice of her body. Still, it was nice to have the added daylight for setting-up.

But it was boring to wait for darkness to begin a paranormal investigation.

She wandered the hall, double-checking each room for anything they might have missed. Not surprisingly, Laz paced the hall, right behind her, quadruple-checking.

Crock leaned casually against the wall, watching them in his cool, detached manner. Nothing showed to reveal his thoughts. Tess was accustomed to full-scale, blow-out arguments with her brother, and her education and military career had taught her to read people, so the fact that she couldn't make out what this gorgeous man was thinking drove her insane. It would be a personal challenge to get this man to crack a smile. Or a smirk. Even a raised eyebrow would indicate basic humanoid behavior instead of plastic aloofness.

She turned her attention back to her mental checklist. Everything seemed to be in order until she opened room twenty-seven. A gasp escaped her as the door swung open. Two men flanked her before the doorknob hit the wall.

"What's wrong?" Crock demanded, glancing around the room.

"Tess? What happened?" Laz's voice held more fear. He would know. He would understand.

Crock—not so much.

"Nothing," she stuttered, trying to turn her shaking tone into a laugh. "It's nothing. I just caught my reflection in the mirror. I thought someone had snuck in here."

It was a little lie—a good one. Really.

Except there was no mirror. She hoped her companions wouldn't notice.

Crock relaxed but his eyes stayed wary as his right hand dropped from the back of his belt to his side in what Tess recognized as a ready stance. An officer had easy access to his gun without appearing to be threatening by propping his gun hand behind his back.

Next to her, Laz tried to shrug off the tension which had his shoulders attached to his ears. Fortunately, he wouldn't demand answers until they couldn't be overheard. Besides, it would take a while to wrap her mind around what she'd seen. The glimpse into the room should have been nothing more than that. Seated on the bed, waiting, were a man and a woman holding hands, smiling at each other.

Laz proved his understanding and loyalty by suggesting, "Why don't you grab some water, Tess. We'll get started once it's good and dark outside."

Tess nodded, stepping back from the doorway. She needed a moment to catch her breath. The first, unexpected sighting always threw her. Laz would finish the inspection.

What she didn't expect was Crock to trail after her.

"Are you all right?"

"Yeah. I, uh—" she tried to think of what to say that wouldn't make her sound like a deranged idiot. "Investigations can get a little intense."

"And you're a little out of practice."

She knew he was guessing, but his tone sounded more like a statement. "Something like that."

He said nothing. Instead, he stretched a long, brawny arm around her to their cooler filled with water and sport drinks. One hand came back with a bottle of each. Tess was surprised when he handed her an orange-flavored drink. "You might need this. You're a little pale."

His bland observation made her realize she was trembling. *Huh.*

She'd avoided anything to do with the paranormal since she was eighteen. The Army hadn't allowed much time to consider what had happened, and she certainly wasn't going to bring *that* little item up to some military shrink. Not if she wanted to remain in the military. Which she had.

Until she hadn't. "Thanks."

Her shaking hands couldn't open the damn bottle. After a moment of fumbling, Crock relieved her of the challenge and cracked the seal.

Tess accepted the bottle and took a grateful swig. When half the liquid was gone, she held the cool plastic to her heated face.

"Are you going to be all right?"

"Yeah."

Crock made a noise that said he didn't believe her. "You know, you shouldn't lie to a law enforcement officer."

Her eyes flicked toward him, but his expression was as stoic as ever. A nervous chuckle escaped her. “Am I under oath?”

“With me? Always.”

Is he…flirting with me?

Before she could contemplate a suitable response, Mikey displayed his impeccable timing and poked his head into the room. “It’s about time to start. Everything’s ready.”

“Coming.” Tess turned to leave, but Crock grabbed her by the wrist. The heat of his hand warmed her to the bone. She stopped, blinking up at him. “What?”

He said nothing for a moment. He simply studied her. “Will you be okay tonight?” he finally asked. “I know a little of what can happen, and I don’t want anyone at risk. I can work this case from another angle if I need to.”

Tess wondered if he was always concerned about involving others in his investigations, or if he was somehow concerned for her. “I’ll be fine. Thanks for caring.”

He held her back for a few more moments, his intent gaze capturing hers. Then he gave a curt nod and released her hand. “Then, let’s get to it.”

Chapter Eleven

Crock watched Tess return to the command center, trying *not* to focus on her jean-clad ass and form-hugging, Army T-shirt. Watching her dark ponytail swing against her shoulders didn't help much either. She was attractive, with the looks and the intelligent sassiness that he really liked. He'd have to work overtime to keep things professional.

Maintaining a safe distance, he followed. The tech nerds were happily checking their gear and chatting about audio equipment. At least it was a conversation he could understand—his dad had been into electronics. He was surprised when Tess offered her opinion on handheld devices and the geeks seemed to respect it.

He wondered, yet again, what this woman was hiding. He'd seen enough to recognize the traits of PTSD. If his suspicions were correct, she'd had issues prior to the military. The military would have only intensified her symptoms depending on her experiences in the field. The last thing this investigation needed was a full-on, freak-out from a woman who knew her way around guns. Perhaps that was why Laz was so nervous about her presence. The man was almost maniacal over his sister's involvement.

It wouldn't be difficult to keep a close eye on the twins. This investigative process intrigued him. It paralleled his experience in crime investigation, but it was the paranormal element that he didn't comprehend. At this point, he didn't have the questions to ask, but one person might be the key to his understanding, and he planned to stick close to her.

He watched Tess hook up her audio and asked Mikey to do a sound check. Then Crock followed her as she went in search of Laz to discuss their approach to interrogating the lampshades—uh…ghosts. Since the duo operated as a unit, Crock decided that's where he'd torture—station—himself.

"What can I do to help?"

Two dark heads with matching dark eyes rose to meet his. Laz glanced at Tess, who shrugged at the silent communication.

"You can operate the thermal," Laz answered, reaching into his back pocket to extract a small, hand-held device which looked like a little radar gun. "You watch for temperature changes here," he pointed to the read-out. "The room temp is set at sixty-eight degrees, but if you see a change, let me know. We'll need to see if you're standing below a fan or getting a draft from a window."

Crock nodded. Since there was no ceiling fan, and the curtains didn't flutter from any breezy vent, that type of interference could be ruled out. The reading was clearly sixty-eight with no fluctuation. He'd seen something like this on a TV show. It didn't seem like rocket science. "What else?"

He noticed Tess had turned away, fiddling with her gadget. She was letting Laz lead the investigation, although Crock suspected she would be equally responsible for any findings. If his attention hadn't been drawn to Tess, he would have missed the small ball of light buzzing around her head.

He'd seen something similar on the night he got shot, but he hadn't given it further thought. He glanced at the others. Neither twin seemed to notice.

Laz remained all business. "We don't know what we'll find, so questioning might be random at first. If Tess or I get something we can work with, I'll get you to ask a few questions. Otherwise, keep your eyes and ears open, and be ready to see if anything needs to be debunked."

Without taking his eyes off Tess and the buzzing orb, he asked, "Like a moving light might be a lightning bug?"

Laz straightened in shock, before spinning around toward his sister. "Yeah, exactly like that. Where?"

"By Tess's ear."

"Tess, do you…?"

She froze, her eyes wide as they swung around and found the floating orb. "Maybe?"

"Shit!" Laz grabbed the thermal from Crock and pointed it at Tess. Crock leaned over his shoulder to see the read-out. The temperature had dropped to sixty-two but was rising.

Crock glanced at the ceiling. No ceiling fan, no air vent. Nothing to trigger a six degree drop in under two minutes. When he looked back at Tess, he saw no sign of a bug or dancing light. Whatever was there was now gone.

Tess was pale, much like she had been after the room check. Before Crock could ask about her, she turned and walked away. Laz's lips were little more than a tight, worried line.

Yeah. I'll be sticking close to these two.

"I assume she's had issues before," Crock prompted.

Laz looked like he wanted to deny the charge, but Crock gave his patented, no-bullshit glare. Instead, the historian heaved a sigh. "It's been a long time. She hasn't said anything in years."

"But she hasn't *done* anything like this in years, right?" Crock knew the answer before Laz gave a shrug. The man didn't know what his sister had seen in the Army. "So, what do I need to look out for?"

Laz pressed his fingers into his eyeballs. "Um, I guess, just keep an eye on her. If you notice anything weird, tell me."

"And if there's a problem?"

Laz's hand dropped, and he met Crock's steady gaze. "Then I'll get her out of here. Although," he hesitated, "I sure as hell don't want to call Gram to come and get her."

Crock let his raised eyebrow ask the question.

"You don't want to know."

As an investigator, he would need to know. From what he'd seen of the grandmother, the answer was no, he probably didn't *want* to know.

Chapter Twelve

"Do you want these, Laz?"

It was just after five when Laz shoved the last of his equipment into his pack. He turned to find Mikey holding two flash drives which held the data from the night's investigation. "Yeah, I'll take them. Thanks." He tucked the drives into the safety of his jeans pocket.

"Holler if you have any problems. See you—when?" Mikey looked like he was having a hard time staying awake, much less able to remember their meeting to analyze the findings.

"Tomorrow. I mean, today," Laz corrected himself, before providing the pertinent details, "Pizza and Corona o'clock."

"Got it. G'night." His equipment tech gave him a vague wave as he followed Jonah out the door without waiting for a reply. It was a Saturday. The pair needed to get some sleep but wouldn't miss an opportunity to review the night's findings over free junk food and cold beer.

Surprisingly, after its rocky beginning, the investigation had gone without incident. A few unexplained knocks and banging doors were typical. Crock had recorded several temperature drops, mostly in room twenty-seven. He, Tess, and Crock had asked questions, but received no audible responses. Overall, it had been a boring night as far as investigations went.

Hopefully, the recorders picked up usable material, otherwise the whole enterprise might be a bust.

Laz doubted the Smith's Crown Hotel was as haunted as advertised, but he still planned to research the history of the site.

He was fairly certain that Tess had experienced no action after that first encounter, and she hadn't been aware of the ball of light Crock had pointed out; however, any questions about what she'd seen would have to wait until Laz got her alone. Hopefully, she wouldn't blow the encounter off as nothing.

While he didn't share—and didn't particularly like—his sister's ability, her sensitivity to the dead was responsible for his own career and life's work.

Laz hoped Tess couldn't see how much he needed this investigation to work. The pressure to move from adjunct faculty to full-time kept him glued to his research. *Publish or perish* was a professor's mantra. He had a few books and several scholarly articles to his name, but more was expected. A collaboration with the Rangers had the potential to expand his work exponentially and achieve the credibility imperative to getting tenured. But—more importantly—this was his chance to make his work *mean* something. To make a contribution. To make his mentor proud.

"I think that's the last cable." Crock strode in and handed over an electrical cord which someone had missed. "What's next?"

Laz envied the man. He was dog-tired, but the Ranger looked like he was as fresh as he was the night before. "Nothing much. We'll meet this evening to sort through the videos and audio for evidence, then we'll go from there. If you'd care to watch, we'll be at our house around six-ish."

Crock rolled his broad shoulders to work out the kinks. "Sounds good. That'll give me a few hours of sleep and some time to catch up at home and the office. Can I bring anything?"

"Unless you want something fancier than beer and pizza, you're good."

A sleepy voice piped up from the corner. "Gram and Tila were making brownies when I left. There should be plenty."

Laz and Crock glanced at the woman tucked into a corner chair, half-asleep. The last time Laz had checked, his twin was snoozing in a huddle. The goosebumps on her arm made him cover her with a blanket. That was over half an hour ago, and he had heard nothing from her since.

Thank God.

No nightmares to explain to a Texas Ranger.

"Okay, then," Crock replied, rubbing his left leg. "I guess I'll see y'all later. Good night."

"Night." The twins chorused and watched as Crock left the room, leaving them to finish up. For the first time, Laz noticed a slight limp in the Ranger's gait.

It's none of my business.

Laz turned and studied Tess as she unraveled herself from the blanket and chair to stretch. Jealousy shot through him. He would have been stiff as a brick if he'd fallen asleep in the tiny armchair, yet Tess seemed to not have any issues. "Don't you have a crick in your neck?"

She twisted her head around. Laz was satisfied, hearing a few crackles. "Not too bad," she mumbled. "I'm used to catching sleep when and wherever I can.

Sorry about that."

"It's all right. We were done." Now that they were alone, he could ask, "What did you see?"

"Huh?"

Obviously, her brain wasn't firing on all cylinders yet. "Earlier. When we went into the room? I couldn't ask you because Crock all but glued himself to your side."

"Oh." She blinked a few times, trying to recall. "A man and a woman. Nothing scary. They sat on the bed, holding hands. They were cute."

Cute ghosts. Great. That'll look impressive on a report.

Laz sighed. "At least we know they're here."

Tess yawned. "We'd better get home. We can figure this out tomorrow."

"You mean today."

"Whatever. Did you plug the ice machine in?"

"Yeah," he said, "and I cleaned up the water on the floor."

Tess nodded. "No zap?"

Laz remembered his hand. "No zap."

The elevator was at the other end of the hall, so they decided to take the stairs. As they entered the stairwell, a chill shot through Laz's body.

"Did you feel that?" he asked.

Tess hesitated on the landing. "I felt—something."

"What do you think?"

"I think—" she shook her head to clear it "—that I need to be more alert to figure it out. Come on. I'll need you to drive."

She continued down the stairs, leaving Laz staring after her. Tess never let him drive her beloved jeep.

The chill settled in the base of his spine before dissipating into nothing. It was creepy, and Laz'd never experienced anything like it before. As he followed Tess, he made a mental note to research the phenomenon later.

****

Laz pulled out of the empty parking lot, quickly shifting through to the higher gears as he headed for the highway. He rarely drove a standard, so he wasn't surprised when Tess complained. "Easy on the stick! I don't want to replace the clutch anytime soon."

Laz ignored her. He knew why she was concerned. Without a steady job, every expense dipped into her savings. He wanted to reassure her, but that wouldn't change anything. He wasn't too far off from the same situation. Adjunct faculty and history were not high-dollar professions.

Hell, I still live with my grandmother.

He had opportunities to travel during the handful of years he'd played minor league baseball and while in college. The past several years had been spent closer to home. His sister had travelled to places he'd only read about. "Tess?"

"Hmmm?"

"You haven't talked much about the Army," he began. "I mean, when we talked last summer, you seemed happy and mentioned plans to re-up, but then…."

She remained quiet for a moment. He was afraid she wouldn't answer. "Yeah, I know."

He waited. And waited. Nothing. "Tess, I…"

"Look, I did what had to be done, but I can't talk about it."

Laz barely caught his twin's whisper. He could sense her fatigue and—something else. "I know some things are classified. I get it. But you're hurting. I just want to know why."

The passenger side remained quiet, but he felt the change. He suddenly wished he wasn't driving. That was an easy enough fix. Pulling the vehicle onto the shoulder, he shut off the engine and turned to face his sister. "Tessie?" he probed again.

Her face was turned away, her elbow propped against the window frame with one hand covering her mouth. Laz knew she was fighting tears.

Tears she would refuse to shed no matter what. He gave her time.

"I…uhm…" her voice shook. "I didn't know…."

He knew. Somehow, he knew. "A guy?"

She nodded, still refusing to look at him.

Laz unlatched his seat belt and hopped out of the jeep. He jogged around to her door, yanked it open, and hauled Tess into his arms. Stroking her hair, he mumbled what he hoped were soothing, but meaningful assurances. Her body trembled with the effort to hold back the tears she hadn't shed since their father's death. He had only one option—start talking. "I hooked up with Miranda while I was finishing my dissertation. I thought she was *the one*, you know? I couldn't wait for you to meet her."

Tess went still but said nothing. He kept going. "When she found out she was pregnant, I got really excited. Mom was pissed, though." He forced himself to chuckle. No one knew the details between him and Miranda. But if anyone needed to know, it was Tess. She would understand.

"Everything was good, until—well, I didn't realize she was drinking and doing drugs behind my back. I got scared when Tila was born a few weeks early. There was concern about drugs in her system and fetal alcohol syndrome, but all her tests came back fine. The doctors wanted her to stay in the NICU to gain weight. CPS got involved because of the drugs. I had to get tested and prove that I was responsible enough to get custody."

Laz paused to swallow the lump in his throat at the thought of what might have happened. "Miranda wanted nothing to do with a baby. By the time Tila was big enough to come home, Miranda was gone. I haven't seen her since."

Tess hugged him tightly but still said nothing.

He withheld a sigh. Heartache was something he understood. If he had nothing else, he had Tila.

And Tess had him.

Chapter Thirteen

"Get your lazy ass off my bed!"

Crock snapped his fingers to call the pit bull from its cozy nest in the middle of Crock's pillow. Whistling didn't work either. Not counting the bubble of drool coming from the dog's mouth, he got no response. Typical.

He was too exhausted to play games. "Damn dog."

It was almost ten in the morning by the time Crock dumped his pack on the bed. The snoring canine sprawled on his pillow refused to be disturbed. He swiped a hand over his weary face, scrubbing the scruff on his cheeks and chin. It reminded him just how long it'd been since he had been home.

Before he could do anything else, he forced himself to take care of business. Gemma wasn't staying with him at the moment, but that was no excuse for not securing his weapons and ammunition.

The uneven thump of his boots on the hardwood floors confirmed what he felt—he was dead tired, his leg ached, but his brain was wired. Sleep would have to wait until after one well-deserved beer, the breakfast burritos he'd picked up on the way home, and a few minutes of quiet relaxation listening to the ducks quack as they paddled around his pier. That should be sufficient to shut down his mental gears. And keep the eerie laughter that had haunted his dreams since his injury at bay.

After putting the weaponry in the gun safe in his home office, Crock headed back to the adjoining bedroom. As always, he passed his hand over the shadowbox by the door. This time, however, he didn't spare the energy to study his father's or his grandfather's legacies.

"Come on, Slug." Crock poked the dark blue-gray hide of his dog, but the seventy-pound lump still didn't budge. Slug was in for disappointment—the usual fight for the pillow would have to wait for another day. "I know you're not dead. Move."

Shoving the beast got an eyeball opened, but nothing else.

"Okay, fine. I guess you don't want food."

That did the trick. At the sound of the magic, four-letter, F-word, the dog shot off the bed and beat him to the kitchen in record time.

Moving at the slower pace his leg muscles demanded, Crock limped through the quiet halls of his home. It was unusual to have the house to himself, with no pressing crises, but he'd earned a little bit of peace.

Accompanied by the sound of inhaled dog food via slurping snorts, Crock grabbed two beers from the fridge and the takeout from the counter before wandering out to his sanctuary—the back porch overlooking a peaceful cove off Lake Grapevine. He pulled up his chair before spotting a worn pair of boots propped on the railing of his neighbor's back porch.

"Hey, Hell!" he called out as he parked his tired ass in the seat.

The boots shifted a bit as their owner, Jake Hellier—known to all as Hell—peered around the post.

"Whatzup, Crock?"

"Never heard that one before," Crock grunted at the other man's attempted twist on a cartoon classic. The man seemed to think his ongoing joke was funny. Of course, Crock spent an equal amount of time spinning the irony of Hell's name and his most frequently used curse word.

Shifting his seat so he could face the water and talk to Hell at the same time, Crock toed off his boots and cracked the knuckles of his toes with a satisfied groan. He propped his tired feet on *his* railing while Jake Hellier hoisted his carcass onto *his* railing so they could catch up.

"Jeez!" Hell complained, "why didn't you warn me?"

"About?"

"Those feet, man! They smell like warm farts on a warthog."

Crock hid a grin as he slipped off one sweaty sock and chucked it at his friend, who batted the innocent cotton into the backyard. "What are you doing that you know what a warthog's ass smells like? Getting friendly?"

A middle finger was his only answer.

There was a truce while each man sucked on their respective drinks.

Hell finally broke the silence. "Where's Gemma?"

"I think Mom took her shopping." Crock answered, rummaging in the bag to pull out a bacon and egg burrito the size of his head. He peeled the foil away, dipped the end of the folded tortilla in a container of salsa, and inhaled a sizeable chunk of heaven.

"So, you're batching it today?"

"Guess so," he mumbled around the spicy breakfast goodness.

"You got any more of that artery-clogging shit?"

Crock didn't stop chewing as he reached back into the bag for the chorizo and egg burrito that Hell lusted over. He threw the foil torpedo to his friend.

"And it's still warm!" Hell crowed.

"That'll cost you extra."

"Put it on my tab."

Nothing was said for several minutes while the two men stuffed their faces.

Swallowing the last morsel, Hell broke the quiet, "Wrangled any cattle rustlers lately?"

Crock smirked at the obligatory work inquiry before answering, "Nah. How many kittens did you rescue from a tree today?"

"Hey! Those little old ladies make damn good cookies." Hell wadded his trash and aimed for a trash bin off the side of his deck. He missed. "The cats are a little less appreciative, though."

Crock snorted. "The cats can get their own asses down from the tree. As for the little old ladies, they just like watching a fireman's ass go up a ladder."

Hell laughed. "True that. So, how's the leg?" his tone turning somewhat serious. His friend had helped with Gemma and his mom while Crock was laid up. "Is it holding up against all the trials and tribulations of Ranger-hood?"

A groan escaped before Crock could catch it. "It's doing okay. I sure as hell couldn't get up a damn ladder yet."

Although it sucks sweaty donkey balls if I can't even get up a set of stairs without hanging on to the railing. Crock kept his whining to himself.

"Good thing you don't have to."

The door creaked behind him followed by the click of claws on wood, announcing the arrival of Slug. The dog heaved a sigh as he plopped down on the deck beside him. A loud belch coincided with a noxious fart.

"Ah, shit! Slug!" Crock sputtered and gagged. Slug gave him the innocent gaze of the guilty. "Gemma's been feeding you her beans again, hasn't she?"

It took a minute for Hell to stop laughing while Crock tossed a rubber bone into the yard. Slug wasn't interested.

"It's been a while since I've seen you. Got any interesting cases?" Hell asked, still snorting. He was always curious about Crock's cases. A dozen years older than Crock, the man had started a career in law enforcement before transitioning to the fire department. The combined certifications made for a professional who could interact on both sides of an arson investigation.

Jake had seen a thing or two over his thirty-plus years in the business. That experience had become a resource that Crock valued and didn't hesitate to exploit.

"Captain saddled me with a cold case."

"Well, that oughta keep you out of trouble for a minute."

"You'd think, wouldn't you?" Visions of naked grandmas danced in his head as he emptied his beer and reached for another while simultaneously throwing a chew rope for Slug. The dog didn't care about the rope either.

"What kinda trouble can you get into going over

old files?" Hell demanded.

"Get out of there!" Crock pried Slug's nose out of the takeout bag which held his trash. Greasy foil and napkins weren't on the dog's high-priced diet. "The case isn't so different from the case that got me a mucked-up leg."

"Yeah?" Hell grunted, shifting his position on the rail. "Tracking a sick kidnapper and killer into an abandoned building is no different than solving a—what? Forty-year-old missing person?"

"A twenty-odd-year-old suspicious death." Crock hated to think about the investigation he had botched by shooting himself in the leg. The attention his injury received gave the suspect a chance to get away. His fellow officers were still hunting the asshole responsible for the disappearance of at least ten girls. He still had trouble swallowing his stupidity.

Instead of re-living the guilt, he tucked his garbage out of the way and grabbed Slug's squeaky rat. The dog's ears perked up at the sight of his favorite toy. Crock pitched it toward the pier, and the pit bull flew off the deck after it. The resulting squeaks startled the ducks, which stole the pit bull's attention. The ducks would keep the dog entertained for a minute or two, as long as his other neighbor's goose didn't get into the act. If that goose got riled up, Slug would likely wind up with a beak-shaped hole in his hide.

Watching Slug's antics, Crock casually asked, "Have you ever run across anything paranormal?"

"You mean ghosts and shit?"

"Yeah."

Hell didn't answer right away, but he seemed to give serious thought to his answer as he reached into the small cooler he kept by his chair. He took his time popping open the cap before saying, “There’ve been a few times when I didn’t have a good explanation for what happened.”

“Like…?” Crock prompted.

His neighbor’s graying, dark head thumped against the support post. “There have a been a few times—well, one time in particular—that I felt a presence. On the side of the road.”

“What happened?”

“We were cleaning up an accident out on 183. It was after midnight, one of those crashes where the idiot had too much tequila and went east instead of west at a hundred miles an hour. Anyway, I was walking around, cleaning up some debris, when I felt something shove me. I stumbled at the same time a pickup swerved around the engine.”

Hell stopped, his voice dropping to an emotional low. “Damn truck flipped over and would have crushed me if I hadn’t been pushed to the side.”

Crock felt a chill run down his spine. “When was this? What part of 183?”

Hell took a swig of his drink before answering. “It was about five years ago near Belt Line.”

The shiver turned to a frozen blast. *It can’t be.*

“You okay?”

Crock glanced up to find Hell watching him. “Yeah. I’m fine.”

“The hell you are.”

“Well, if you’re so sure I’m not, then why’d the hell did you ask?”

“Because I know you too well, son.” Hell set his half-empty bottle on the railing. “Isn’t that the area where your daddy died?"

"Yeah." Crock said nothing for a minute. "That was his territory."

"Thought so." Hell stretched his lean body but winced and grabbed his left shoulder.

"What's wrong with you?" Crock didn't mind pointing out the older man's weakness if it drew attention away from his father's death.

"Ah, I strained my shoulder the other day. I've got a few days to let it rest. It'll be fine." Unfortunately, Hell had other ideas about the direction of the conversation. "That'd be kinda crazy if your daddy's ghost kept me from getting flattened on the side of the road."

Crock didn't think it'd be crazy at all. It would be just like Samuel H. Ward to keep an eye on the stretch of road he'd protected for many years, first as an Irving police officer, then as a state trooper.

"I'm working with a paranormal team," he announced before Hell could say anything else.

Hell grunted, "Good luck with that."

"Why?" Crock liked to think he was open-minded and seeking answers to a cold case from a non-traditional source seemed like a great idea.

Hell chuckled, picking up his beer. "The dead can't exactly testify in court."

"No," Crock admitted, "but it can lead me in a direction that might have been missed in the original case."

Hell waved his bottle, encouraging Crock to keep talking about the investigation.

"It's been interesting. It's a brother-sister team. Twins. I spend half my time keeping them separated."

"What are they? Kids?"

At times.

"Nah, in fact the sister is pretty nice. Recently out of the Army, knows her firearms, and can take her brother down in a heartbeat." He didn't want to admit anything more—like the fact that he was interested. *Very* interested.

Hell snorted and proceeded to push his buttons. "Sounds like my kinda woman. Can I get an intro?"

"Sure. Right after I maim you for breaking Gemma's heart."

It was no secret that his baby sister had a major crush on Hell, and that Hell treated Gemma Rae like royalty. His neighbor was one of the few people Crock trusted to take over Gemma's guardianship if something happened to him.

Hell flipped him the bird while laughing. "You'd have to catch me first. I guarantee you'd lose with that leg of yours. So, what's a chick like that doing messing with ghosts?"

Taking a healthy swig of his brew, Crock wondered the same question. "I'm not positive, but I think she's got some abilities, but her brother doesn't seem to share them. I suspect that he started investigating when they were teenagers, trying to understand what she was seeing. It backfired on them, and she ran off to the Army."

"And now she's back and ready to prove herself," Hell finished. "Or she already did that in the Army?"

"Something like that," Crock agreed.

"So, what's ghost hunting like?"

"A whole lot of asking questions to an empty room in the middle of the night and hoping like hell that no one outright answers you back." Crock quickly filled him in on the previous day's investigation and findings.

"Have fun. It sounds like you've got your hands full."

"You can say that again."

Chapter Fourteen

"You are an idiot, Laz Corona." Tess cursed as she lunged for the pizza boxes plummeting to the floor. She missed the first one but snagged the second before it crashed. Not that it would matter—the pizza was ruined.

"Well, shit," Laz huffed, his elbow clinging to the remaining two boxes tucked sideways under one armpit. His other hand was occupied with a case of beer. "What was I supposed to do? Balance them on my head?" he groused as he headed to the kitchen.

Tess followed and dumped the boxes on the table. She rescued the remaining pizzas from her brother, praying that the one closest to his armpit wasn't hers.

"No, but you could have rung the doorbell. Or—here's a novel idea—put down the damn beer." Tess cautiously opened the box and groaned. Inside lay what was supposed to be a cheese pizza—except the cheese was supposed to be on the crust and not on the box top. "What a mess!"

Grumbling under her breath, she grabbed a knife and began scraping cheese off the box top, while Laz got busy loading the beer into the fridge.

Tess cringed as she cracked open the second box and found her favorite—pepperoni, green olive, and spinach—in an unappetizing, squashed mess. "How in the hell am I supposed to eat this?"

A spoon appeared in front of her, so close to her nose that Tess felt the tip graze the inside nose hair. “EWW! Gross! Get away from me, eejit.”

“So, y’all fight even without an audience? That’s good to know.” A deep voice came from the doorway.

Tess spun around to find Crock in his usual stance, with his usual stoic expression, leaning against the door frame, as usual.

Annoyed to have been embarrassed, yet again, in front of the man, she grabbed the offending spoon from her brother and tossed it into the dishwasher. “Oh…ah…hi! We didn’t hear you come in.”

An eyebrow lifted. “Your grandmother met me at the door. She looked like she was doing some kind of ritual around the porch. Never seen anything like it, but it smelled to high heaven.”

Tess sent a panicked look to her brother who was already moving toward the front door.

“I’m on it.” A shout cut through from the living room. “Gram! What’re you do—oh, shit! What’s the sulphur for?”

Tess could tell that discussion was *not* going to end well, so she did her best to distract the Ranger. “Uhm…okay. Would you…uh…how ‘bout a beer?’”

When in doubt, a little Texas hospitality went a long way.

His expression never changed. “Sure. I’m not on duty.”

She dug in the fridge, only to realize her dumbass brother had left the cold brews behind the newer, warmer bottles. Questioning her twin’s intelligence, Tess dug around until she found a cold one.

“We aren’t normally such nitwits,” she started.

"For some reason, our family loses its mind whenever you're around."

"I've noticed."

Nothing. He gave her *nothing* to work with. She felt like she needed to explain a little bit. "Well, uhm, Gram is an…*interesting* individual."

"I gathered that."

Tess gave up. She moved back to her chore of scraping cheese off the box top. In a weak attempt to be humorous, she said, "I hope you like your pizza in chunks."

Crock reached over to take the last box. "What happened to them?"

"The brilliant and talented Dr. Lazaro Corona strikes again."

"Ah."

Nothing more was said. Nothing more *could* be said.

A small voice intruded on the awkwardness. "Can I have pizza now?"

They turned to find Tila standing in the doorway. Although relieved to see the child fully clothed, Tess wasn't sure what she was seeing. "What are you wearing?"

The child simply shrugged. She appeared to have raided every closet in the house for today's ensemble: Tess's best red heels, Gram's floppy gardening hat, and her daddy's rattiest T-shirt. The depiction of ears of corn screaming and running away from a microwave popping popcorn was hilarious, but not what a small girl would wear as a dress. Tess could only hope her niece had underwear on but was thankful that her ass wasn't displayed for the world to see.

"Pizza," Tila demanded.

Tess returned the child's glare, waiting until Tila folded.

"Please?"

Tess removed a plastic plate from the cabinet and placed a small, mostly intact, slice of cheese pizza on the plate. Tila scowled at the appearance of a couple of carrots next to her pizza. A masculine throat cleared, silencing the protest before it began.

Smart kid.

Tila turned toward Crock and glared.

Not so smart kid.

"Go." Tess ordered, hoping to keep a three-year-old from smarting off to an officer—although jail time might do some good. "Eat. Maybe Grammy will read you a story."

The promise of a story did the trick. Tila flounced out of the room with a parting shot. "We're going to finish *Frankenstein*. Then we get to start *Dracula*."

Silence reigned until Crock spoke up, "Did she…?"

"Yeah."

"And your grandmother is…?"

"Yeah."

He was quiet for a moment. Then, "No wonder."

"Yeah."

Crock shook his head and grabbed an adult-sized plate from the stack on the table. Mikey and Jonah stumbled in after Laz, and soon the kitchen was brimming with testosterone, pizza, and beer.

Tess settled back. Her plan for the evening's entertainment was to ogle a cute, seemingly intelligent lawman—who filled out a pair of Levi's quite nicely—

and watch three idiots at work. At least one of the idiots thought it was work. She wasn't sure Mikey and Jonah believed in the paranormal; the geeks mainly liked to play with the equipment and see what they could get the technology to do.

As she'd suspected, nothing of interest came from the overnight investigation: a few unexplained bangs and creaks, a shut door later found open, and footsteps. Nothing that related to Crock's case.

Eventually, Mikey slipped into a two-beer stupor. It didn't take many times hanging out with the socially awkward techie to realize he had zero tolerance for alcohol. Crock helped Laz steer the stumbling drunk to a chair in the corner, supplied with a couple of bottles of water and a slice of his preferred veggie pizza.

"Why'd we get a vegetarian?" she asked. She didn't mind, but everyone else was a devout carnivore.

Laz detangled himself from Mikey, who was trying to kiss his food. "He says meat upsets his stomach."

Tess eyed the geek as he attempted to relocate the pizza into his mouth. "But he ate a buttload of tacos last week."

"Gram convinced him she made the taco meat out of cauliflower and spinach, with *mole* sauce to give it the meat color."

"Huh." *Kudos to Gram.* "So, any upset tummy because of too many tacos?"

Laz loaded his empty plate with the last piece of meat-lover's. "He didn't complain about anything. He's a freaking hypochondriac. He thinks it makes the woman more sympathetic."

Tess snorted. "Does it work?"

"Nope. Dude hasn't had a date in years."

"And what if he actually has an issue with beef?" Crock, ever the voice of reason and caution, wanted to know.

Laz shrugged. "He eats anything and everything when he's over here and has never had a problem. If he did, Gram would fix him up with one of her remedies."

The discussion was heading into dangerous territory. Gram used herbs and oils for her concoctions. As a practicing Native American healer and medicine woman, among other practices, she could treat physical and spiritual ailments in any manner she chose. Some methods were shadier than others. Tess decided it was time to change the subject before Crock asked too many questions that might get him hexed.

Before she could say anything, Jonah piped up for the first time all evening. "Hey, check this out."

The trio gathered around the cameraman. They'd already gone through the video once, but Jonah was doing a second sweep. On the screen, Tess saw herself standing in the doorway of room twenty-seven.

"That's the corner camera?" Crock asked.

"Yeah. I mean," Jonah stuttered, "yes, sir." He wasn't used to talking to anyone, much less a Ranger.

Nothing further was said as they watched the video. Jonah froze the feed and pointed. "See? There."

It took a couple of reviews to see the anomaly. Exactly where Tess had seen the couple sitting on the bed, a wave of white mist brushed by the screen. The entire clip lasted less than a second and was easily missed the first time. It became hard to breathe. Confirmation of what she'd seen was rare, even if it was faint.

"I don't get it," Crock said. "What am I looking

at?"

No one answered right away.

"That haze, right there." Laz pointed to the screen. While Crock studied the spot, Laz turned to Tess. "Is that where you saw them?"

The Ranger glanced up, his eyes narrowed. "Saw who?"

Tess remembered that Crock had left before her conversation with Laz. She briefed Crock on the sighting.

Crock studied the video again. "That's promising, right?"

Laz answered for her. "Yeah, but they didn't say anything. We'll have to find a way to build trust. They might communicate with us then."

"I was thinking," Tess waited until both men turned their attention to her. "We could probably do a session at the graveside. Do we know where they are buried? Or were they cremated?"

Crock thought for a moment. "I'll have to double-check where they're buried. If you can give me a day, I'll get the information on Monday morning, and we can head there in the afternoon."

Laz piped up, "I've got meetings on Monday. And I need to research the history of the hotel. The manager mentioned some other deaths."

Tess shrugged. "That doesn't keep me from going." Ignoring her twin's annoyed look, she turned back to Crock. "That'll work."

For Monday. Tomorrow is another story.

Tess's brain plotted while she agreed to Crock's plan. What he didn't know wouldn't hurt him.

The sooner they got answers, the sooner the sweet couple could rest.

Chapter Fifteen

Tessie sat up and looked around the room. She didn't know what woke her, but she was scared. It was quiet and dark, except for a tiny bit of light that came from the window. Enough to make the tree outside put creepy shadows on the wall. Daddy said the tree and moon played at night to give her silly pictures when she couldn't sleep.

Mommy didn't like that story. Tessie had heard Mommy and Daddy fight over it.

Lazzie was asleep in his bed, tucked in with his stuffed monkey. Mommy wanted her to act like a big girl, and big girls didn't cry or wake up their bubba or anyone else in the house when they got scared.

She shivered. Cold air blew from the fan, but her hair was sticky and wet. Searching around, she found her pink blanket and Teddy across the room. Tessie wondered if she'd thrown the bear in her dream. She didn't remember the dream, but Opa said that he didn't always remember his dreams either, so that was okay.

Tessie checked the floor for monsters before sliding out of bed. She didn't want to get caught. Mommy would be mad and yell at her. Quietly, she crept over to Teddy and picked him up.

A squeal startled her. Tessie hid her face in Teddy's tummy and bit his soft fuzz to hold back a scream. She froze, afraid to move, then slowly lifted her head and turned to see what was there. The only thing she saw was the tree outside scraping the window. The creepy shadows waved on the wall.

Silly pictures.

Mommy would say it was the wind.

Tessie studied the window and the tree, willing it to make the noise again. Just so she could be sure. She could hear the wind. It whistled. She would have to ask Daddy how the wind could whistle if it didn't have lips. He would know. He knew almost as much as Grammy.

The tree bumped against the window, making the same noise. She relaxed, relieved to know the noises were only from a tree. Mommy might be proud that she had figured it out on her own.

But Tessie couldn't tell Mommy. She'd get in trouble.

With a hug for Teddy, Tessie turned back to her bed.

And screamed.

Tess woke with a strangled gasp. The sheet was tangled around her legs and soaked with sweat and tears. Her nightshirt was also dripping wet. Goose bumps rose on her skin as she slowly recognized the familiar hum of the ceiling fan. Shivers caused by the cold air blowing on her drenched body and the shocking return of an old nightmare drove her from the bed to turn off the fan.

With the motor silenced—*blessed silence*—she slumped against the wall, eyes closed, and drew an unsteady breath. It'd been years since that dream had disturbed her. In the Army, she'd stayed focused on her work and education to the point of exhaustion. Dreams—and her curse—didn't bother her as much.

This one must have been triggered by last night's investigation.

She opened her eyes when she felt steadier and glanced around. The clock told her that she'd been asleep for only a couple of hours. The room was lit by the full moon peeking through her blinds, highlighting the orderly clutter. Unlike the room she had shared with Laz at the age of four, no one else was responsible for cleaning her room. Her commanding officer wouldn't be impressed. The pile of clean, folded clothes on the chair patiently waited to be hung in the closet. Books were stacked on the bedside table. The one she'd been reading when she fell asleep was partially tucked under her pillow.

Teddy was on the floor. Again.

Tess never knew how her old bear found his way from her bed or nightstand to the floor, but it was a frequent enough event that she didn't worry about it.

Not anymore.

Gathering her wits, she stumbled to the small, Jack-and-Jill bathroom that she shared with Tila, washed her face, and pulled out a clean T-shirt from her dresser. After a brief check to make sure she hadn't disturbed her niece, Tess changed the sheets on her bed. Her ability to move quickly and not wake the household had been perfected over many years. It was another lesson she'd learned from an early age and honed by the military.

Thanks, Mom.

A tap on the door proved there was one who would always know what she tried to hide. Tess wasn't surprised to find a sleepy Laz braced against the doorframe. His dark hair stood in random spikes all over his head. It wasn't his best look.

"It's nothing, Laz. Go back to bed."

"What do you mean 'it's nothing'? The hell it is. You haven't had a nightmare since you've been back."

If it wasn't the middle of the night, he might have been yelling. The whisper-shout mixed with his I-just-woke-up-and-my-vocal-cords-are-still-snoring voice. Not a good combination in her not-so-humble opinion.

"Go back to bed, Laz."

"Shit, Tess. You remember how those dreams hit me. What was this one about?"

Yeah, she knew. It was part of their weird twin-dar. While he couldn't experience the dream, her twin felt the fear and anxiety coming from her. And he didn't like it. Not one bit. Which was why she'd tried to block the connection to keep him from worrying.

She considered lying, but he would know. "It was the old house."

"Our room?" Too many real nightmares had happened in their parents' old home. Laz always wanted clarification.

"Yeah. The shadows."

It had been more than shadows. It was a warning.

Laz was quiet for a moment. If his eyes weren't searching the room for the dangers he couldn't see, she would have thought he'd gone back to sleep standing in her doorway.

"Ted's on the floor."

"Yeah. I'll get him." There wasn't much else to say. Tess felt his regret for letting her back on the team. "It's not your fault, Lazzie. I want to help out."

His hand ran through his messy hair before he pushed away from the frame. "I know, Tessie. I just...."

She knew. They both would change a lot of things if they could. And there was only so much she could share with him. With anyone.

As if he could read her mind, Laz asked, "You saw some stuff in the Army, didn't you?"

Her jaw clenched, as it usually did when asked about her military experience. There were too many things she didn't want to relive, even for her twin. Swallowing hard, she shrugged off his concern as she bit out, "Some."

If she thought he would let it go, she was sadly mistaken.

"I want to help you, Tessie. I can listen if you need to talk. No judgements," he promised. "I'm here for you if you need me."

The tightness of her throat threatened to choke her. "I know, Lazzie." It took a moment to regain control. "Go on back to bed. I'm good."

A long, tanned arm reach out and snagged her around the neck. The quick embrace was reassuring. They might fight like twins, but they loved each other fiercely and didn't want the other to feel alone in their suffering.

"You're going back?" He pulled back to meet her eyes but kept his hands on her shoulders.

She hesitated. "I need to go to their gravesite, but yes, I'm going back to the hotel."

"Okay, I'll go…"

"No." Tess stepped back, looked him in the eye.

"But…"

She cut off his protest. "I'll be fine. It's just two ghosts, and they'll be more willing to talk without an audience."

Laz didn't like it, but tough. "You'll call me before you go over?"

"I can do that."

He grunted, "You'd better."

"Or else?" she tried to lighten the tension by teasing him.

It worked. "Or else I'll sic the law on you."

Tess didn't tell him that wasn't a threat in her book. Instead, she gave him a grin.

"Night, Tessie."

"Night, Lazzie."

Life was good when they let down their guard and called each other by their childhood nicknames.

She closed the door on his retreating backside before retrieving Teddy from the floor. Tess put him in his place on the second pillow on the bed. Checking the room, Tess convinced herself that nothing was wrong but muttered a quick prayer of protection anyway before crawling into bed. She was strong—stronger than before—but she couldn't take any chances.

Not with her history.

This time, she couldn't run.

Chapter Sixteen

Crock sucked on a coke while waiting for the inevitable. This was not how he planned to spend a Sunday afternoon, but he fully expected one sexy ghost-hunter to make an appearance.

From what Laz had said, the family went to church and lunch every week under threat of God's and Gram's wrath—with the greater threat coming from the matriarch of the family. Afterward, Laz usually planned to spend time with his daughter, leaving his grandmother and sister to their own devices.

In other words, up to no good.

Thank God, there was a fast-food restaurant across the street from the hotel. Sure enough, after the last fry and before the last slurp, a familiar all-terrain convertible pulled into the hotel's parking lot.

From his vantage point inside the iconic fast-food joint, he watched Tess Corona hop out and head into the little hotel with an overnight bag in hand. His gut was on target. Again. After she'd tried to hide her little freak-out session in the hotel, followed by video confirmation of whatever she'd seen, he'd known she would come back. She couldn't *not* come back.

He took his time wiping the salt and grease from his fingers. After depositing his trash in the waste bin, Crock fished the keys from his pocket and strode out to his truck. He drove across the street to the hotel where he had a brief conversation with Mary who eagerly gave him the information he already knew. He headed down a familiar hallway.

Crock ignored the plastic *Do Not Disturb* sign on Room 27 and banged on the door. A loud *thump* was immediately followed by creative cursing.

It must be a family trait.

"Uh…who's there?" The female voice on the other side of the door sounded wary.

"The Easter Bunny. Open up." He counted to four before he heard the latch turn. "Sunday is supposed to be a day of rest," he snarled when she cracked open the door. "What in the hell are you doing?"

Tess stared at him. He could only image what she was seeing. Probably one pissed-off Texas Ranger. She also didn't seem surprised to see him. Or, more likely, she expected *someone* to follow her.

"I'm following up on a theory." Her tone sounded official, but she acted like some guilt-ridden kid trying to hide her drug stash. "And if you're the Easter Bunny, where's my chocolate rabbit?"

Crock grunted before pushing his way into the room. He ignored her last comment. "What kind of theory?"

"That's on a need-to-know basis."

Bravo, sweetheart! He raised his eyebrows with his patented do-you-really-want-to-go-there-'cause-I-can-pull-out-the-handcuffs look.

He was a little disappointed when she didn't respond to his challenge. Instead, she checked the hall—probably for her brother—before closing the door.

"Well?"

"I…uhm…" Tess looked like she was searching for a plausible excuse. He wasn't having any of that bullshit.

"Do you want to dig that hole deeper? Or should I tell you what you're up to?"

"Sure, go ahead." She crossed her arms over her breasts.

He stared at her. Tess straightened, set her hands on her jean-covered hips, and glared back.

Stifling a snort, Crock laid out his suspicions, "Here's what I know—you used to run audio to Laz's video. You were incredibly successful because you can hear the spirits and have an actual conversation with them. Judging from your reaction the other night, you probably see them as well. You ran off to spend a decade as Uncle Sam's good, little minion because one of the little darlings spooked you."

Tess gaped at him like a hooked fish. He must be pretty warm.

Crock gave her a second to tell her side. When she remained silent, he kept going, "I don't have a problem with you having extrasensory skills, or whatever the hell you call it, but I'm not letting *anyone* go rogue on *my* investigation. You keep me in the loop, or we are going to have a major problem. Got it?" He gave her his best impression of a drill sergeant.

The military minion in her snapped to attention. "Yes, sir!"

"At ease, soldier."

Damn, she's cute. He refused to let his expression show his amusement. "Now, how close was I?"

"Uhm…" she hesitated. Based on what he'd seen with her brother, Crock was certain that Laz didn't even know all the details. “Maybe sixty-four percent. I…”

She was interrupted by pounding on the door. Crock knew who it was but was prepared in case it wasn’t. His right hand slipped behind his back by habit as he checked the peephole. Sure enough….

“Dammit, Tess! You were supposed to call me.”

Crock relaxed at the sound of a familiar, but furious, yell. He raised an eyebrow at her before opening the door, moving out of the way as her brother stormed into the tiny room. “What in the hell are you thinking?” Laz demanded.

Tess squared up her five-nine to face the six-foot-one-inches of her twin’s fury. “I tried to call you…”

“Bullshit!”

“…and I guess your phone was turned off.”

“That’s a load of crap!” Laz yanked his phone from his pocket. “See, it’s—well, shit.”

Tess smirked. “Way to go, Einstein. You forgot to charge your phone, again.” She waltzed over to her pack on the bed and unzipped a side pocket, pulling out a charging cable. “Here.”

Laz was grumbling in several languages as he plugged in and waited for the phone to restart.

Crock was impressed—at least Tess gave the appearance of trying not to gloat. Her effort was worth a few points in his book.

“See! I did so try to call you.”

And there went the points. Laz growled some more—this time, a murder-and-mayhem glare was involved.

“Okay, that’s enough, you two. I’m not here to referee your teenage spats.” Crock perched on the corner of the desk, effectively putting an end to the argument. "Tess was just about to tell me about why she high tailed it to the Army after something went wrong with one of your investigations. And," he added, turning to her, "how in the hell did you come up with sixty-four percent?"

He didn't get an answer.

The grumpiness vanished from Laz's face to be replaced by guilt. "It was my fault…."

"The hell it was!" Tess fumed.

Crock pressed his fingers into his eye sockets. He understood the brother's sense of responsibility—he had plenty of his own when it came to his sister—but Tess was a grown woman who knew what she was doing.

Thankfully, she hurried to tell her story before he tried to stab himself with a pen. "You're right. I *can* hear ghosts. Sometimes I can see them. We were investigating an old house in Weatherford. It wasn't anything fancy—a serial killer had lived there and buried the bodies in and around the carport—but *something* was there, and it didn't like me. That's about all there is to it."

Crock lowered his hand from his eyes to stare at her. His eyes slowly travelled over to Laz who didn't look happy. "That's it?" he asked with more than a little bit of disbelief.

"Uh, yeah."

He hadn't expected her to share everything. But that was a bit less than he'd expected. He wondered if she understood what happened. Or worse, she'd repressed it.

That could get ugly if left to fester.

Crock resumed his usual stance: arms folded, legs

spread, no-nonsense gaze focused on his target. This time, he aimed his laser beams at Laz. "And…?"

"I told you…" Tess started to protest.

Crock shot back. "You had your chance. Now, it's his turn,"

With a huff, she plopped down on the corner of the bed. He halfway expected her to stick out her tongue.

Laz didn't answer right away, but finally admitted with a defeated shrug, "That's all she's ever told me about it."

"And you bought it?" No response followed. "Look. I've seen the two of you work together and argue until I want to shoot one or both of you. Y'all have some kind of psychic communication thing that I don't understand, but I've seen with twins before. So, let's spill your guts, then we can get this show on the road."

Crock stared at the glowering pair, daring them to keep messing with his mind. He had a case to work and working with paranormal investigators was already raising a few eyebrows. The sooner they got their shit together, the sooner he could get the answers he needed.

"We call it our twin-dar." Laz broke first. "I don't get more than a sense of how she's feeling. If she's happy or sad or scared, I'm aware of it. If she's hurt, I know about it."

He'd expected more than that. Crock nodded his understanding. "And when she senses a spirit? Do you get that as well?"

Laz pushed away from the wall that he was holding up. "I'll get a chill or feel something brush by, but I can't hear or see what she does."

Crock studied his boots, thinking. "What did you feel during that last investigation? The one before she left town?"

Shoving his hands in his pockets, Laz glanced at her before speaking, "She was terrified. Something happened, but I couldn't tell what. It felt evil."

"Any guesses as to what that evil was?"

"My guess would be a shadow person," Laz admitted.

Crock felt like he was finally getting somewhere. He'd heard of shadow people before but didn't remember where and wasn't exactly sure what they were. That was a question for later. "Then what happened?"

"Then she shut me out."

Crock could see that being excluded was more painful for Laz than whatever evil he'd sensed. "Is she shutting you out now?"

Laz stared at his sister. "She's trying to."

"It's not you, Lazzie," Tess whispered, anguish lacing her words.

"I know, Tessie."

Crock was reaching his limit for family dramatics, heart-warming or not. "Okay, then, moving on. Tess, was it a shadow person?"

She passed her hand over her face. "I guess…I think so, but there was something else. I don't know what it was."

"Any guesses?"

Her head moved side-to-side. "I don't really remember."

Crock was no psychologist, but he could sense when someone was omitting important details. He doubted Tess would lie outright. If she could fool her brother, then he'd have to pay close attention to what she *wasn't* saying.

Crock glanced at Laz, who looked worried. "That may be why you were blocked out. *She* blocked out the whole incident."

Her brother didn't look comforted by the information. Before Laz could answer, Tess threw herself across the room with a yelp.

Chapter Seventeen

"Breathe, dammit! Before you pass out."

Breathe, he said. Tess struggled to obey Crock's demand, fighting the blackened spots which danced in front of her eyes. She remembered jumping off the bed, but now found herself sitting in a chair, with her head shoved unceremoniously between her legs.

Not exactly how she had envisioned the events of the evening transpiring.

Coming back to the hotel had been one big-assed mistake. First, she'd spent a hundred bucks—that she couldn't afford—on a hotel room just to chit-chat with a couple of ghosts. That expense, mixed with her purchases for a rare evening alone, meant her jobless streak was draining her funds faster than she'd like. Tess hoped Laz appreciated her sacrifice and would loan her some money if she got desperate.

After securing the door, she had searched the room. Finding nothing that would interfere with her private séance and spa night, she set out the candles stashed in her backpack. The citrus and sage scent might not do much for a spirit or two, but she needed to do something about the musty smell in the room. The ambience, plus the wine and cookies she'd bought, would keep her company for the long, boring hours of ghost-hunting time.

Besides, she could always pretend she was meeting

a certain hunk for a fun-filled evening. Which became the second reason why she'd made a big mistake.

Fifteen minutes ago, when she'd opened the door, she'd hoped to find some random, drunk guy named Crock come to play instead of one pissed-off Texas Ranger named Crock come to take over.

No such luck.

Although angry lawmen did seem to do something for her dormant libido. Especially ones in snug pants and western-style shirts with the sleeves rolled up to show off tanned and muscled forearms. Maybe it was the cowboy hat that did it for her. Definitely the hip holster.

Mistake Reason *Número tres*—well, she was smart, but obviously not that smart. Challenging the man that her plan wasn't any of his business. Tess knew she'd made a tactical mistake before the words were out of her mouth. Of course, this man needed to know. It was his case. Fortunately—or unfortunately—he didn't pull out the handcuffs. Instead, she got a raised eyebrow and a glare to match. Oh, and a lecture. That was fun.

Since his facial expressions gave no hint of his mood, she was learning that his eyebrows asked the questions, while his eyes gave away his level of irritation. Right now, they told Tess that arguing with a stump was not something she wanted to do all damn day. Her psychology degrees had earned her the privilege of learning interrogation techniques in the Army. Both on the giving and receiving ends. She'd earned herself a spot as Crock's receiver-of-shit list.

But damn, he's sexy when he means business.

Now—the *pièce de résistance*—let's act like a

damn fool because a ghost decided to get her attention. She hadn't freaked out like that since she was a toddler. She needed to write a book: *How* Not *to Impress a Hot Guy*. Yeah, that sounded like a great title.

"I'm okay." She tried to sit up, but firm hands kept her down.

"Breathe, slow and deep."

She tried. It was hard to tell if the shallow gasps were from her meltdown or from being folded into a pretzel. She'd never been good at yoga. Tess concentrated on her breathing. It was difficult, but she managed to get more air into her lungs, making her feel a little less like a weakling. As her vision cleared, she had a spectacular view of the dingy green carpet and a pair of really nice, shiny cowboy boots next to Laz's grubby sneakers.

Getting her hands on her thighs enabled Tess to push up against the weight sitting on her back. This time the hands didn't shove her back down. Dizziness struck once she was upright. A powerful hand steadied her shoulder. Her eyes focused on the bathroom's toilet roll holder to keep the room in one place.

"Why's she reacting like this?" Crock demanded.

"Shadow people terrorized her when we were little. The few times we've run across them, Tess had a panic attack."

Laz's voice came from her left side. Tess realized it was his hand holding her shoulders.

"I'm no doctor, but I'd say she's got a touch of PTSD." Crock registered his opinion.

A touch of…the gasps for air changed to hysterical giggles, followed closely by sobbing hiccups. Instead of being forced into a seated headstand again, Tess found her face pressed into a hard chest that smelled like her brother's favorite aftershave. She ought to know—it was an easy birthday and Christmas gift to send from overseas. He must have received buckets of the stuff from her over the years.

A warm hand brushed her hair back. "Tessie?"

She shook her head. There was no way in hell she could face either her twin or the sexy Ranger after making a complete fool out of herself. Not to mention she probably now had a blotchy face and racoon eyes.

Some all-knowing and totally understanding individual pressed a damp cloth into her hand. Without raising her head, she tried to erase any evidence of freak-out.

When her skin became raw, Tess pulled away from the hands which continued to stroke her head and back. A cold bottle of water met her lowered gaze, and she accepted it gratefully. A few minutes later, she felt almost human.

Crock crouched next to her. "You okay?"

"Yeah." *Imminent death by embarrassment, but otherwise okay.*

Laz wasn't so easily appeased. "Get your stuff. We're done here."

"No, we're not," she grumbled.

"Yes, we are."

"No, we're not."

"Yes…."

"For fuck's sake!" From his language, Tess hazarded a guess that Crock had finally reached his limit. "Both of you, shut it or I'll arrest you both and put you in the same damn cell, in the middle of nowhere, in August, with no air conditioning, and feed the damn key to a pissed-off rattlesnake."

Tess and Laz shared a look of shock, then burst into laughter. It was several minutes before they gathered what was left of their dignity. Their companion clearly thought they had lost their minds.

"Are y'all through?"

Tess swiped the tears away. "Yeah. I think so."

"Good. Maybe now I can get some work done," grunted the Ranger.

Trying to swallow her residual giggles, Tess pulled herself together. "I'm sorry."

Crock eyed her. "Are you going to tell us what happened to trigger that spectacular little episode we just witnessed?"

"Do I have to?" The accompanying glare convinced her that yes, indeed, she had to. "They were just trying to get my attention."

"Who?"

Tess looked around the room. Sure enough, there they were. "The couple that was here the other night."

That got Crock's attention. "A couple? Of ghosts?"

She stood, unsteady but brushing away the assistance offered by both men. "I'm good."

Tess turned toward the older couple waiting patiently in the corner. Instead of answering Crock, she addressed the spirits. "Hello. I'm Tess. I saw you before and came back to visit. Who are you?"

The pair said nothing.

Behind her, Crock became restless, but Laz drew him out of the way and against the wall. Tess saw a small device emerge from her brother's pocket. He came prepared to record the event. Returning her focus to the spectral hosts, she used his calmness to direct the conversation. "They're with me and are interested in what you have to say," she reassured the pair. "Are you the Greens?"

The couple gazed at each other and smiled. The man took his wife's hand. The warmth the dead pair had for each other made Tess envious. Maybe true love wasn't a figment of Hollywood's imagination.

"Dr. Green." Tess wanted to give the dead the same respect they had received in life. "You may remember my brother, Lazaro Corona."

Laz stepped forward. He couldn't see his old mentor, but he trusted Tess enough to speak to the dead man. "I never truly thanked you for everything you did for me, Dr. Green."

The male ghost eyed Laz. *"Teach. Truth."*

Tess glanced at her live companions. She never knew if others heard what she did or not. Apparently, they hadn't, so she relayed the words for their benefit.

Laz nodded, still speaking to their hosts, "That's what you hammered into my head—history is about truth and needs to be taught so that future generations will learn what really happened."

"Truth."

The words resonated in Tess's head. A feeling of sadness and—guilt surfaced. She frowned, trying to understand.

"What'd they say?" Crock wanted to know.

She held up her hand, motioning for quiet. "Do you need the truth?"

"Truth. Peace."

"You need the truth to be at peace?" Tess guessed. Ghosts typically used sparse, cryptic words, making the interpretation a guessing game. "What is the truth?"

The man motioned to her, and the pair disappeared. Tess didn't understand until she heard a loud *thump* in the hall.

"What in the hell was that?" Crock demanded.

At the same time, Laz spun around, searching for the noise. "What are they doing?"

Tess headed for the doorway without answering.

"Tess?" Laz sounded concerned. Crock's contribution included plenty of swear words involving stubborn women not communicating with the investigating officer.

"Hush!" She proceeded to ignore them both, although she did make a mental note to crucify one cute Ranger. *I'll communicate on his ass!*

Without further griping, the men followed her from the room. Once in the hall, Tess glanced in both directions until she located the couple. They stood at the end next to the stairwell exit. Light from the window behind them made it difficult to see them.

She approached the pair cautiously, not knowing what their intent was. When she drew close, the man lifted his hand and pointed to the door.

"The stairs?"

He nodded. *"Truth."*

She glanced back at her brother. "Laz? Didn't you feel something when we went down the stairs the other night?"

It was Laz's turn to nod. "Yeah. I don't think we want to go back in there."

Crock stepped around her to get to the doorway. "Is there something in here?"

Tess checked with the ghost of Dr. Green. "He keeps saying *'truth'* and pointing to the door."

She heard Crock mutter something that sounded like "here we go again" as he opened the door.

****

A cold flush surfaced at the base of Laz's spine as Crock swung the door open. The man's hand hovered near his gun, but Laz figured that was out of habit more than the actual need to shoot something. Bullets didn't typically bring down ghosts.

Cautiously, the Ranger stepped onto the dimly lit landing and looked around. Laz felt the cold spread throughout his body. He'd never felt anything like it before.

"Be careful," Tess whispered. "It doesn't feel right."

Laz noticed that his sister had moved closer to the steps. He reached out and pulled her back. "Uh…don't, Tess."

"Why not?" Her eyes flashed with irritation.

He shrugged. "I'm not sure. I just…I don't want you to go in there."

No matter what happened, he didn't want her in the way of spirits or bullets.

She rolled her eyes at him and ignored his warning as she stepped to the railing. It was a small consolation to see her holding on to something relatively solid.

Crock carefully climbed a few steps toward the third floor but stopped halfway up. "It feels pretty normal up here, but the air down there feels heavy."

Tess glanced at where the ghosts presumably waited. "He's indicating down."

Crock moved back to the landing and started down the steps. Stopping a few steps before the mid-floor landing, he halted. "It feels colder. You don't have that thermal on you, do you?"

Laz shook his head. "No, just the recorder. We can try that. See if we get anything?"

Crock turned around and climbed back up. "You're the expert."

Laz moved forward to hand over the device. Crock's right boot barely settled on the top step before slipping off. He teetered on the second stair, caught between balancing and falling. Gravity won.

"Shit!" Crock yelled.

Laz jumped forward to grab Crock's flailing left arm, catching some of his heavier weight. The bigger man managed to catch hold of the rail with his right hand, and with Tess's hand grabbing his shirt to help, the Ranger swung around, landing butt first on the step.

"That went well." Laz wheezed as he rubbed his lower back. The cold flared to a burning sensation. He didn't think he'd strained anything, but the incident happened too quickly to know for sure.

"Yeah." Crock looked a little pale and was also breathing hard. "Good catch. Thanks."

"Any time."

Tess appeared next to Laz. "Are y'all all right?"

Having her so close to the stairs made Laz nervous. Reaching out a hand, he kept her from going near the stairwell.

"Give me a minute." Crock answered her question. His right hand kept hold of the handrail while the other massaged his left thigh.

Tess stared at him. "This has happened before."

Laz watched a rigid mask drop over Crock's face as he shut down. The Ranger shook his head as if to clear it, then stretched his left leg out. Gingerly rising from his seat, he gripped the rail firmly. He refused to make eye contact as he limped to the hallway, favoring the left side.

Tess started to say something, but Laz gave her a warning glare. She closed her mouth but stared at him.

He didn't know what she was looking at, but for some reason her attention made him irritable. "What?"

"I…it's nothing." She hesitated. "Why are you rubbing your back?"

"Don't worry about me. I just pulled it when I grabbed Crock."

Her eyes flicked to his right, then her face transformed from concern to confusion.

"What are they saying?" Laz knew the ghosts were talking. He glanced around to find the recorder lying at the bottom landing, smashed to pieces. It was a good recorder, too. "Well, fuck." He turned back to see Tess watching him. "What?"

"I don't know," she answered slowly, "but I think we might need to get out of here."

Laz jerked his head in agreement. "Let me grab this." He didn't give her time to protest. Instead, he sailed down the stairs, swept up the pieces of the recorder and ran back to the landing.

****

Tess wasn't sure what she was seeing. Laz seemed like himself—but not.

The ghost of Dr. Green continued to point at his former student, then to himself. Given the spirit hadn't spoken more than a couple of words, she knew she'd have to figure out the answers on her own.

"Ow!" Laz's hand gripped her upper arm hard enough to create a bruise. "What are you doing? That freakin' hurts!"

"Sorry." Laz released her but didn't look like he was sorry. If anything, he looked annoyed.

Rubbing her arm, she waited for him to leave the stairwell before following. Crock stood outside in a trance-like state, staring down the hall.

Laz paid no attention to the Ranger as he brushed by him on his way back to room twenty-seven. "You coming?"

Crock woke from his transfixion. "Are we good?"

Personally, Tess didn't think anyone was good, but she gave a shrug and a curt nod. Her séance and spa night was officially a total bust, but she still had wine to drink. It was time to put the kibosh on this shit show before someone—or something—got any crazy ideas.

She turned to the ghosts. "Will you join us?"

They floated in place for a moment before blinking out of sight. The duo met them in their original spot in the room, standing by the bed. Before Tess could ask a question, the man mimicked writing.

"He's writing something." She turned to Crock, who had moved in behind her. "Did he leave any kind of note?"

Crock nodded. "There were several letters and legal documents that surfaced during probate."

Turning back to the ghost of Dr. Green, who now jabbed a pale finger at Crock, Tess said, "I think they might be important."

Crock pulled out his pocket notebook and made a note. "A document examiner has them now. There's a question of authenticity."

The ghost mimed writing and opening a book before pointing at Laz.

"You wrote to Laz?" Tess asked. "That one is legitimate? And something about a book?"

Laz perked up, sounding more normal than he had in the stairwell, "His books? No one knows what happened to his library. He had some treasures in his office. Can he tell us where they are?"

Instead of answering, the man seemed satisfied and stepped back. The wife moved forward and pointed to the night table.

"The table?" Tess moved toward the bedside stand. A standard hotel lamp, a notepad, and an information placard were the only items on the surface. The lamp was old, but the electronic outlets at the base told her it hadn't been there for twenty years. She could see nothing that might indicate what the spirit wanted. "I'm sorry. I don't understand."

"Tess?" Worry laced Laz's voice.

The woman became agitated. Before Tess could react, the ghost rushed toward her. An icy blast hit her with a physical shove. Shocked by the contact and the impact, Tess reached her hand out, catching the edge of the nightstand.

"No! Please don't! Danny! Danny! Help me!"

The woman screamed as she fought against her captor. In her struggle, she stumbled. She would have fallen into the person holding her, but they shoved her away with enough force to spin her around. With a final cry for help, the woman fell. Her head struck the edge of the nightstand with a sickening thunk.

The scream stopped.

"Tess?"

"What is it?"

Tess stumbled back, gasping for air. Whimpers

filled her ears. Hands grabbed and steered her to sit on something soft. It took a moment, but she finally recognized the hotel room. She was seated on the bed.

In a state of numbed shock, she stared at the faces swimming before her. Bile rose in her throat, forcing her to swallow several times. Her gaze drifted from the wobbly men before her to the nightstand.

The vision replayed in her mind's eye. Then again. And again.

Her gut protested as she slid off the soft surface.

The smell of vomit greeted Tess as she slowly became aware of her surroundings. She sat on the floor with a wastebasket cradled in her lap. Fortunately, it had captured the contents of her stomach. Strong hands kept her from pitching forward into the soupy mess. Another hand pressed a cool cloth to the back of her neck. Someone held a glass of water to her lips and forced her head back. Instead of drowning, Tess had enough sense to take some water in her mouth.

"Swish it around, then spit," a voice commanded.

She tried to follow orders. The water dribbled from her non-functioning lips instead. The damp washcloth moved to wipe her mouth. After a few more-or-less coordinated gulps, Tess looked around. She couldn't focus on the concerned faces positioned on either side, so she risked a glance into the corner of the room. The couple was no longer there.

Searching the room, she found only a residual sense of paranormal presence. Disappointed, she turned to her concerned companions. Her eyes met the green-tinted gaze under Crock's raised eyebrows.

When her voice returned, she croaked, “How did Mrs. Green die?”

She already knew the answer.

Chapter Eighteen

"Gram!" Laz yelled as he stormed into the house.

His heart rate still hadn't settled, and he was on the edge of a full-blown freak-out. He couldn't remember ever feeling this strange mix of fear, agitation, and anger. Throwing up or throwing furniture might be in his near future. He was fighting to stay in control.

"Hush, you idiot!" Tess hissed. She was supported by Crock since her legs were prone to buckling. "You don't want to wake the demons."

It was almost midnight. It had taken Tess nearly two hours to recover enough to stumble out of the hotel. Despite her protests, an executive decision was made to leave her Jeep behind. Her brother and Crock would retrieve it later.

Crock dumped Tess in the closest armchair. "Do you two really need to argue, right now?"

Laz left Tess to explain their weird family situation to the Ranger. He'd debated all the way home about bringing Gram into the picture. But he needed answers to too many questions. He did heed his sister's warning as he headed for the kitchen.

At the doorway, he called in a softer voice, "Gram?"

"I heard you the first time." Gram shuffled into the living room from the back of the house where her lair was. Her long, silver-streaked black hair was plaited into one long, thick braid, and she wore an old, chenille housecoat that he remembered from high school. "You wake up that child, and I'll make you wish you could pee normal again."

Laz sighed with relief. If anyone could give them an idea of what had happened, Gram could. If she was in a helpful mood. "Tess saw something."

Gram didn't look impressed. "Tess sees a lot of things. The Army even said she passed the eye exams. I was real excited, I tell you." Her tone declared anything but excitement. Annoyance, yes. Excitement, no.

"No." There were days that he wanted to beat his head against the wall. This was quickly becoming worse than that. "She had a vision of something."

"Are you going to let her tell me about it, or are you going to pretend you know what's going on and waste my time?"

Yep, this is a drown-myself-in-the-toilet kind of night.

Tess spoke up, "Gram, I met a couple of ghosts."

Gram glanced over at his twin with a suspicious gleam in her eye. "Were you drinking?"

"Uh, no. Should I have been?"

"Hell, yeah! Tequila makes everything more fun." Gram moved into the living room and sat in her favorite, tie-died swivel chair. The one Laz tried to cover up each time he was in the room. "Now, Laz, be useful and get me a beer, and then Tess can tell me about these ghosts."

"Gram, now isn't the time…"

"Remember what I said about peeing like a normal person? Now, get me a damn beer, Lazaro Arthur Corona Junior."

“Yes, ma’am.” He hated it when she used his full name. It usually preceded some really, uncomfortable curse. And he was fond of peeing normally.

Laz returned with four bottles of beer and passed them out. Gram was eying their guest. Crock started to decline, but, after a glance at the old woman, he wisely changed his mind. Laz didn’t blame him. Gram was a lot to take without alcohol on board.

Once everyone was happily sucking on their bottles, Gram continued with her pleasantries, “So, you gonna officially introduce me to the cop or what?”

“Gram,” Tess took over, trying to soothe the old witch, “this is Crock Ward with the Texas Rangers. He’s been here a couple of times now.”

“Yeah, but you two try to lock me in the pantry when he’s here.” Gram took a swig of her beer. “What do you think about that, Mr. I’m-a-badass-Texas-Ranger? Isn’t locking an old woman in a closet against the law?”

Crock thought for a minute. “Depends.”

“All righty then.” Laz broke in before the handcuffs came out to play. Gram probably had her own set. “Tess, why don’t you tell Gram what you…uhm…saw?”

Tess was holding back. Laz and Crock had only heard the generalities, but he’d been anxious to get his sister out of that damned hotel room. And get answers.

Answers that Tess refused to give.

The voice recorder burned a hole in his pocket. He couldn’t wait to analyze the recording. After everyone was in bed, Laz planned to hide in his office, after downing a couple of pain killers for his throbbing back and get to the bottom of Tess’s experience. He prayed there was nothing that would make her run away again.

Gram didn't ask any questions during Tess's story—which wasn't anything more than he'd heard the first time. And the second. Gram's eyes wandered around the room, studying each person. Her dark eyes settled on Crock. "What are you looking at?"

Crock watched quietly from his seat near the window. His barely touched beer bottle rested on one knee. Hazel eyes focused on Gram, but the man didn't respond to her belligerence. Laz should have warned the Ranger against getting into a staring contest with the old woman. Gram *knew* things when she stared at you. It was akin to having your soul sucked out through your eyeballs.

Of course, Crock was accustomed to staring people down. He did it for a living. Rangers probably took classes on laser vision and other superpowers. Laz wasn't sure whom he should lay odds on. No one moved for an eternity. The air thickened with tension and a fair amount of fear from the twins. Just before the atmosphere erupted into a mushroom cloud, a miracle happened—both parties blinked.

Eruption averted.

Gram turned and addressed Tess as if nothing had happened, "So what do you want me to do about your little vision?"

Tess looked shell-shocked. "Uhm…it's probably nothing, so…?"

Gram snorted. "It's nothing only if you don't want to do something about it."

Crock spoke up then. "Would someone please tell me what's going on?"

"How the hell should I know?" Gram had no

respect for law enforcement. “Tess is the only one who saw anything, and she’s not sharing at the moment.”

“So, exactly what am I supposed to do with this?” Crock grumbled.

“How in the hell should I know? I’m just an old woman, but if you ask me—oh, wait, you *are* asking me. Well then, you probably shouldn’t play around with shit you don’t understand. Unless you want to understand—then, be prepared.”

In her own cryptic way, Gram was telling them she was bored and going back to bed. “If y’all’re done wasting my time, I’m going to hack into someone’s computer and rob a bank.”

Crock’s eyebrow shot up, his expression more of amusement than concern, but Laz quickly assured him—just in case, “Gram doesn’t know how to turn on the computer, much less how to hack into a bank.”

“Says you.” Gram’s parting shot was accompanied by a one-fingered salute as she ambled back to her room.

“Is she always such a delightful individual? Or was this a special occasion?” Crock asked. His expression never changed.

Tess answered before Laz could think of a good response, “Special occasion. Usually she’s worse.”

“Good to know.” Crock didn’t look convinced.

Tess’s head dropped against her seat with a groan. Laz didn’t need twin-dar to know she was exhausted and more than a little upset. He also knew he wasn’t getting anything else out of her tonight. “Why don’t you go on to bed, Tessie. We can hash this out tomorrow.”

Her head rose and her weary eyes met his. “You

sure? We haven't figured this out yet."

"And we won't figure it out when we're about to drop either," he reminded her. He wasn't going to admit that he was wired up and might not sleep for a week. Not when she was on the verge of collapse.

Crock returned her gaze in his usual, stoic manner. With a sigh, Tess stood and bade them goodnight.

Once she was gone, the Ranger leaned forward. "What'd your grandmother mean by all that—whatever it was?"

Laz sighed heavily. "Gram thinks Tess isn't utilizing her *gifts* like she should. She gets pissy when something happens."

"Do you have any idea what happened tonight?"

"Not a clue." Laz shoved a hand through his hair. He and Tess never discussed their twin-dar with outsiders. No one knew how it worked, but one thing was certain—they each felt it in a different manner. But whatever Tess saw was something else entirely. It was nothing like her nightmares. He had no indication of what she'd experienced. "She's never mentioned visions, just hearing and seeing the ghosts."

"And what did you sense? From her?"

Crock's questions made him reexamine the experience. "I don't…I'm not sure. It was like she went blank."

A blond eyebrow arched upward. "Blank?"

"Yeah. She wasn't there." And that right there was what scared the hell out of him.

"Any theories?"

"That's what I hoped to get from Gram." Laz admitted, thoroughly disgusted with his grandmother's lack of interest. The old biddy might be nuts, but he'd learned to respect the unknown from her. And from what they could determine, Tess's gifts closely followed Gram's.

Crock sat forward, placing his all-but-full beer on the coffee table. "What is the deal with your grandmother? Y'all act like she's got dementia, yet you go to her for answers, and she shoves it in your face."

Laz rubbed his face in frustration. The man was way too perceptive, but there were things that couldn't be shared. Not without permission.

"Gram basically raised us. She's…her side of the family is Comanche, with a mix of Navaho and Caddo. And my grandad was a mix of Central and South American cultures. I started studying our history as a kid, and it led to what I do professionally. Gram is basically my source for all things unusual because she comes from a long line of spiritual healers and mystics. She's studied as many of the current and ancient rituals as she could get her hands on."

He stopped to take a deep breath, trying to keep from saying more than he should. How could an outsider possibly understand that Gram was the quintessential grandmother—most of the time. From his earliest memories, she'd baked cookies, read to them, and let them finger paint and eat mud pies. He was thankful that Tila was having those same experiences. Gram was truly great with children—until she wasn't. That was the woman that most outsiders encountered—the evil *bwitch* more likely to shove small children into an oven than to stuff them with sweets.

Crock filled in the rest. "So, your grandmother has abilities which Tess probably inherited, but doesn't fully understand. I assume it takes time and practice to hone these skills, and that's why Tess is having problems right now. She didn't use her ability in the service."

Laz gave him a nod. "I guess the sensitivity is making up for lost time."

"Can your grandmother help her?"

Laz laughed. "Yeah, she can. Gram tried to teach her after we came to live with her, but Tess blew it off. Hell, middle school had enough weird going on without dealing with psychic weirdness."

"But if Tess asked…"

"It'll have to be Tess's decision." Laz rolled his head, trying to release some of the tension making his head and neck ache. The thumping in his low back had spread. "Gram has always said that a mystic has to find their own way using their own skills. There's only so much that can be taught."

Crock leveled his hazel gaze on Laz. "Do you think Tess wants to learn?"

"I don't want…"

"It doesn't matter what you want, Laz," Crock interrupted. "I know you don't want a repeat of ten years ago, but it looks to me like her skills are manifesting whether either of you want them to or not. And if she doesn't take control, then bad things can and will happen, like tonight's little episode."

Laz knew the other man was right. It was Tess's decision to face her demons. Literally. They weren't in middle school anymore. There were things he couldn't protect her from—including herself.

"You're right. It's not going to be easy," he admitted. "We've been through a lot together, but she'd been through more than that by herself."

Crock wouldn't understand half of what he meant. Nothing would keep him from protecting Tess, but that didn't give Laz the right to protect her from the demons which haunted her. Her nightmares alone reminded him that she was never free. Perhaps if she faced her fears, she could finally make some decisions about her life.

At the very least, that might get their mother off her back.

Crock handed his remaining beer to Laz as he unfolded himself from the chair. "Then, I'm calling it a night." He stretched a few kinks out of his lean body before heading to the door. As he stepped onto the front porch, he turned back. "I've got an idea which might help Tess with her decision. Mind if I try?"

His gut reaction said *hell, no*. Laz realized trusting others to help his sister was just as frightening to him as watching her experience the unknown. He still didn't know what Tess would want in this situation. Without an answer, he gave the only response he could.

"If she's willing." Laz glanced at Gramp's old mantle clock. "Tomorrow. I can't ask her to do anything else tonight."

"Fair enough. I've got to go to the office in the morning. I'll come by after lunch."

Laz waited until the Ranger drove away to shut and lock the door. His hand fisted against the solid wood door. He didn't want this. At all.

He banged his fist against the door, then went to his office, knowing he wouldn't sleep. At least, he knew Tess's nightmares wouldn't be what kept him up.

It would be his own memory of her sitting on a dingy hotel floor, shuddering helplessly and puking her guts out.

Chapter Nineteen

"And I believe you've met Sergeant Crock Ward. Crock, you remember Claudette Hudgens, currently in administration at TCU."

Crock choked as he swallowed the chunk of brownie he'd just bitten into. Fighting through the sudden pain in his throat, he glanced up at his boss's unexpected appearance. In front of his desk stood Childs and a familiar administrative assistant.

I didn't think Childs would work that fast. Standing, he brushed the crumbs from his fingers and pants before greeting her. "Mrs. Hudgens, it's good to see you again."

She took the offered hand and gave a stiff nod in greeting. "Sergeant Ward."

"Please, call me Crock." He watched her eyes dart around the room, landing on a bulletin board of mug shots. The board identified the most-wanted criminals in the United States, not just those wanted in Texas.

Her eyes returned to his and narrowed. "That won't be necessary, Sergeant Ward."

Crock resisted the sudden urge to find something which required his immediate attention and leave the grown-ups to their business. Instead, he put forth his best effort. "I hope this visit means you will consider joining our ranks."

"I have yet to make a decision."

Yes, Mrs. Hudgens would make a fabulous addition to Company B. Any hardened criminal would spill their worse secrets under her silent glare, saving time and tax-payer dollars. Hell, she might put him out of a job.

As if she wasn't the most intimidating person in the room, she changed the subject. "I trust you found Laz?"

With her unexpected aloofness, he had a sinking feeling that this interview hadn't gone well. A quick glance at his captain confirmed his suspicion. Crock nodded. "Yes, ma'am. Eventually. And I had an interesting introduction to his family."

"I thought I recognized those brownies." Mrs. Hudgens nodded to the plate, eyeing Childs's thick, brown fingers trying to steal one from the plastic-covered plate. He yanked them back under the weight of her disapproval.

She continued, "Domatila Corona is an excellent baker, and Laz always brings treats for his students on exam days. I believe she adds something extra to the batter. It makes the students seem less stressed."

Still eyeing the sweets, a funny look crossed Childs's face as he realized what Mrs. Hudgens suggested. He quickly recovered and, recognizing an opportunity to prove he could be a gentleman, liberated a chair from another desk and held the seat for the lady. He settled onto a spot with one hip perched on the corner of Crock's desk.

"So, what can you tell us about the Coronas?" the captain asked. "From what Crock has told me, they seem to be a family of characters."

Crock sat down. He hadn't told his boss much, but Childs was always one step ahead of his investigators.

He wondered what the admin's take was on the twin terrors who pulverized his sanity. He leaned back in his seat, rubbing his eyes. They had begun to cross from reviewing old case files—yet another "perk" of restricted duty.

Mrs. Hudgens answered, "Laz is particularly proud of his family name. He's traced the origins from Mexico back to Italy and Spain. You are correct," she added, "they are an—*interesting* family."

Crock grinned, adding for Childs's benefit, "Laz has an adorable little girl and a twin sister who's recently out of the Army. They live with their grandmother. So far, I've seen them at their best—hunting dead people and arguing."

Childs looked amused. "Typical sibling rivalry?"

Crock's grin turned to a grimace. "Something like that. I had to keep them from killing each other the other day. They were rolling around on the floor, strangling each other over a recorder."

"What are they? Twelve?" his boss snorted, fingers inching toward the brownies.

Crock pushed the plate of treats to the corner of his desk and away from the wandering hand before he glanced back at their guest. He gave her his most inviting grin. "Do you know much about Tess?"

Mrs. Hudgens remained perched on the edge of her seat. Crock imagined that was her permanent state. "I've only interacted with his sister a few times since her return home. She's a guarded one."

He supposed that was one way to describe Tess, although Mrs. Hudgens could put anyone on their best behavior with a glance. "What do you mean?"

"She seems rather intelligent but isn't interested in

small talk. While Laz will talk your ear off, Tess sits back and watches."

He could see Tess as a watcher. Her eyes certainly watched him whenever he was in the room. Of course, he was guilty of doing his own watching.

Mrs. Hudgens glanced at her watch. "Oh, my. I'm sorry, gentlemen, but I must get back to the school for a faculty meeting. If you need anything else from me, you may call."

Both men stood and shook her hand. Childs offered to escort her to her car, but she stopped him. "Thank you, Captain Childs, but I can find my own way. I'll be in touch regarding your kind offer."

With that, she was gone.

For a moment, neither man moved.

"Well, you certainly justified your paycheck," grumbled the captain as he swiped a long-awaited brownie from the pile.

Crock shot him a grin. "You mean *again*. I knew you'd like her, but I earned my paycheck with that brownie you just stole."

A sigh of contentment escaped from the captain. "Man, this is awesome!"

Crock smothered a chuckle. "Tess called them pot brownies."

The enraptured look on Childs's face fell. "Do they have pot in them?"

"Don't ask, don't tell." Crock laughed, enjoying his boss's reaction.

He'd asked Tess that exact question when she shoved the plate into his hands after the pizza-analysis party. The look on her face was hilarious. Based on her stuttering response, the dessert was named for the little cast-iron pots they were baked in. Obviously, she'd never considered whether the favorite goodie contained marijuana or not. And after Mrs. Hudgens comment about the students being relaxed for exams, Crock was willing to bet the elder Corona occasionally used CBD oil in her recipe.

Having dealt with the older woman and glanced at the pictures on the mantle, Crock gathered the grandmother had herself a great time during the seventies. And—since he was a smart man—he didn't ask too many probing questions.

"Do we need to bring her in? And do we need to do a drug test?" With eyes wide and a nervous hand swiping his in-need-of-a-shave bald head.

Unable to resist, Crock grabbed another brownie from the stack. He swore it would be the last one. "That's a battle I'm not going to fight. The woman's a shaman, so she's got a defense—although *medicinal-purpose brownies* is a bit of a stretch." It was time to let his captain off the hook. "Considering Laz's little girl was eating them by the fist-full, I'd lay good money they're pot-free."

Although there might be a time when I need something more than alcohol to deal with the Coronas. He kept that thought to himself.

"You…you son of a donkey's uncle!" Childs sputtered for a moment, before settling down with an appreciative grin. "Sounds like I need to meet these characters."

Crock nodded, still chuckling. "Take a flask. You'll need it."

Child's slowly resumed chewing, even as he reached for another helping. Knowing the captain, the plate would be licked clean in another minute or two. There was only one way to keep the glutton at bay. “Save a couple for Gemma.”

The captain froze in mid-reach. Crock watched in amusement as Childs halted and carefully counted the remaining brownies before removing the smallest one. He neatly arranged the last three treats, then re-wrapped the plate with plastic wrap like it was a precious gift. The package was topped off with a pink sticky-note that had a heart with *BJC* written on the inside.

His boss was a certified asshole.

Gemma was special to Company B, if not the entire Department of Public Safety. When she came to visit the office, all lesser tasks such as interrogations and investigations ground to a halt. After the injury which had sidelined him for a few months, Crock was thrilled to have his partners care so deeply for his sister. A week didn’t go by without someone from the company checking up on him and Gemma to make sure their needs were met. It would have happened regularly if it’d just been his sorry ass, but they spent more time and effort caring for Gemma than they did him.

His weekly wellness visits didn’t include gifts of pink lemonade cupcakes or trips to get frozen yogurt with sprinkles. He barely got a *hello*.

But he had adamantly refused the mani-pedi offered by the two female Rangers who had stopped by to take his mother and sister for a girls’ day out. Gemma wanted to paint his toenails a hot pink.

Oh. Hell. No.

A man could get jealous of his baby sister. Crock wasn’t that man. The sweetest girl in the world could bring two hundred badass Rangers, including his captain, to heel. That didn't bother him one bit. If anything ever happened to him, Gemma Rae would be well taken care of.

"How's the Green case coming?"

Childs's subtle reminder to get back to work brought him back to harsh reality. "Slowly. We made contact with both—uhm—entities, but they haven't said much yet."

It was awkward talking about ghosts with his boss, but he couldn't report on what happened yesterday. Tess had given them little to work with. He hoped that would change when he met up with the duo after lunch.

"There's no info on a possible cause of death, correct?"

Crock hesitated before answering, "We have a potential weapon, but there's no way to prove it."

Childs waved his crumb-covered fingers in the universal *just give me the info* manner.

"Tess had an—encounter," Crock didn't want to call it a vision because it seemed to be much more than that. "Sounds like there was an altercation, and Mrs. Green might have been shoved, hitting her head on the bedside table."

The captain brushed brownie crumbs from his hands before crossing his arms. "What's on the death certificate?"

Noting his boss didn't ask about how he obtained the information or Tess's encounter, Crock pulled his case file over and flipped it open. A picture of the couple lay on top. It was a studio picture, typical of what could be found in a church directory. He set it aside, uncovering an official record. "Subdural hematoma secondary to blunt force trauma."

“A piece of furniture would certainly do the job,” Childs mused, “and you’re right, any evidence would be long gone by now.”

His boss didn’t seem to require a response, so Crock continued to flip through the file in hopes of anything catching his attention. Underneath the death certificate was a later picture of Dr. Green, probably taken as a faculty photo a year or two before his death. His eye was drawn to the oddly shaped age spots scattered on the man’s face and hands.

He glanced at the captain before handing the two photos over. “Does anything stand out to you?”

Childs brushed off the last of the brownie crumbs from his hands before laying out the pictures on the desk. “Doc is a lot older here. He’s developed a skin condition.”

That’s what Crock thought. He pulled his laptop over and opened the browser. “I don’t think that’s a natural condition.”

His boss quickly caught on. “Arsenic?”

Finding the symptoms of arsenic poisoning confirmed Crock’s suspicions. “Yeah. ‘Raindrops on a dusty road.’ Those dark spots on his hands and face are typical. Redness. The crusty brown patches.”

“Unless you’ve got an MD in your pocket, you’d have to get that verified,” Childs said as he compared the photos with the online references. “The spots do look similar.”

Crock went back to the case file, searching for more information. “There’s no coroner’s report on the husband. Wonder what the death certificate gives as cause of death.”

Childs grunted. “At his age, probably natural

causes. There wouldn't have been an autopsy due to his age and lack of suspicious circumstances. We might need to dig up the body."

"Maybe." The exhumation process was time-consuming and required a court order—which required evidence they didn't have—or the deceased family's approval. The nephew and niece hadn't been cooperative with his initial questioning. While they were eager to dig up Mrs. Green for her jewelry, Crock had a feeling they wouldn't be thrilled to bring up Uncle Dan. Especially if they had any involvement in poisoning him.

"Meaning—what?"

"Hell if I know," Crock admitted. "The man was in his eighties. The manager said Dr. Green wasn't feeling well when he checked in and didn't show up for breakfast. And arsenic is in a lot of everyday foods, including wine."

Childs mulled the information over before asking, "But…are we talking about a second homicide or was Dr. Green a foodie who liked a bottle of wine or two with dinner?"

"The family said he was a staunch Baptist who didn't drink."

"The same could be said for my daddy, but he knew how to tie one on every now and then," Childs muttered as he flipped through the rest of the file.

Since his boss rarely shared personal information with his coworkers, Crock decided it was best not to respond. Instead, he kept his focus on the investigation. "I guess that's one of the questions that might get answered by our paranormal team. Unless there's something hidden in those letters."

The captain leaned back from the file. "You don't have the copies?"

"I haven't seen them."

"How did that happen?" Childs demanded. "I'll see if the court's document examiner can make copies and send them over."

"That'd be great. Or I can meet up with her." Crock wondered if Tess might be able to sense something from the letters. Something made him hesitate. He flipped through the sparse remnants of the file, studying each document. "No word on the missing evidence box."

"Nope. It's still MIA."

Well, shit. He glanced up at his boss. "I'll have to backtrack and verify Dr. Green's alibi."

Childs leaned forward. "The school should have a list of faculty and staff at the time. Maybe even a list of his students."

Crock agreed. "It's a long shot to find anyone who remembers one class twenty-odd years ago. Without that evidence box, the entire case might need to rechecked."

"Great googly-woogly! That'll take a minute, and I've got the family breathing down my neck."

His boss's version of cursing up a storm would have made Crock chuckle, but only if he had a death wish. "I don't have a lot to go on. There're several items missing. There's no information on fingerprints. There's mention of hair samples from the husband and wife, but no DNA report. We're not talking about the 70s here. Forensics was a thing, even in the 90s."

Childs took the file and flipped through it again. "The lead investigator was McDonald out of Fort

Worth. I knew him. He had his flaky moments, especially toward the time of his retirement, but he wouldn't have made those kinds of mistakes."

Crock didn't recognize the officer's name. "Is McDonald still around?"

The captain stood slowly, shaking his head. "Cancer got him maybe ten years ago or so."

Crock watched Childs walk away. He leaned back in his seat, wondering what his next step needed to be. Either McDonald was incompetent—which he knew Childs wouldn't swallow—or something had happened to the file in the twenty-something years it'd been stored. The missing box probably held the answers he needed. With his recent experiences with the Coronas, he wasn't willing to rule out a paranormal heist of some sort.

At least he could possibly retrieve some of the missing information. Crock also needed information on the other reported deaths at the location. That was an area he hoped Laz could help with. He just hoped that somewhere he'd find the key to unlocking the mystery.

And he knew the right person to help fill in that particular blank.

Chapter Twenty

Tess cursed all dust bunnies. How ten million of the nasty little critters came to nest behind the fridge, she'd never know. And what in the hell was that fuzzy grunge?

She'd already scrubbed the inside of the fridge and the oven within an inch of their lives. A cobweb hanging onto the corner of the ancient refrigerator had caught her eye, forcing her to pull the appliance out from the wall. Nothing had prepared her for the scum hidden from view.

"What in the hell are you doing?"

Tess glanced up to find a horrified Laz and a familiar, sexy Ranger staring at her dusty, dead bug-covered ass hanging out from behind the refrigerator.

"Cleaning, Einstein. What did you think I was doing?"

Laz's wide-eyed gaze swung around to meet Crock's, who held up his hands in a 'don't look at me, she's your sister' protest before disappearing back into the living room.

"Uhm…Tess?"

"What?"

"Are you okay?" Laz sounded nervous.

Tess crawled out from her hole. "I'm great. Help me move this beast back."

"I can do that," he began, "if you tell me what's got

you in super-clean-up mode."

Tess glared at him. "What makes you think something's wrong? Nobody's cleaned back there since 1985. It was disgusting."

Laz positioned his body on the hinge side of the fridge and pushed it back. "You only clean when shit's flying, and even then, you don't clean behind heavy appliances."

He was right, but Tess had no intention of telling him that. "So?"

"So, we need to figure out what happened, so it won't happen again."

Tess shoved on her end, and the heavy appliance groaned as it slid into position. "It won't happen again."

"How do you know that?"

"Cause I'm done with investigating." She should have learned that lesson the first time. Or the second. Probably by the third.

"Tess…." Laz protested.

"No, I'm serious, Laz." Tess washed up, vigorously scrubbing under her nails. She needed a good manicure. Maybe she'd take Tila for a girls' day out. She needed a refresher on what girlie stuff entailed. "I should have remembered, but I guess I needed a reminder. If I don't go looking for ghosts, I won't find any ghosts. Easy."

"But…."

"But that won't be enough." A deep voice came from the door.

Both twins turned to find Crock leaning in his usual stance in the doorway.

"What won't be enough?" Tess demanded, flinging water from her hands before reaching for a dish towel.

"My understanding is that you will continue to develop as a sensitive. Spirits will hunt for you," Crock responded, seemingly unperturbed by her defensiveness.

Tess wanted to deny that little truth nugget but knew better. "Where'd you pick up that intel?"

"The net," he said simply. "That and your grandmother mentioned something about it as she was leaving."

She exchanged a glance with her twin. "Did you know she was heading out?"

"Nope." Laz tried not to look worried. "She's probably going to burn down someone's house or steal a car."

Crock eyed them, before continuing, "I'd like to ask you to stay with the investigation, at least for a little while longer."

Tess grabbed three water bottles from the now-sparkling fridge and passed them out before plopping down at the kitchen table. "Nothing good comes from that type of work. I wind up with ghosts feeling me up and telling me their creepy secrets. And now…well, I'm done with all of it."

Laz stopped her. "I listened to the audio last night."

She doubted he could hear what she'd seen. It didn't work that way. "So?"

"There's a woman's voice." He pulled a recorder from his pocket and hit *play*.

Tess froze as her own voice filled the room. *"The table? —I'm sorry, I don't understand."*

A faint growl filled the silence.

"What was that?" Tess demanded.

Crock glanced at her, surprised. "It wasn't part of

your vision?"

"No." Tess hadn't heard anything but the woman's screams.

Laz shushed them. "There's more."

The growling was followed by the sounds of Tess stumbling into what she knew was the nightstand. She heard her own gasping breaths.

"Tess?" Laz's voice came from the recorder. He sounded worried.

As did Crock. *"What is it?"*

The next words were breathy and quiet, but there was no mistaking a woman's voice. The message was too garbled to make out the words.

The sounds of her own retching, mixed with her brother's and Crock's frantic responses, almost made Tess want to vomit again. She took a slow sip of water in hopes of keeping the bile down.

Thankfully, Laz shut off the recorder. "I couldn't identify the growl, but I worked out that last bit. She seems to say, 'W*itness murder. Help us. Help them.'* We know you saw something, Tess. I know you relived it in your dreams all night long."

Tess glanced up. His worried eyes told her the truth: she'd kept him up—again.

"So, what do you want to know? That I witnessed a murder? Yeah, I'm now a witness. How are you going to explain that in court, huh? 'Miss Corona, would you please tell the court what you saw?' 'Well, let's see. I had a vision of a man attacking a woman twenty years ago. She was yelling for help, and he shoved her into the nightstand. No, I couldn't identify the guy.'" Tess snorted. "Yeah, I think it really matters what I saw, don't you?"

As expected, Laz stared at her with his jaw hanging open. Crock looked much more thoughtful.

After a moment, Laz rubbed a hand over his face. "A twenty-year-old murder. And you saw it happen."

Tess didn't answer. She didn't need to.

It was Crock who broke the tension in the room. "That's actually very helpful."

"How?" Tess and Laz asked in equally shocked unison.

Crock sat back in his chair with his arms crossed over his chest. "All we had was that Esme Green died from blunt force trauma to the side of her head. Her death was ruled suspicious, but now we know it was murder. No weapon was ever found, but then no one considered a nightstand as the murder weapon. And now we know the assailant was a man. That's three huge breakthroughs."

Tess sniffed, "Well, that narrows the suspect pool to what—fifty percent?"

The Ranger's broad shoulders lifted. "It's more than we had. And that's better than a poke in the eye with a big stick."

"Well, I sure as hell don't like it," Laz registered his complaint.

"It's not for you to like or dislike," Crock remained calm as he took a swig from his water bottle.

"While y'all are liking and disliking this shit, I'm the one who gets to actually witness this woman's death. Yay me!" Tess punched her fist into the air. "No, thanks. I saw enough of that kind of bullshit in the Army. I'm done."

That shut the guys up—for a moment.

Crock spoke first. "Will you try something for

me?"

Tess shrugged, taking another sip from her bottle. The cool water soothed the dust scratching her throat. "As long as I don't have to move from this chair, sure. Why not?"

The Ranger set his bottle on the table and reached for his gun. Tess could see the Texas Department of Public Safety insignia mounted on the top. It wasn't a flashy weapon, but the .357 meant business. Crock pulled the slide back, cleared the chamber, and removed the magazine before holding the gun out to her.

Tess hesitated. She had no idea what he was up to. "What's that for?"

He said nothing but waited for her to take hold of his gun.

Slowly, Tess reached out and took the weapon in her hand.

Glancing around the room again, he was certain that no one was there. He was alone.

"Where are you, you bastard?" he muttered under his breath.

A scratching noise came from the hall. Cautiously, he left the room and moved back toward the stairs.

"No!"

A disembodied whisper came from the ether. Something pulled at his arm. Crock froze, glancing around.

Nothing was there.

An invisible force shoved him into the wall.

"Stay," *the voice muttered again.*

He turned. Nothing was there.

One final check of the hallway before starting down the unlit stairs confirmed the place was empty.

Two steps down, a dark form moved away from the wall. His gun hand came up, his finger hovered near the trigger. "State police! Don't move!"

The shadow didn't move.

"Who are you? What do you want?"

No answer.

The shadow rushed toward as an icy hand shoved hard against his back.

He was falling. Maniacal laughter filled his ears.

BANG!

Tess gasped, thankful that she was sitting down. The sensation of falling was real, as was the pain burning through her left leg. The gunshot seemed real enough to check her hand to make certain she hadn't accidentally squeezed the trigger.

All was blessedly silent.

She glanced around. Two blurred faces swam in front of hers. Gaping holes replaced their mouths.

Her hearing returned slowly. The blessed silence was no more.

Laz was shouting, "Shit! What happened?"

"Are you all right?" Crock knelt next to her chair. He took the gun from her nerveless fingers, while his other hand kept a firm hand on her shoulder for support.

"W-what?" Her voice sounded odd to her until she realized her hearing was still dulled. She hadn't actually fired the weapon. Had she?

"Here."

Her water bottle appeared in her hand. Her hands shook so badly, she couldn't twist the top. Laz did the honors. Half the bottle spilled onto her shirt as she tried to take a gulp.

A rough hand wrapped around to steady her hand.

"Take it easy, now."

Tess looked up to see that the hand belonged to Crock. Her eyes closed as the cool water slipped down her dry throat.

"You're okay." Crock's calming voice helped to ground her.

"What…?" Laz began.

Tess opened her eyes to see Crock waving Laz's concern away. "Give her a minute."

Which was about how long it took for her vocal cords to work properly again. "I'm okay."

It was enough to cause an explosion.

"What in the fuck were you thinking? After what happened at the hotel, you want to hand her your fucking weapon? For God's sake, how many…?"

"You might want to stop right there before you say something you shouldn't." Crock gave her brother an icy glare, his tone hard.

Both men stared at each other, neither willing to give in.

"I'm okay." Tess repeated, this time a bit louder, hoping to break up the tension in the room.

Laz didn't take the hint. "What happened?"

Tess's eyes met Crock's blanked face. He wasn't going to give any clues if he had any. "I'm not sure."

"Well, you saw *something*. You almost passed out." Laz demanded.

Tess sat back. She emptied the water bottle, giving herself a moment to think. Unable to read Crock's face, she wasn't sure how much of his experience she could share. Not that she understood what she'd seen.

"The gun went off," she stated.

Her twin stared at her. "That's it?"

"Well…yeah." Tess hesitated. "My hearing…it's like the gun went off, and I wasn't wearing earplugs."

"You weren't wearing…" Laz ran a hand through his hair. "You weren't…"

"Okay," Crock broke in, "I think we've established she wasn't wearing ear protection. Neither was I, for that matter. Just my comm wire. Let's move on, shall we?" He turned to face Tess. "Tell me what you saw."

Tess took a deep breath. "You had your gun out, clearing the floor. At the top of the stairs, you heard a noise, but as you turned…" She couldn't keep going.

Crock waited.

"It pushed you." She barely heard her own whisper. Shaking the fear away, Tess straightened and said, "So, I'm getting visions when I touch certain things. I mean, you obviously didn't die, so it's not about death, but about…"

"What happened." Crock finished for her. His eyes never left hers. "Did you see what it was?"

Tess jerked her head up and down.

"Do you *know* what it was?"

Tess swallowed, then nodded.

A flicker of emotion lit Crock's eye, but before she could tell what it was, the light was gone. "What was it?"

"I…" She didn't want to say.

He must have seen the protest in her face. "I need to know, Tess."

It was fear she'd witnessed in his eyes; the same hidden fear which now laced his tone. Crock wasn't emotionless. He was incredibly controlled.

Tess pulled away. She rose on shaky legs and stumbled to the other side of the room. What had happened to him was no different than what haunted her nightmares. She couldn't keep her own fear out of her voice. "I don't want to do this anymore. I can't."

"Tess…" Crock rose from his kneeling position.

"No!" Laz stepped between them. "Whatever is happening, she doesn't need to do it anymore. No investigation is worth her experiencing others getting hurt."

Heavy breathing echoed throughout the room.

After a long moment, Crock spoke again. "I understand. I do. But I would ask you to reconsider. There are thousands of unsolved murders and deaths. Cold cases. Some have elements that can't be explained by any normal method." He paused, letting the information sink in. "It's my job to see if I can get answers—closure for these families. I've experienced the paranormal. You just witnessed part of it. I almost became a victim because of a…whatever the hell it was."

Crock moved closer to her, resting one hand on the counter. "If you have psychometric abilities, then I'm asking you to consider—*consider*—helping me, in whatever capacity you are willing to." He glanced at Laz. "Both of you. You're a team, right?"

Tess tried to say something, but the lump in her throat was thick. She glanced at Laz, who seemed to be waiting for her decision, although his protest was written all over his face.

All her life, she'd run from the shadows. Laz could only share so much, but he had tried his damnedest to protect her from the unknown. She had wanted to prove she was stronger, both to her brother and to herself.

It was past time to woman up.

"It was a dark shadow," she murmured. "Actually two of them. The one on the stairs distracted you while the one in the hall grabbed for your gun. They're evil, and they wanted you to die."

"So, the gun…?" Crock began.

"There was nothing wrong with it," Tess took a deep breath before continuing, "You were in a low ready position. Your finger didn't squeeze the trigger. The shadow shot you."

Crock's eyes closed. "What about…?"

"A ghost shoved you down the stairs," she added, anticipating his question. "A young girl who was one of the victims. She was trying to get your attention and tried to protect you from the shadow people."

Tess watched as a shudder quaked through his body. She understood how he felt—to finally know what he'd experienced. Full comprehension didn't matter—a name did.

When his eyes opened, she saw the depth of his gratitude behind his words. "Thank you. I can work with that."

Chapter Twenty-One

Crock drove her out to the cemetery. He didn't know what she was looking for, but he hoped there would be at least one or two answers that might give them a better direction.

He'd sworn to Tess's brother that she wouldn't be in any danger of shadow people, and both men strong-armed a vow from a reluctant Tess to share any and all visions and sensations. Laz was pissed about staying behind but agreed to wait for Jonah and Mikey to enhance the audio he'd captured the night before and to research the other reported hauntings in the hotel.

Nothing else was mentioned about her vision or his injury. There was nothing to say. He didn't know Tess well, but it was already evident to him that—despite the crazy family vibes—she was a very private person.

He respected that.

It was amazing that she'd been able to hear his gun go off and feel the pain in his leg. Her reaction to the vision did concern him. For someone accustomed to gunfire and extreme situations, whatever happened when she touched an object was enough to send her into a full-blown panic attack.

The silence in the cab was becoming weird, so Crock decided to satisfy his curiosity. "What'd you do in the Army?"

The woman beside him tensed; wariness laced her

next words. "I…uhm…a little bit of everything."

While he didn't expect a detailed job description, a normal person would at least give a generalized idea of their duties. Apparently, there were land mines in Tess's past, and he'd just found one.

Crock barely took his eyes off the road to glance at her. "You know I can tell if you're lying or not."

"It's not that difficult to tell when someone's lying."

"Oh, really?" he demanded. "What makes you say that?"

His mood was lighter than it had been in a long time. Knowing that he hadn't accidentally shot himself in the leg like a dumbass and that the gun he'd lost trust in was safe to use made his year. Hundreds of questions flitted through his brain, especially surrounding his injury. According to Tess, a child's ghost tried to save him. He wondered if the girl he'd seen before he passed out was a real manifestation, or simply the product of the intense pain playing tricks on his brain.

Maybe someday he would know the answer.

"You act like a big, badass Texas Ranger, yet you drive a girly truck."

Shock must have been written all over his face because her smirk lit up the cab. He fought to hide his own grin. He had no doubt that Tess lived to annoy her brother for no other purpose than she could. The military would have only reinforced her ability to knock a man off his high horse.

And he applauded her ability to deflect the conversation away from anything that might compromise her many secrets. He willingly let it slide—for now. "How the hell do you figure?" Crock demanded. "There's no way this truck is *girly*."

"Yes, it is."

"How?"

It was her turn to be smug. "The color. Most guys would go for black—maybe white or silver. If they want color, it's going to be something bright, like a fire-engine red or yellow. Burgundy is a *pretty* color." Point made, she sat back. "So, why do you drive a pretty, girly truck?"

"It's state issued. It is *not* girly," he growled.

Tess grinned. She obviously liked to win. "Whatever. Why?"

"My sister picked it out."

Tess's ears perked at the tidbit of juicy detail. "You let your sister pick out your truck?"

Crock held back a groan. He didn't share his sister with outsiders. They tended to pity him or smother him. Or—like his last girlfriend—force him to choose between her and his responsibility. Family would win every time. Somehow, he thought Tess would be different.

"Yeah. I had to compromise. I was due for an upgrade and was given a choice of a dark gray or the red. She thought she needed a custom, purple paint job. The red was a compromise."

"She *thought* she needed purple? I need to meet this girl who needs a customized truck." Tess sounded impressed. "But again, why?"

He gave a shrug. "She might be slightly under the impression that it's her truck."

Tess laughed. "You are nothing but a big softie."

"No," Crock had *never* been accused of being a softie before. "I am nothing more than a stupid, stupid man who loves his baby sister." He paused, hiding a sappy smile, and said, "but don't tell anyone."

Tess's grin was plastered to her face. "I wouldn't dream of it."

****

Tess held her breath as the truck pulled off the Farm-to-Market road and into the graveled area for an older, but well-kept, cemetery. An arched sign over the gate announced Marystown Cemetery, and a Texas historical plaque marked the site's importance.

While not large by metroplex standards, it was about two or three acres of a quiet, tree-enclosed clearing dotted with granite stones of varying heights. Styles ranged from the late 1800s to more recent additions, including obelisks, Woodsmen of America tree trunk columns, and historical markers. Cedar and oak trees dotted the otherwise plain field of graves. The cemetery was surrounded by chain link fencing.

Crock pulled up next to the gate which was secured with a chain and padlock to prevent unauthorized vehicles from driving onto the property. A smaller gate next to the archway opened to allow visitors to walk in.

Tess hopped out of the truck and inhaled the clean, cedar-filled air as she surveyed her surroundings. Fortunately, the humidity wasn't awful, and the temperature was a mere ninety degrees. In another month, it would be miserable out in the open, with the only shade from a handful of trees. She'd always loved the peace and tranquility of cemeteries, especially the older ones, although she considered funerals to be morbid displays of shared grief and not true celebrations of life.

Before leaving for the Army, she and Laz had

made a pact that if one twin died, the other would throw an epic party. Laz's would have barbeque and chocolate chip cookies served at the Texas State Archives. Her own funeral would be held on a beach somewhere—maybe South Padre Island—with hamburgers and hot dogs grilled over a campfire, followed by Gram's homemade banana pudding.

Of course, Gram would be long gone. Hopefully. Tess wasn't going to place money on that old bat dying first.

While Crock strolled around his truck to meet her, he fiddled with an app on his phone. "Find-a-Grave doesn't have the GPS coordinates listed. We might have to split up to find them."

"They're over there." Tess didn't need a grave tracker. She pointed to the far southeast corner at a grouping of stately granite head stones and wasn't surprised to see the eyebrow raise.

"Is grave hunting another one of your hidden talents?"

She hid her smile, moving toward the gate. "You might say that."

Crock held out a hand to stop her. "Are you okay with this?"

She looked at him, confused by his sudden concern. "Why wouldn't I be?"

He glanced around the quiet cemetery. "You've had some bad experiences with the dead. I didn't think about…"

"What a cemetery might do to me?" Tess finished for him. It was her turn to quirk an eyebrow at him. When he returned his gaze to her and gave a curt nod, she went on, "Nothing can happen here. Most of my issues have been with ghosts who haven't moved on, or other evil weirdos."

"So, it's not *all* the dead?"

Crock was making an effort to understand, which gave her a thrill. No man, other than Laz and her father, had ever been truly interested in her, certainly not enough to ask about the abilities she'd kept hidden for most of her life.

"Not all, no. These," she gestured at the surrounding graves, "for the most part, are at peace. Their souls have moved on."

"And the ones who aren't at peace?"

Tess shrugged and resumed walking. "That's why Laz and I hunted ghosts."

"To do what exactly?" Crock asked, following close at her heels.

"I don't know." That was a question Tess had never asked herself. Laz had started the investigations in order to better relate to her sightings. While she didn't mind talking to the ghosts, the conversations created more questions than answers. Questions she ultimately didn't want to know the answers to.

Before Crock could dig deeper into uncomfortable territory, they arrived at their destination. A few short minutes of looking around brought their search to a double headstone. At the top of the rosy-pink stone, *Green* was etched in a simple, block script. The names and dates of Esme and Daniel were cut into a gray granite inset below the family name. Between their names, double rings gave the date of their marriage. A matching polished granite bench was placed at the foot of the graves, also engraved with the family name.

Tess appreciated her companion's restraint as he

stepped back and allowed her to walk the perimeter of the plot without subjecting her to a multitude of questions. As she expected, there were no spirits here, offering cryptic messages from the beyond. There was, however, an unnatural disturbance surrounding the marker, indicating the dead had not crossed over yet. It left a gaping hole in the otherwise peaceful cemetery.

"What do you think?"

Tess turned to face Crock. He stood by the bench in his standard pose—legs apart, arms crossed, shaded eyes, and an unreadable expression. "There's not much here."

"But there is something?" His question was more like a statement of fact.

She wasn't sure she wanted to commit to an answer, mainly because she wasn't sure. "I think so. It's confusing."

An eyebrow lifted over the sunglasses. "Maybe it'll help to talk it out."

Crock's suggestion was more than a suggestion. She hadn't liked the promise he and Laz forced on her. Tess took a deep breath. "Because their souls aren't at peace, there's a void here."

"Meaning?"

She huffed in frustration. "Meaning…hell, I don't know. What do you feel when you stand by a grave? Like that one," she said, pointing to a neighboring headstone.

The eyebrows creased, but Crock dutifully stepped closer to the designated marker. After a moment, he answered, "It feels…quiet, I guess."

Without her prompting, he moved to a few other graves before coming back to her side. "They all feel the same."

"How about the Greens?"

He moved close enough to lay his hand over Dan's name. "It's kind of…empty."

Tess watched as his hand travelled up to rub the center of his chest. "And how do *you* feel?"

"I'm not sure. Maybe a little anxious?" He didn't sound certain.

She understood. Most of the time, she had difficulty discerning how she felt around spirits. "Now, how about Esme's side?"

Crock's hand hovered over the wife's name. "It still feels empty, but…almost content."

"That's what I got, too," Tess said. "That's why it's odd. She was the one with the unsolved murder. Yet, she's more at peace than Dan."

"That doesn't make sense."

"No, it doesn't," Tess admitted.

Crock's eyebrows hunched together in a universal sign of confusion. "How am I able to sense all this?"

"My guess is that you have some degree of sensitivity yourself, which might be why those shadow people went after you. And—as someone who likes order—the lack of a soul at rest makes you uncomfortable."

His head lowered to allow his eyes to meet hers over the rims of his glasses. "You sound like you've used that psychology degree a bit."

"A bit." Tess tore her gaze from him. She had never told her family what her job was in the military—or even the truth about her education. She certainly wasn't going to admit anything to this Ranger, no matter how much she wanted to jump his bones.

A sudden chill raced up her spine. Goosebumps rose on her arms. Shivering, she rubbed her skin.

"How can you be cold?" Crock asked as he caught her arm and drew her over to the sun-heated rock bench. "It's like ninety-odd degrees out here."

Something told her she did *not* want to touch the bench. Tess tried to pull away before her butt hit the stone, but gravity wasn't cooperating.

The heat of the mid-afternoon May sun disappeared to the cool gray fog typical of a Texas October morning. A familiar man placed bright flowers by his wife's marker before settling onto the bench. A groan, followed by a pained sigh, escaped. One spotted hand rubbed his aching knees.

"Good morning, my dear. I'm sorry I missed coming by last week, but I have good news." He inhaled deeply, then exhaled with a wheezing cough. It took him a moment to regain control, and he gave the headstone a smile. "It's time, Esme-Belle. Everything's ready. We shall dance on our anniversary and be a family again."

The vision disappeared as suddenly as it appeared. Tess gasped and leapt up only to find her face planted against a different type of rock—the muscled kind.

"What was it?"

She shook her head, willing herself to not faint, cry, or further embarrass herself in front of this man again. She didn't understand her visceral response to the visions. There was absolutely no reason for it.

Not wanting to admit to weakness, she reluctantly pushed away from Crock's chest, and forced her unsteady legs to move. She stumbled closer to the Green's headstone. At the moment, between another vision and residual sensations, emotion seemed the lesser of two evils.

As her hand brushed the rough granite, Tess sensed sorrow mixed with guilt that her brief vision had hinted at. She glanced down and found that her hand had landed above Dan Green's name. Moving her hand to cover his wife's, the feelings lessened. They returned when her hand returned to hover over Dan's.

"Tess? Talk to me," Crock's tone told her he was concerned. "What's going on? You saw something."

Tess jerked her head, but she didn't want to talk about the vision. Instead, she focused on the granite beneath her hands. "I'm not sure. It's like Dan feels guilty."

Crock stared at her for several seconds before stepping next to her. "Guilty about what?" He placed his hands on the maker next to hers. "I don't feel anything but the emptiness."

She thought he sounded a little disappointed. "You mentioned that his death was ruled heart failure?"

"Yeah." Crock stepped back and assumed his usual stance. "That's what the death certificate said."

"That's not what happened."

The sunglasses were yanked off, and she met the fire of Crock's green and gold gaze. "Then what *did* happen?"

She noticed he didn't question her about her conclusion. "Dan may have planned his death, but I can't be sure."

Crock was quiet for a moment. She couldn't tell if he believed her or not. He finally muttered, "But how can I confirm that?"

Relief flooded her, replacing her anxiety. "I'm not

sure. I'll know when I see it."

Feeling better, Tess turned away. Two identical, flat headstones caught her eye. Covered in the remains of cut grass, she bent down to brush them off. The first read *Francine Esme, Daughter of D.M. and E.F. Green.* The second was for *Michael Daniel, Son of D.M. and E.F. Green.* The children were two years apart in age, but they had died within days of each other.

"...and be a family again."

Dr. Green's words sent a chill through her spine, making her shudder in the heat. She felt Crock's presence, silently witnessing the Greens' heartbreak with her. Children's markers always tore at her heart.

Taking a deep breath, she knelt in the grass and placed her hands on top of the graves. Acknowledging the encompassing peace, she said, "Francine Esme and Michael Daniel Green, you are not forgotten."

With her eyes burning, she took an unsteady step back from the slabs. A strong hand wrapped around her waist and centered her. It remained there as they turned and walked slowly back to the truck.

"That was beautiful, but why...?" Crock left his question hanging.

Tess smiled. "I read a book for one of my psychology classes. It was by a neuroscientist named David Eagleman. He said there were three deaths: when the body stopped functioning, when it's buried, and the last time the name is spoken."

"That's pretty deep."

"Very," Tess agreed, the heaviness in her chest making it hard for her to go on, "It mirrors *Día de los Muertos* and All Saints Day. We celebrate the memories of our loved ones. I think of my dad,

Gramps, and my…" she stopped before she said something that needed to remain buried deep within her soul, "my ancestors. One day, no one will be around to tell their stories." She swept a hand across the many graves around them. "All of these people had lives, yet does anyone remember them?"

Crock stopped, placing his glasses on his head before moving in front of her. He took her hand. "Does the loss of their stories make them any less at peace?"

Tess's eyes landed on his hand. She remembered another who had held her hand, who had cared enough to do so. The pain surfaced but withered quickly. What she thought she had been a part of was gone. It never should have been. Now, she could appreciate the warmth of the man beside her and prayed there were no hidden agendas or major secrets hiding behind his concern.

She'd had enough of that.

Tess gave Crock's hand a squeeze and met his calm, hazel gaze. "No. They are still at peace."

"Then maybe it's enough that they were remembered by those that mattered, for the time that it mattered."

Tess glanced away and let her gaze survey the cemetery. "I suppose."

"Look," he pulled at her hand to draw her attention back to him, "their stories are not forgotten. We've all got family stories that live on. Sure, there are stories that have been forgotten, but many haven't been and get passed on to the next generations. That's life. But that's why we're here, doing what we're doing. People like Esme and Dan—their story isn't finished. It's our responsibility to help them get answers and find their peace."

She understood what he was saying—but… "It's just difficult for me to fathom that kind of nothingness."

He gave her hand a squeeze. "From what I'm starting to understand, it's not nothingness. Peace isn't nothing."

Tess dropped her eyes to where he held her hand. A different sensation settled over her—one she almost didn't recognize because she'd never felt it except in cemeteries. He was right; peace wasn't nothing.

Peace felt pretty damn amazing.

Chapter Twenty-Two

With Tess's feelings fresh on her mind, they left the cemetery and returned to the hotel. This time, Tess studied the historical plaque by the front door. Settlers by the name of Smith had been massacred by Comanche raiders. To survive the loss of her husband and older sons, the family matriarch opened a boarding house which later became the Smith's Crown Hotel and Saloon.

Tess glanced around. No saloon.

Crock stepped up behind her. "What are you looking for?"

She pointed at the sign. "There was a saloon here."

"To bad there isn't one here now," he grunted.

Tess had to agree. She wanted to ask, but—remembering the chatty hotel manager—she reined in her curiosity.

The information forced her to look at the hotel under a different light. The scarred check-in desk could have once been the bar. Some of the rooms, including the one Dan and Esme died in, had the feel of a nineteenth century boarding house. And a massacre might explain a few of the reported hauntings.

Unfortunately, room twenty-seven was occupied. The chatty manager, Mary, caught up with them as they headed to the second floor.

"They are a lovely, young couple who came here

on a ghost adventure," Mary rattled on about her newest guests. "They were thrilled to learn about the investigation and would *love* to meet the Ranger handling the case."

Tess watched Crock's body stiffen as the elevator shuddered open. A fascinating shade of pink rose from the back of his shirt. She could only assume that, while Crock enjoyed his job, he wasn't comfortable with the legend status associated with the title of Texas Ranger.

She understood. She wasn't comfortable with people thanking her for her military service.

Crock steered the conversation back to his case, "You mentioned Dr. Green wasn't feeling well. Can you recall any other details about his illness or his death?"

"Oh, yes," the woman answered. "When he checked in, He was pale and in pain, but he insisted on taking the stairs. I wasn't too worried until he didn't show up for breakfast the next morning."

"And you sent the housekeeper up to check on him?" The woman nodded. "Do you recall what time that was?"

Mary thought for a moment before saying, "It was close to check-out time, so around ten-thirty or so."

"And how long did she take to report back?"

"No more than fifteen or twenty minutes, I'd say."

Tess watched Crock's eyebrow begin a slow ascent. "Did you call 911 or did the housekeeper?"

Mary smiled. "I did. While we waited for them, I cleaned him up, and…are you all right, Sergeant Ward? Oh, dear. Did something get in your eye?"

Tess barely contained her snort of laughter at the look on Crock's face. The eyebrows were twitching like crazy, and an angry flush creeped from beneath the collar of his pearl-gray shirt.

She assumed the interrogation before Crock could do anything drastic, like arresting a sweet, grandmotherly hotel manager for evidence-tampering. "Why did you feel that was necessary, Mrs. Dunham?"

"Well, when I arrived, he had bloody foam coming from his mouth and nose, and he was covered in vomit. And he had soiled himself." Mary's head swung back and forth from Crock's rising irritation and Tess's calm amusement. "Dr. Green was a very dapper gentleman. He wouldn't want anyone to see him that way."

Fortunately, the slow-moving elevator opened at that moment, and a grumbling Crock bolted from the small car. Tess offered the flustered manager a smile.

"Did I do something wrong?"

Tess led the distressed woman off the elevator. "It's best to let the professionals do any clean-up. Things like blood and vomit—and yes, even diarrhea—can give them an idea of what happened. It's information that might alter how they proceed."

"But the poor man was dead!"

Tess turned to Mary, stopping several doors from where Crock was pacing on the other end of the hall, muttering to himself. "In the event of an unexpected death, the responders have to contact the medical examiner or coroner to determine the manner of death. Details like that help them decide if further investigation is warranted."

It had been a while since Tess had needed to educate a well-meaning civilian on death protocols. She wasn't too rusty.

"Like an autopsy?"

"Yes, ma'am."

"I'm so sorry," Mary appeared distressed, with tears sparkling in her eyes, "I didn't realize…. He was such a sweet man. I just wanted to show his body the respect he deserved."

"I'm sure you did, but," Tess added gently, "next time someone passes in your hotel, please just leave everything as is, and let the responders do their jobs. They have been trained to treat the deceased with due respect."

Mary pulled a tissue from her pocket and wiped her nose. She gave a nod and a watery smile. "I will."

"Thank you." Tess turned toward Crock to see him back to his unruffled, stoic self. From the raised eyebrow, she knew he had overheard her explanation and Mary's promise. She quickly reviewed the conversation and realized she might have given away more of her past than she intended.

Not giving him an opportunity to interrogate her, Tess moved down the hallway, stopping at each door to be certain there were no hidden spirits. A reassured Mary 'entertained' them with anecdotes of the pseudo-celebrities that had stayed in the hotel and surrounding area, including the history of Caddo Peak, the sandstone mound northwest of Joshua. The rocks had been carved with names, the earliest of which was dated 1836. Tess doubted the information was pertinent to the investigation.

They were about to leave the floor when Tess remembered the stairwell. With Crock in tow, she headed down the hall. The door felt lighter than she remembered.

Crock obviously felt the same. "The air isn't as

stifling as it was before. Why?"

Mary piped in, "After you were here the other night, I asked Charles to clean up the stairwell and the basement. Maybe he finished."

Tess exchanged looks with Crock. With the cobwebs and rat pellets hiding in the corners—to which the manager was seemingly oblivious—the handyman hadn't been in the stairwell in quite a while.

"Whatever was here the other night, isn't here now." Tess searched the steps and landing for any signs of paranormal activity. Without equipment, she had to rely on her intuition. She felt nothing of the thicker sensations which had almost sent Crock down the steps at their previous visit.

Slowly, she made her way to the lower landing.

"Careful," Crock called softly.

Tess glanced back at him. He was also remembering his near crash landing. She gave him a nod before moving to the next set of stairs. Footsteps told her that Crock was making his way down the steps as well.

"I don't know what y'all are doing, but if you're going to be a while, I'll meet you downstairs in the lobby." Mary called after them. "My knees can't handle those stairs anymore."

Crock assured her they could manage without her, then waited until they heard the elevator ding in the distance before asking, "Anything?"

"Yeah." Tess couldn't give him more but continued down to the lower levels toward the unlit basement. "What set you off?"

He grunted, "Sorry about that. This case has more holes than the Byron Nelson," referring to the area's biggest golf tournament. “There’s missing evidence, so when I hear that the professor’s body was tampered with, it irritated me.”

Tess acknowledged his frustration but continued downward. The closer they drew to the basement, the less lighting was available, and the more Tess sensed a presence.

“They’re down here.” Tess stumbled when she hit the last step. She bit back a yelp when Crock’s hand grabbed her arm. He was closer than she expected.

“Sorry.” He didn’t sound sorry.

“I’m okay. Watch that last step.”

She pulled out her phone and hit the side button to light up the screen. Switching to the flashlight app, she scanned the gloomy basement. It wasn’t a large space, but the sight of unused cleaning equipment, broken furniture, and debris scattered around made her glad she had the app.

A second light lit behind her as Crock pulled out a small flashlight. He located a light switch and flipped it on. A single uncovered bulb woke up to illuminate the darkness.

“I don’t think Charles does much of anything down here,” Tess muttered.

Crock grunted, “I’d have to agree with you. I doubt he even keeps his drug stash down here.”

Tess stifled a snort of laughter. A small scratching noise shifted her attention to a poorly lit corner of the basement. She picked her way around the room, trying not to disturb anything. Crock moved to explore the opposite side of the space.

A wooden workbench sat in the corner, covered with an inch or two of dust. Holding her phone up high,

Tess peered over the surface and found nothing but rusted tools and rat feces. She swallowed her disgust and shifted her attention to behind the bench. At first, she saw what looked like a rope. The rope moved out of sight and was replaced by glowing orbs of light.

The orbs squeaked.

Tess jumped back, clamping her hand over her mouth to hold back a screech. Her heart decided to shift into a higher gear than normal. A crash sounded behind her. She turned to find Crock attempting to get to her side. In his rush, he'd knocked over an old metal chest filled with unused—and unusable—tools.

"What happened?" he demanded when he finally got to her, grabbing hold of her arm.

A long, thin line of blood emerged along his forearm.

"I'm all right. Sorry about that. Do we need to get you a tetanus shot?" she asked, pointing to his arm.

He stopped and looked down. "Ah, hell! No, I'm good." A folded bandana emerged from his pocket, which he used to blot the injury. It was only a scrape. His attention turned back to her. "Why'd you scream?"

Tess tried to pull her shit together, breathing deeply. "It's no big deal. I'm a bit edgy down here. I should have expected to find a rat down here."

Crock leaned over to see for himself. "Yeah. I'm sure the health department might have something to say about that."

She agreed. *Not my circus, definitely not my rat.*

Tess turned her back on all vermin-related issues, but the sight which greeted her froze her in her steps. "They're here."

"Who?" Crock was still distracted by the rat.

"The Greens."

He spun around to look where she pointed into the murky corner by the stairs. From what Tess had seen so far, the Ranger could discern balls of light where ghosts moved, and, with the poor lighting, he might be able to follow their movement.

Keeping her eyes on the couple, she shuffled forward to keep from knocking anything over.

"Hello, Dr. and Mrs. Green," she greeted them as gently as she could. In her peripheral vision, she saw Crock pull out his phone. She assumed he would try to record the conversation.

Her questions came naturally—so naturally, she let the conversation flow. She focused on Dan Green. The sadness and guilt she had felt from his gravesite pulsed through the wisps of his presence in the room. In contrast, Esme's smiling spirit held no sorrow, only love for the man by her side. Tess pondered how the spirit of a murder victim could be that peaceful and happy.

The ghost of Dr. Green gave Tess a nod as if acknowledging her unspoken question. He then turned to his wife and placed his hand to her cheek. She smiled, took his hand, and together they faded into nothing.

"They're gone," she told Crock.

He stopped the recording and hit replay.

"If you don't mind, we had a few more questions for you."

Silence.

"We visited your grave site today. It's a lovely pink marker. Did you pick it out for your wife, Dr. Green?"

Nothing.

"Dr. Green, I felt unexpected emotions at the cemetery. Is there something I should know? Something about your death? Or your wife's?"

"Yes."

Tess's eyes shot up to catch Crock's. He appeared as shocked as she was thrilled.

"Your death?"

"Fa...t." Static interfered with the full response.

Crock stopped the recording. "What was that?"

"He said 'fault.' When I asked what he meant, they got all lovey, then disappeared."

"So, what you felt at the cemetery…?"

Tess shrugged. "I think we need to keep searching. But—" she was quiet for a moment. "—he's expressing a lot of guilt. I think the deaths are somehow related."

"What makes you say that?"

Tess wasn't sure how to answer. If it was Laz, he would have understood that sometimes she had a sense of how things happened. She knew Crock didn't…couldn't operate without concrete evidence. And concrete was something she did not have.

"What's your gut tell you?" he asked.

Surprised, she glanced at him. He stared back, expecting an answer. "Well…I, uh…" She took a deep breath, trusting that he wouldn't think she was nuts. "He feels guilty about something. I'm not certain if it's his death, or hers, but he believes he is responsible for both."

Crock said nothing for a moment. "That might mean his death was a suicide. I can buy that. Not taking medication when needed—or taking too much."

"Or, taking something that was contraindicated."

"There are lots of possibilities," Crock agreed. "I

need to talk with the coroner, but arsenic might have been involved."

"Arsenic takes time to build up toxicity. But maybe that's what he wanted—to die slowly." Tess was shocked, not by the possibility that Dr. Green committed suicide, but that Crock had accepted her suspicion with an intent to follow-up on it.

"Now, why do you think he was involved with his wife's murder? All the reports suggest he was nowhere near here when she died."

He trusted her. If he kept this up, she'd fall in love with more than just his truck.

She sighed. "I don't know. It's just a feeling based on their interactions. She doesn't act like a typical murder victim."

"Fair enough." Crock glanced at his watch. "If we're done here, I want to do a perimeter check before we head out. I think there's an exit at the top of these stairs."

Tess followed him as they retraced their steps. She didn't realize how chilled she'd been in the basement until she stepped out into the Texas afternoon heat.

Crock didn't insult her abilities by asking her to wait while he did his survey. At the back of the building, they found the hotel's maintenance man, Charles, leaning against the dumpster and staring at the brick wall of the building.

Before they could say anything, the scruffy, young man in his mid-twenties looked up at them and muttered, "That's one *big* cockroach."

Tess thought the kid appeared stoned, but when she turned to look at the brick wall herself, she nearly jumped into the reeking dumpster. On the wall, amongst the ancient graffiti, a *huge* cockroach clung to the wall. Its antennae waved at them.

A huge, friendly cockroach. Yuck! She quickly checked the size of Crock's boot. Not big enough. He probably wouldn't appreciate bug guts smearing the shiny, leather sole either. There were no other usable weapons in the near vicinity, which was surprising given how run-down the area was.

Unnerved, Tess decided she'd had enough of critters for the day. She grabbed Crock's arm and dragged him away from the killer bug.

The drugged-up Charles followed them out of the alley.

****

Crock had no clue that talking with ghosts could be so exhausting.

After an enlightening conversation with the marginally enlightened Charles, Tess concluded that the handyman was a medium, or at least a sensitive, who used drugs to mask the weird things he couldn't explain. As a result, the boy's comments about drugs and death led Crock to call in a mental health unit to address his suicidal ideology. Tess admitted she wasn't skilled enough to help Charles with the psychic element—that was more Gram's realm—but she promised him to get him some information.

One detail bugged him. Tess obviously felt the same way.

"I think Charles might have confirmed our suspicions," he began.

"You mean the idea that Dr. Green planned his death, if not actually committed suicide?" Tess rubbed her head. "Charles mentioned he had discussed the possibilities with the dead couple on several occasions."

"Yeah, that one." Crock shifted in his seat to steer with his left hand. His right hand tapped on the console as he thought through what they knew. "The man was in his eighties. His wife was dead. He had no surviving children. His niece and nephew are acting like greedy little twits about the will. But why would he wait twenty-odd years to take his own life if he felt he had nothing to live for long before that?"

Tess shrugged. "I don't know. What if there was something about her murder? Was he trying to do his own investigation?" But that wouldn't explain his sense of guilt. She was missing something—something important.

Crock shot a glance at her. "What makes you say that?"

"Dan Green was a historian, but he dabbled in folklore. He supported Laz in all his research over the years. It seems like he would have done his own analysis to find Esme's killer along the way."

"So, why would he suddenly decide it was time to die?" Crock demanded.

At least the man was open-minded to her ideas. "Maybe he'd had enough. Maybe it was time to…" her voice trailed off as a thought struck.

"What?"

She shook off her hesitation. "I'd have to ask, but Laz had published an article about pairing paranormal investigations with folklore or legends to get to the 'truth.'" Tess used air-quotes to emphasize her brother's work. "It's probably one of the articles which led you to meet with him in the first place. Dr. Green was an advisor on the project and was listed as a contributor. If Dr. Green thought Laz was better suited to get the answer to his wife's death—"

"Then Dr. Green would be willing to let another historian—one he trusted—do the work while he joined his wife," Crock finished. "It's an interesting concept. Is there any way to get confirmation? It's hard enough to get one or two words recorded."

Tess didn't answer right away. "There might be a way. Or at least, I could try."

"And what's that?"

"When I touched your gun, I got a vision of your encounter. It…wasn't the first time that happened." Crock gave no response other than the raising of an eyebrow. She quickly added, "What if I tried handling something of Dr. Green's? Something associated with his death?"

Crock thought for a moment. "The only thing that might fit would be the letters written before his death. The only problem with that is the originals are being checked out as possible forgeries. I'll have to check on their status."

****

After listening to Crock make several phone calls, Tess was convinced they were heading in the right direction.

The handwriting expert had completed an initial analysis of the letters and will. Crock arranged for Tess to look at copies of the letters to see if there was any helpful information. In the meantime, her companion was in full interrogation mode. "What was the other incident?"

"What other incident?"

"Tess…" Crock warned.

She heaved a weary sigh. "Last week—the day of the investigation, in fact—I was at Tila's former teacher's apartment. She was fired the day before on flimsy grounds. When I got there, she showed me some documents. Apparently, Karlyn actually owns the daycare, but the director had paperwork drawn up, changing the name."

She proceeded to tell him about the vision and the couple she'd witnessed talking about the documents.

"Could you tell who they were?" Crock probed.

Tess rolled her eyes. "The woman was the new director. No idea about the man. I didn't recognize him."

"Can you describe him?"

"He was seated. I didn't see the woman." She paused before adding, "I'm almost positive the paperwork was forged. The will was a copy, but it felt like it was legitimate."

Crock grunted, "Okay, so you've got a built-in forgery detector. That certainly makes my job easier."

"It's not admissible in court," she reminded him.

He shrugged. "But it saves me time and expense in getting things analyzed."

"So, you just have to haul me around on all your cases."

He glanced over at her. "Yeah, that's *so* not going to happen."

His statement wiped the smirk from her face and was replaced with her lips pursed and pulled to the side. She followed up with a one-finger salute.

Crock grinned, catching the offending hand in his grip. "Enough of that." His smile faded. "Do you remember any details?"

Tess thought back. She had been shocked by the vision, but now she focused on the few details which stood out. “He was bald. Stocky. Oh! He had rings on his fingers.”

An eyebrow lifted. “What kind of rings?”

The image in her mind sharpened its focus on the man’s jewelry. “They’re large and chunky, like an animal head. Probably silver. I think they match.”

The second eyebrow rose to meet its twin. “Can you tell what kind of animal?”

Tess shook her head. “Maybe some kind of predator, like a wolf or bear. Sharp nose, bared teeth. There might be stones for the eyes. I can’t be certain.”

“That’s a good description.” He stopped at a light. “I’m not sure what we can do with that information, but it’s a start.”

“I know. Karlyn is screwed unless she can prove the papers are forged,” Tess said on a sigh. “Not only that but a lot of changes have pissed off the parents. The state is investigating the complaints.”

“Is she getting an attorney?”

“She needs to, but I haven’t talked with her since Friday.” She paused before admitting, “I thought I’d see if you had any recommendations.”

“I might know a lawyer or two. She should probably file a report with the police.” Crock took one hand off the wheel and rubbed his lip, thinking. “Hell, a case like that might even work its way to our fraud investigator.”

“Would that be in the Ranger’s jurisdiction?”

He glanced at her with a slight lift in the corner of his lip. “The state of Texas is our jurisdiction.”

Tess stared at him. “What about other federal

agencies?"

"What about them?"

"Wouldn't a fraud case be more for the FBI or the Secret Service?"

"We often work together."

"Ah."

Like most people, she'd never considered what the Texas Rangers did beyond catching the bad guys. Unlike most people, she had an uncommon wealth of knowledge about the workings of federal investigations, but she'd never worked with any entity close to home.

Texas has its own way of doing business.

Crock steered the conversation in a different direction. "What'd you get up to in the Army?"

Out of habit, she answered, "A little of this, a little of that. I did what had to be done."

A soft snort answered her. "That sounds like a motto of some sort. The question is—whose motto?"

"The Army's."

"Isn't the Army's motto 'this we'll defend'?"

This guy knew too much. "Uh…yeah."

"So, what was your rank?" Crock kept his eyes on the road, but his tone indicated he expected an answer. It was how Tess would expect his voice to sound during an interrogation.

Two could play that game. "Special Agent Corona, sir!" she barked, adding a salute for fun.

Crock tried—really hard—to keep a straight face. The way his cheek sucked in told Tess that he was biting the inside of his cheek. She leaned forward to catch his eye. *That did it.*

He suddenly veered the truck off the road and swung into a convenience store parking lot. She hopped out of the cab before he could lock her in and followed him inside until he slammed the men's room door in her face.

Tess darted into the ladies' room which backed up to the men's room. All she heard through the grungy, tiled wall was water running full blast into a sink and a flushing toilet.

She grinned.

After determining the ladies' toilet wouldn't leave her with any communicable diseases, Tess took care of her own business and wandered back into the store. She found Crock, with his sunglasses firmly in place, buying two bottles of water and a bag of roasted peanuts.

"Do you want anything else?" Except for a heaving chest and a slight wheeze, neither his tone nor his face gave away any sign of lost control.

She didn't mind. She had accomplished her goal—Operation Crack-That-Nut was a success. "I'm good, thanks."

He handed her a bottle and headed out of the store. Silence followed them back to the truck. The man held her door open, which she thought was awfully nice of him. She hadn't experienced many *gentlemen* in the military. Everyone was polite, but equality was the expectation. Not many doors had been opened for her—not since her father's death.

She smiled at a memory of her daddy holding a door, escorting her on a father-daughter date. Shortly before his death, he had taken her to a little Italian restaurant with small candles on the table. Daddy had listened to her talk about her friends and her dreams. She realized now that he was teaching her how a man should treat a woman.

There had been too few of those dates.

Tess shook away the bittersweet memory and turned her attention to the one who triggered it. Having learned his lesson, Crock didn't ask her any more questions on the way back to her house. Tess liked to think she'd rendered a Texas Ranger speechless.

Crock pulled in front of the house and got out. Before she could get the door open, he had come around to hold the door for her. Tess wasn't sure how to respond, but she did feel a little more feminine with that small act of courtesy.

At least she did until the screaming started.

"Crock! Wait!"

Her legs weren't as long as Crock's, but she was fast. She managed to catch up with him at the front door. He'd already unholstered his weapon and was prepared to charge through the door.

"Wait!" she shouted. "It's not what you think."

More shrieks came from inside. And yelling. And crashes.

Crock turned to face her. "What in the hell is it then?" he demanded.

That stumped her. "I don't know, but I'll let you shoot anything that I don't recognize."

"Promise?"

Instead of answering, Tess unlocked the door and cautiously opened it. The door was yanked out of her hand. Tila ran out, screaming at the top of her lungs.

"Keep it away from me!" The child spotted Crock and ran to hide behind him.

"Keep what…?" Crock jumped back and nearly fell over Tila as a bloody object raced between his legs.

"What the fu—?"

"Gram!" Tess yelled, hoping to cover the Ranger's unintended expletive.

A demented, old woman rushed through the door with a bloody butcher knife in hand.

"Where'd it go?" Gram shouted.

Crock reached out and grabbed Gram's arm to keep her from swinging the blade in his face. Unfortunately, fresh blood flew off the knife and splattered onto his pristine western shirt.

"Well, shit."

At the same time as Crock resumed his cursing, Gram struggled, yelling, "Let me go, you jackass! I've got a dead chicken to catch!"

Chapter Twenty-Three

Crock wasn't sure if he should go ahead and check into a mental health unit or wait until he was sentenced to a high-security facility. Hell, he might even drive the hundred and sixty-odd miles to the state hospital for the criminally insane in Vernon, just to save tax-payer dollars for the transport expenses.

Only the thought of Gemma Rae kept him from doing anything … unfortunate.

Instead of throttling the female members of the Corona family, he'd wasted an hour chasing a headless—or nearly headless—chicken. He didn't look too closely. He'd simply handed over the bird to meet its final fate.

Then came the calming of a hysterical child who demanded bushels of chocolate, with a strawberry milkshake on the side, in restitution for her mental anguish. He needed a large bottle of Texas bourbon to salve *his* mental anguish.

After assuring him that there was no Satanic, animal-sacrificing ritual, Tess explained that her great-uncle was a farmer who often brought his sister-in-law fresh meat. Crock guessed that what he'd witnessed was about as fresh as one could get.

With said chicken now on its way to the poultry afterlife, and its carcass relieved of feathers, well-massaged with assorted spices, and shoved into the oven, Crock had been convinced by the females to remove his shirt so they could ogle his abs—correction—*scrub* the dirt, blood, and grime out before it—the shirt—was ruined. There was some hope for his dress shirt, but his cotton undershirt resembled a crime scene or zombie victim.

He made a mental note to burn the damn things when he got home. There was also a high probability that he wouldn't be eating chicken anytime in the foreseeable future.

The phone conversation with his captain had been almost as fun as chasing the chicken. The asshole had nearly busted a gut when Crock called in an incident report. His captain was on his way to witness the aftermath for himself.

"Hey, Gram! When's dinner going to be done?"

He didn't hear the response, but it wasn't important. It would be a while before he ate anything again. Crock was ecstatic that Tess finally asked a question that wasn't directed at him, his comfort, or his workout routine. She was doing her damnedest to *not* stare at his chest since he'd removed the stained shirt. The grandmother wasn't as discreet.

He'd checked his truck for a replacement shirt but remembered the bag of spare clothing had been removed for washing and had yet to be replaced. Fortunately, Laz had come home from whatever errand he'd been running, rolled his eyes at the mayhem, and provided Crock with a T-shirt which sported a purple frog in full baseball gear. Although a little tight, it at least kept one precocious three-year-old from poking his bare six-pack.

That same, delightful child, who—not two hours

earlier—threw a fit about the demons of Hell chasing her around, now sat quietly in her great-grandmother's lap with a stuffed alien tucked in her skinny arms. He was afraid he was beginning to understand this family. And he was beginning to like them. That terrified him.

Laz walked in with refreshing, adult beverages in hand, which he proceeded to dole out to the grown-ups.

I might be working with nutcases but thank God they understand the curative properties of alcohol.

Crock estimated that a few dozen beers *might* help him recover from the last few hours. He hoped his boss would be willing to drive him home.

The thought had no sooner crossed his mind when the doorbell rang. Laz was closest and greeted the captain with typical Texas hospitality. "Hey! Come on in. Want a beer?"

Childs started to refuse but was interrupted by a precocious imp and a stuffed alien. "What's under your hat?" Tila demanded.

Crock knew the gruff Ranger liked kids and waited to see what his captain would do. "My head," Childs answered with a blinding white smile dedicated to the child. "Who's your friend?" pointing to the skinny, green doll.

"Mr. Snotbubble," the little girl answered.

Crock forced back a snort of laughter. Gemma Rae had barely been able say 'dolly' when she was three, much less come up with an off-the-wall name for a toy. "You shouldn't wear a hat in the house. Grammy says it's not nice."

"Your Grammy is a smart lady." Childs smiled as he reached up to remove his pristine white cowboy hat.

It wasn't often that Crock saw the man with any

fuzz covering his bald head. The man was meticulous about his hygiene. Crock wondered what had happened that his boss hadn't taken care of that tiny detail in what appeared to be several days.

And the kid offered her expert opinion on his appearance, "You look like a dandelion."

Crock suddenly realized he shouldn't drink while in the Corona household. Beer burned when spewed through the nasal cavity. His coughing and sputtering snorts drew Childs's attention. To the sight of Crock lounging, beer in hand, in ill-fitting, non-regulation attire.

"I'm off duty." Crock choked out in response to the disapproving glare.

"Uh huh. Then so am I." Childs growled, holding back his own amusement. As Laz shoved a bottle into one meaty hand, the captain waved an accusing finger at Crock. "What's with the Chippendale look?"

"Remember that phone call?"

"The one that brought me to this fine establishment? Something about rats, cockroaches, and chickens?"

"That's the one."

"Say no more." The captain glanced at the beer in his hand, shrugged his massive shoulders, and settled into a corner of the sofa. After introductions were made all around, he gestured out the door. "Why are y'all burning tobacco in seashells on the porch? Is that supposed to cover the sulphur smell?"

"Yeah, Gram," Laz said, "I thought I got rid of all the sulphur. Why does the front door smell like rotten eggs again?"

His grandmother reached for a second beer, but her

grandson held it out of reach. It only took one evil-eyed glare for Laz to hand it over.

Her black eyes glanced around the room before she finally drawled, “We’ve got pests. I’m trying to get rid of them.”

Crock wondered if she was referring to him a pest, but before he could ask, Tess spoke up. “Did we get an infestation of termites or something?” She sounded exhausted.

I don’t know why she’s so tired— I was the one chasing after the damn chicken. She was too busy laughing her sweet ass off.

Crock drained the last of his beer and picked up the fresh one waiting for his attention. His boss caught his eye to which Crock gave an indifferent shrug.

The elder Corona finished a swig of her drink before responding, “We don’t *now*. But that wasn’t the kind of pests I was using it for.”

Tess set her bottle aside. “What kind of pests?”

“Well, I’m looking at several right now.” The smirk on the older woman’s face changed as her eyes glanced over her family. “I probably need to get some more sulphur. And sage. Maybe then you won’t ask as many questions.”

Crock heard the buzz of a dryer. He rose, but Tess was faster. She returned with his shirt before any further insults could be exchanged

He headed to the downstairs bathroom to change out of the stripper-T. A heavy sigh escaped as he took in the laundered shirt in the mirror. Between lemon juice, meat tenderizer, and bleach, the fairly new shirt would never again be up to the Ranger’s dress code. The pale gray was now permanently marred with bleach spots and smelled like lemons and whatever god-awful girly perfume was in the homemade detergent.

Resigned to pick up some new shirts for work, Crock returned to the living room to find his boss questioning Tess about her military experience. He hoped Childs had better luck. As a former military man and with twenty years in the Texas Department of Public Safety, the man was accustomed to getting information, no matter how evasive the subject.

And Tess wasn't willing to give up her secrets.

He propped himself against the door frame and waited for the expert interrogation.

"Crock tells me you were in the Army," Childs began.

"Yes, sir."

"And you have a degree in psychology."

"Yes, sir."

"What'd a psych degree get you in the Army?" he asked before lifting the beer bottle to his lips.

Having never seen Childs take a drink of anything stronger than coffee, Crock swore the man only wet his lips with the liquid before realizing what he had in his hand and quickly set it down.

"I did what had to be done." Tess still wasn't giving anything away.

"Where were you stationed?"

Tess paused before answering, "Virginia."

Childs's lips lifted slightly. "Really? I've been to most of those bases. Where were you? Langley? Fort Lee?"

"Neither, sir."

"Quantico?"

Her dark eyes flew up to meet Child's amused gaze

but held onto her secrets.

"Seems I got a base hit." Childs leaned back with a smirk as his gaze slid to meet Crock's. "There aren't many divisions of the military that use Special Agent instead of rank. Crock mentioned you were well-versed in murder victim behavior and standard death scene procedures, and that you did a thorough job of questioning your target—although I don't understand how you can question a ghost. The fact that you were based in Virginia and just spouted off the CID motto—I simply filled in the gaps."

Criminal Investigation Division. That explains—a lot. Feeling like a dumbass for missing the obvious, Crock considered the questions Tess had asked and her attention to detail. With her knowledge and skills regarding the dead, he could only imagine the types of cases she dealt with in the Army. Especially if she spent time overseas.

He turned his attention to Tess. Since meeting her—had it only been three days?—he had been intrigued. Knowing that she had law enforcement experience only intensified his interest. The woman could relate to the job. In his experience, that understanding was a rarity.

"Wait just a damn minute!" Laz piped up. "For over ten years, I've been trying to figure out what in the hell she's been doing. I know Tess's been all over the world, but she never gave any details. And you've been here, what? Ten minutes! And you just…."

Tess broke in as Laz seemed to run out of verbiage. "I couldn't talk about much of my work. It was mostly classified."

"But to not even say which division you were in?"

If the red face was any indication, Laz was pissed. "I was worried, dammit! It drove me insane to hear you were in Tokyo one month and Afghanistan the next. Was your position so secret that you couldn't even share it with me?"

"I couldn't say anything because I have a stupid habit of telling you too damn much," Tess snapped. "Besides, you would have tried to justify my job to Mom, and we all know what she would have done."

"What? That she would have worried about you? Or been proud?"

Crock watched as Tess's entire body froze. The only thing that moved was the flash of fury and pain in her eyes. Apparently, her brother had said the wrong thing.

And Laz knew it. "I'm sorry. Shit! I didn't mean to—I meant that I was proud but scared for you. I just wanted to know *something*."

It was a full minute of silent, sibling communication before Tess closed her eyes and took a deep breath. When her eyes opened, she glanced at her grandmother before looking around the silent room.

"I'm sorry," Tess whispered, her face etched with caution and regret. "There was very little I could say about my work, so I chose to say nothing. I'm sorry you were worried. There were times—well, let's just say I wasn't behind a desk. My undergrad was in psychology *and* criminal justice, and I—have a master's degree in forensic psychology. I was a special agent who did a lot of investigations, profiling, and some undercover work. I was—*versatile*."

Crock didn't like the sound of that. From what he knew of the Army and its specialized divisions, versatility meant secrets and danger. Visions of espionage and takedowns danced in his head.

She continued, “I had to deal with a lot of scummy people and situations that I’d really rather forget.”

No one moved. Nothing was said. The tension remained thick until, finally, Tila crawled from her grandmother’s lap and shuffled to Tess’s side. Her tiny arms held out the stuffed alien. Tess responded by pulling the child onto her lap. They sat together, cuddled in the knowledge that all was good—if not a little weird.

The older woman slapped the arm of her tie-died recliner before standing. “Well, enough of that sentimental shit. Who’s ready for fresh, roast chicken with all the fixins’?”

Shudders flew up Crock’s spine as he shot to his feet. “Whoa! Look at the time!”

Chapter Twenty-Four

After a total of five beers—one plus a bit at the Coronas and four while regaling his neighbor with the events of the day—and not enough water or food on his stomach, Crock met the next morning with an early start and a couple of painkillers. He had to make a dent in his to-do list before collecting Tess for a visit with the document examiner.

Fortunately, the TCU campus was practically empty. Crock knew summer school—or mini-mester, or whatever the hell it was called—was in session, but apparently not many students roamed the campus during that time. With no Mallorys tagging after him, he was able to go directly to his target—Mrs. Claudette Hudgens—with neither help or hinderance.

She sat at her desk, looking the epitome of professionalism, with a portly, older man in an ill-fitting suit standing over her. The way the admin glared and leaned away from the man told Crock that either the man had severe onion breath or Mrs. Hudgens was displeased by the invasion of her territory.

Maybe both.

A look of relief flashed on her face when she caught sight of Crock. Before she could greet him, the man straightened and eyed Crock suspiciously. "Sir, this is a school campus. We do not permit handguns. You will need to leave, or I will be forced to contact campus security."

Mrs. Hudgens was quick to correct him. "Dean Johnson, this is Sergeant Ward with the Texas Rangers. Sergeant Ward, this is our Dean of Humanities, Dr. Terrence Johnson."

The look on Dean Johnson's face didn't change, even at the sight of Crock's badge and credentials. "What on earth would bring a Texas Ranger to our campus?"

Crock raised an eyebrow. "An investigation."

The other man scoffed, "What investigation? I haven't been informed of any investigations involving TCU."

"The school is not under investigation." Crock decided he was pretty much done with the pompous asshole, but he needed to play nicely. "I'm working on an unsolved case, investigating the death of Esme Green, the wife of Dr. Dan Green."

Dean Johnson laughed. "You can't possibly think anyone at TCU had anything to do with her death."

Crock narrowed his eyes at the man's assumption. "I never said that, sir."

"Then what exactly are you saying?"

"That I am investigating an unsolved case."

Dean Johnson waited.

Crock waited.

Johnson cracked first. "I have other business to attend to. If you will excuse me."

"One question, if you don't mind, Dr. Johnson." Crock stopped the man once his hand reached for the door to an inside office. When the dean turned, he asked, "Were you with TCU in 1995, when Mrs. Green died?"

Dr. Johnson straightened. "I was a member of faculty at the time, yes. Why?"

"I may have some questions for you regarding the events surrounding that time."

"I fail to see how I can be of any help." A fine sheen of sweat glistened on the dean's forehead. "I am a very busy man, Mr. Ward."

"Sergeant."

"I beg your pardon?"

"It's *Sergeant* Ward." Crock kept his tone calm but firm. He wasn't even sure he needed to speak with the man. But the guy was being an ass, and he was feeling ornery. "I thought you might have a…unique perspective of the circumstances during that time."

"And if I don't."

Crock pretended to consider his answer. "Then I guess I will have to thank you for your time and continue with my investigation."

The man sputtered—obviously frustrated by not getting to throw his considerable weight around—before giving a curt nod. "Well, I guess that would be all right. After all, Dr. Green was only absent for the one class."

Crock fought his eyebrows into submission. He didn't want to appear too interested and scare the man away from giving valuable information. "Did you cover a class for him?"

Dean Johnson sniffed. "Of course, Dan was my mentor, as well as my friend and coworker. If he needed to pick up an anniversary gift for his wife, I was perfectly capable of covering for him."

Crock's notepad magically emerged from his pocket, and his pen was already making note of the dean's revelation. "Do you recall the time?"

The dean eyed the notebook with suspicion. "Why are you writing that down?"

"Just making a few notes." Crock clicked his pen. He wondered if the school kept records of class schedules for over twenty years. It would be a massive headache to figure out what classes might fit with the timeframe. "I never know what information might become important."

"Of course, it is important!" the man huffed. "I didn't think I would get lunch that day because of that class, but Dan brought me a sandwich as thanks."

Or, instead of going through ancient files, I can get the information I need from the pretentious, and unwitting coworker. "How did Dr. Green appear on his return?"

As expected, Dean Johnson's feathers were ruffled. "The man was a professional. And a friend. He apologized profusely for my inconvenience, then proceeded with his day. His distraction was expected. They had planned for their thirty-fifth anniversary for months—returning to their honeymoon suite as they did every year. He wanted this one to be special."

Unbelievable. Crock did his best to keep his temper in check. He hoped that the timeline was off and simply missing from the investigation file or tucked into the missing evidence box. He might be able to forgive that sin. But if the original investigators failed to follow-up on this smoking gun, that the professor had plenty of time to get to and from the hotel, then Crock—and his boss—were going to throw a holy conniption fit. Any other cases those officers might have mishandled would be suspect. With the investigating officer dead, he prayed that rest of the team had long retired and weren't still mucking up investigations.

"Thank you, Dean Johnson." Crock gave the man a genuine smile. "You have been a great help today."

The man's eyes widened in surprise, then quickly narrowed. Without acknowledging Crock, he turned to his waiting admin. "Claude, I will need that power point by the end of the day."

Her hand twitched, leaving a slight wobble in her otherwise precise handwriting. "It's already in your inbox, sir," came the calm response.

The door didn't hit the Dean as he fled the room, but there was a cloud of dust left in his wake.

Crock bit back a triumphant grin. *Asshole.*

Under control, he turned to face the unruffled admin. Before he could speak, an unexpected interruption bounded through a door behind the secretary's desk. Crock smothered a groan. "Hello, Mallory."

"Sergeant Ward!" the student gushed, dancing from one foot to the other. "I was hoping to see you again. I did some research on the Texas Rangers."

"Mallory…."

The puppy was as enthusiastic as ever and either didn't hear or didn't listen to Mrs. Hudgens.

"They were founded by Stephen F. Austin in 1823 to protect the Republic of Texas from—"

"Mallory!" Mrs. Hudgens would not be ignored.

"Yes, ma'am?" The puppy stilled and turned her wide-eyed attention to the woman who was apparently her boss.

The admin proceeded with her patented, quiet authority, "I don't believe Sergeant Ward is here for a review of his employer's history, as fascinating as it is. If you are through arranging those files, you may deliver this paperwork." Several folders appeared in the older woman's hand. "To the President's office."

"Yes, ma'am." Mallory accepted the pile, but eyed Crock with adoring puppy eyes.

Before she made it to the door, Crock caught her attention. "I'm sure you've done some excellent research, Mallory. If you are interested in further information, there's a museum in Waco dedicated to the Rangers history. It also has a research facility where many of our archives are held. You might check it out." He didn't add that much of his family history resided within those hallowed walls.

Her face lit up with excitement. If she had a tail, it would have been a blur. "Thank you, Sergeant Ward. I'll look it up."

After the student disappeared, he turned back to the admin. For the third time, he was cut off—but who was counting.

"Thank you for your patience, Sergeant. Was there something you needed?" Mrs. Hudgens stood at her desk as if nothing was unusual.

Relieved to finally get to the point, Crock began, "I actually came by to see you, Mrs. Hudgens."

"I will be happy to assist if I am able, Sergeant Ward."

An idea sat brewing in his head since he'd realized the file held no mention of Dr. Green's alibi being confirmed. The interaction with Dean Johnson confirmed his suspicions. "You worked with Dr. Green?" he began.

"Oh, yes. Until his death."

"How long have you worked here?"

Mrs. Hudgens studied him. "I started at TCU in 1994 as a student intern. Dr. Green was already a tenured professor. Dean Johnson was adjunct faculty at the time."

"So, you probably met Mrs. Green."

She nodded. "Esme was sweet. She was a professional dancer and taught modern dance on an adjunct basis. I even signed up for her classes for credit."

Crock tried to envision the prim woman before him doing any form of modern dance. He gave up quickly. "Were you interviewed after her death? I didn't find your name among the notes."

Mrs. Hudgens shook her head. "No, I wasn't interviewed. I was a student worker. But, if there is a list of staff members or students, I would be listed under my maiden name—Collins."

Crock still held his notepad and pen, ready to record anything helpful. "What do you remember from that time?"

"I remember that day clearly. Dr. Green came with a package that morning, well before his ten o'clock class. He said it was their thirty-fifth wedding anniversary and asked if I wouldn't mind wrapping her gift for him. Since I was in his class after lunch, I offered to deliver it then."

The hotel manager had said that Dr. Green arrived at the hotel, gift in hand, only to find his wife dead. According to Dean Johnson, the professor had left his mid-day class to get a gift.

"What happened next?" he asked her.

"It was rather odd," she mused, "I wrapped the gift,

took it to class with me, but Dr. Johnson led the class instead."

Crock's head shot up. "When did Dr. Green return?"

"It wasn't before three. The class was supposed to end at two, but several of us remained in the room to work on a project. Dr. Green met me here in the office shortly afterward to pick up the gift."

"Did he say anything about where he had been?"

Mrs. Hudgens shook her head. "He was in a hurry to leave. He said he didn't want to be late for his anniversary."

Crock did the math. There were several hours unaccounted for. Those same hours fit the time frame that Mrs. Green was alone in her hotel room. Clearing his throat, he pressed for more. "Did he seem different in any way?"

She nodded. "He was flustered. The dean—that would have been Dr. Taylor—wanted to talk to him about missing class and the students' complaints, but Dr. Green just scheduled an appointment for the following week and left."

"Are there others—either students or staff—who might have information?"

She indicated the dean's office. "The staff has changed several times over the years. Dr. Johnson and I are the only ones remaining from that year."

Crock would have liked to ask a few more questions of the dean, but he had an appointment with a cute, but annoying twin who might go off on her own without him present to keep her out of trouble.

"For the moment, this information gives me a much-needed direction. If I have any further questions,

I will be sure to contact you."

She gave him a tight smile. "Of course. I would be happy to help."

"Thank you for your time, Mrs. Hudgens. Have a good afternoon."

He turned to leave, but the admin stopped him. "Sergeant?"

Crock turned back. "Yes, ma'am?"

Indecision and anguish flickered across her face before resolve took over. "Thank you."

"For what?"

Mrs. Hudgens moved to the edge of her desk, her left hand idly skimming the surface. A simple gold band winked as the light hit the metal. "It was your recommendation that led to my interview with Captain Childs. That position would be perfect…for someone."

Crock released the doorknob and stepped back. "You aren't going to take the job."

"No." She offered a small smile. "I wanted you to know that I appreciated your faith in me, and I wanted you to hear my answer from me, before I spoke with the captain."

"I have to tell you that I'm disappointed." Crock said carefully. Something wasn't right. "May I ask why? Did something offend you?"

"Nothing like that." Her smile dimmed. "There are many reasons, but the main one is that I am settled here."

His internal lie-detector pinged, but his tone never changed even though he wanted to beg her to join Company B. "That's not the main reason, is it?"

Confirmation came when she closed her eyes to shut him out. Something bothered her about the position. He thought she might give a better answer, but time ran out.

"Claude!"

Mrs. Hudgens—who obviously did not care for the shortened version of her name—stiffened at the shout from the inner office. All remnants of emotion disappeared. "It's enough," she answered him first. "If you will excuse me, I must return to my work."

Chapter Twenty-Five

Tess wasn't sure what to expect when Crock told her they were meeting with a document examiner. She had worked with one while in the Army, but he had been thoroughly military. And a total ass.

The tall, older woman who entered the small conference room was infinitely preferable. Impeccably dressed in green and turquoise with matching accessories, Nancy Carter had a slight stoop in her posture and a gentle demeanor which made her seem more grandmotherly than a court-appointed expert. If the woman was surprised to find someone other than a Ranger present, she gave no sign.

"Good afternoon," she said, smiling as she introduced herself.

Crock rose from his seat to shake her hand. He made to pull out her chair, but she waved him away with a gracious smile. "I understand you have a few questions about my report."

"Thank you for meeting with us, Ms. Carter. I'm Sergeant Crock Ward, and this is Tess Corona. She and her brother are consultants on the Green investigation."

"Please, call me Nancy." Her gray eyes twinkled as she addressed Tess, "Corona? That's an interesting name. What kind of consulting do you do?"

Tess wasn't prepared to do more than listen. "Oh, uhm, I, well…"

Crock sat down. "Tess has experience in profiling and brings a unique perspective to the case. She's helping me understand the motives behind what might have happened with the Greens."

Tess was surprised by Crock's response. It was entirely truthful, but sufficiently vague when it came to her involvement.

He continued, "We hoped that your findings might help clear up some of the more confusing elements."

Nancy grinned. "That's a nice way of putting it. This case has more twists and turns than a drunk, baby giraffe."

Tess knew then she had met a kindred spirit. "That's an accurate description. What did you find?"

Nancy reached into her cordovan-colored attaché to remove a packet of papers and a spiral-bound notebook. Tess tore her gaze away from the leather bag which she coveted—a lot—and leaned forward to find the papers were copies. She studied them while the expert flipped through her notes.

Finding the right page, Nancy began, "In addition to the original will, there are two codicils which leave all monies and real estate to his remaining family instead of the university as originally bequeathed, there is an additional life insurance policy dated the week before Dr. Green's death, and three personal letters of intent."

As she mentioned each item, the analyst pointed to the corresponding page. "As you can see, the professor had a distinct handwriting and an articulate style which I would expect from someone of his education and caliber. However, his hand had developed a tremor which made isolating the writing patterns challenging."

Tess idly picked up the copy closest to her. The addressee on the letter drew her attention.

Nancy eyed the sheet in Tess's hand. "I see you found the one which might interest you the most."

Crock's raised eyebrow encouraged her to read the name aloud. "This one is addressed to Dr. Lazaro Corona."

Crock's eyebrows disappeared behind his hairline, while Nancy made a noise with her tongue. "I assume that Dr. Corona is a relative of yours?" she asked.

Tess gave a slow nod. "He's my twin brother."

"Ah," Nancy glanced at her notes. "That letter appears to be…"

Tess completed the expert's statement. "Real."

Nancy's surprised gaze met hers. "It is. How did you know?"

Crock also shifted his attention to her. "Did you see something?"

"No." Tess reassured him but hesitated to continue. "It just feels right." They waited for more until the attention grew uncomfortable. "That's all I get."

After studying Tess for a moment, Nancy's gray eyes looked thoughtful as she selected another page from her file. "How does this one feel?"

Immediately, Tess shook her head. "That one's just wrong."

The expert's lips pursed. "Perhaps you don't need me, after all."

Tess's eyes shot up to meet Nancy's amused gaze. "No, please, I just have a sense of what was Dr. Green's and what wasn't. It's nothing which would stand up in court."

Nancy gave her a soft smile. "What is it you are

looking for here, then? How can I help?"

Tess put the copy down and leaned forward. "I'm not sure. I've had a few experiences…"

"Psychic experiences?" Nancy pressed.

Even though the woman had guessed correctly, Tess didn't feel comfortable telling Nancy about her extrasensory talents. Not when she had difficulty discussing those skills with her own family.

The woman continued with a knowing glance, "In my spare time, I'm a chaplain at Parkland Hospital, and I've seen many things over the years. Some things defy explanation. Very little surprises me anymore."

Her instincts told her to trust Nancy, but Tess still hesitated. Crock's presence helped make the decision to share. "I've been able to visualize events which happened by touching something related to the event. I know it sounds crazy, but I'm trying to figure out how this works."

"Interesting!" Nancy exclaimed. "If you can sense what is a forgery versus what is real from a copy, what do you think you might get from the actual document?"

"I don't know." Tess realized the woman wasn't shocked by her admission. "I haven't handled anything paper-based from this case yet."

"But what you aren't saying is that you *have* handled a forgery before." Nancy shuffled through more papers. "What happened that time?"

Tess glanced at Crock. As usual, he sat back to watch and listen. Only the eyebrow twitch encouraged her to go on. "It was a title transfer for a business." As she told the woman of Karlyn's situation, Tess realized that this woman might be the answer to the daycare issues. "My friend needs help to get her sister's business back. Do you know any attorneys that handle these types of cases?"

Nancy reassured her, "I've worked with many from all over the state. What county was this in?"

"Tarrant."

"The first one who comes to mind is Octavia Brown. I can forward her information to Sergeant Ward if you'd like. I assume this is your case, Sergeant?"

Crock gave a brief nod but said nothing.

Tess sighed with relief. "That would be helpful. Thank you."

Nancy made note of the request in her notebook before returning to the task at hand. She pulled a clear plastic folder from her neat stack. "I have the originals here. Let's see what you can do."

The folder landed in front of her. Tess wasn't sure she wanted to touch the plastic, much less the documents within. Unfortunately, she had a sexy Ranger to test her limits. He grabbed the folder and flipped through the contents. He sorted them before placing them face-down on the table. "Don't look at the content," he advised, "just feel."

She glared at him. The eyebrow lifted. *Do I really want to get into a staring contest with him?*

His eyes narrowed. *No. No, I do not.*

Tess huffed as her right hand hovered over the first document. Nothing. Crock shifted in the seat next to her. *Quit stalling, Corona.*

Her fingers touched the cool paper.

Dan studied the framed picture of his wife. A pen nervously tapped the desktop.

"I'm sorry, my dear. I should have fought harder."

He removed a bottle of pills from a desk drawer.

"But I have it all arranged. I will be able to join you soon. Very soon."

Tess withdrew her hand with a gasp and leapt from her seat. Without thinking, she found herself in the corner of the small room.

"What happened?" Crock's chair scraped the tile as he rose from his seat.

Tess wondered how the room had become so cold. It was when Crock's warm grip pried her shaking hands from her face that she realized she was the only one who was chilled.

"Don't you dare pass out on me."

Pass out?

That was a good possibility. When Tess realized throwing up was equally an option, she looked around for alternatives that wouldn't be as embarrassing.

Nancy came to the rescue with a bottle of water. "Here. Sip this."

A hand, which didn't belong to her, held the bottle to her lips and poured. The water was cold, and a fair amount spilled out of her mouth and onto her shirt. Even though she was freezing, the shock of a damp bra woke her numb senses.

She was leaning against a warm brick wall.

The brick wall spoke, "Are you going to live?"

The body might be warm, but the soul was an iceberg.

"Yeah," Tess muttered, closing her eyes while inhaling *eau d'Crock*. A little bit of spice, a little bit of leather, and a whole-freaking-lot of male. It was nice. Nice and safe. She wondered how long she could make this last.

Hands pushed her back. *Not long enough.*

"Look at me."

No problemo. Tess raised her eyes to meet his. Concern mixed with determination as he scanned her for something—sanity maybe?

"Does that happen often?"

Tess started at the sound of Nancy's voice. She'd almost forgotten she wasn't alone with Crock. "I'm fine."

"Uh huh," Crock grunted. "You know Laz is going to have my head if I take you back looking like you're one step from joining the Greens, right?"

Screw Laz. "I'm fine," Tess repeated. If she was going to continue to do this shit, she was going to have to get a grip or take up drinking as a hobby.

Reluctantly, she shoved away from Crock and faced the other woman who waited patiently across the table. "I'm sorry, Miss Nancy," she began, "having these visions has been a new experience for me. I don't quite have a handle on my reaction."

With a reassuring smile, Nancy gave her arm a squeeze. "That's all right, dear. It can't be easy to witness past events. I can only imagine what that must be like. I hope you never see someone committing a murder."

Tess's smile faded.

Fortunately, Crock changed the subject. A little. "So, what did you get with that letter?"

Slowly exhaling, Tess answered, "Nothing bad. It was Dr. Green. He was at his desk, talking to a picture of his wife."

Crock nodded. "Laz mentioned that he sometimes overheard Dan talking to her photos. What did he say?"

"He said, 'I'm sorry, my dear. I should have fought

harder.'" Tess hesitated before deciding not to mention the pills—yet. She shook her head. "I don't know what he means."

Neither did Crock apparently, but he did look thoughtful. He reached over and picked up the document she'd dropped. "This is the letter to Laz," he said as he scanned the letter. Tess expected an eyebrow to raise, and sure enough, it did. His eye caught hers. "I think Laz needs to see this."

She hesitated before taking the letter from him, anticipating another vision, but apparently the paper had told her everything it needed to. After reading the first paragraph, she stopped. "I think you're right."

"Where is he?"

"He was meeting with a grad student to discuss their dissertation." Tess handed the letter back to Crock who slid it back into its protective folder. "After that, he was going to take Tila to the park."

While Tess pulled out her phone to send a text to her twin, Crock turned back to Nancy. "This one piece is a breakthrough. Do you have any other helpful information?"

Nancy shook her head. A gleam sparkled in her eyes. "All the letters appear to be written by the same hand, as was one of the codicils. The insurance documents and the second addendum are not. I assume the recipient of this letter hasn't seen it?"

"No."

"And have you read the will?" Nancy kept her attention on Crock, "Or the addendums?"

It was Crock's turn to shake his head. "No, I haven't seen any of these. The case file pertains to the wife's death, not Dr. Green."

Tess watched the spark in the older woman's eye glitter before shuffling through the papers on the desk. Nancy found what she was looking for and handed a couple of pages to Crock. His face was unreadable as he perused the pages.

Until both eyebrows rose.

Crock exchanged a glance with Nancy as he handed the sheets back. They said nothing.

Tess waited for him to share the intel.

And waited.

And waited.

Her phone pinged. "Laz says he'll meet us at home in an hour."

"I can only release the originals to the court." Nancy assembled her paperwork. "However, if the sergeant would like me to make a copy for his file…."

Crock gave the document examiner a ghost of a smile which made Tess green with envy. "That would be helpful. Thank you, Ms. Carter."

"Any time." Nancy turned to Tess. "It was lovely to meet you, Tess. I will send you Octavia's information when I return to my office."

Tess reached for the woman's hand. "Thank you so much, Miss Nancy. I hope we get a chance to meet again."

****

After getting the necessary copies from Nancy, Crock led Tess back to his truck without a word. He was more than a little frustrated by her lack of trust, but he waited until she was secured in his vehicle before he laid into her. "I thought we had a deal."

"What?"

Crock wanted to strangle his companion. He gave

her credit for attempting to sound innocent. "You are supposed to share what you're experiencing so Laz and I can help figure out the details." He was proud he didn't yell at her, although he *really* wanted to. "Teamwork. Remember that little concept? I know the Army taught you that much."

"I didn't…."

He cut off her protest. "Yes, you did. You shut down at the cemetery, and you shut down in there. I know you saw more than you admitted. What else did you see?"

"Why should I tell you?" she shot back. "You didn't share that last little bit of info."

Crock thought about the will's codicil. The one Nancy Carter had indicated was real. He hadn't shared it, but it certainly made Dan's death a little more suspicious. And a lot more problematic.

"I have to do some checking. It might be a rabbit hole. But—" he cut off what would be an obnoxiously loud protest from her, "—I *will* share as soon as I can verify what it means."

Tess was somewhat mollified.

"And—" Crock watched mutiny return to her face "—I need to know what else you saw before we leave this parking lot." He met her glare with one of his own.

She finally huffed, then caved. "He had a bottle of pills. He said something about joining Esme."

"And the cemetery vision?"

"Pretty much the same thing." She sighed. "He said he had everything ready. They would dance on their anniversary."

Crock propped his elbow on the steering wheel and tapped the dash with a finger while he considered the new information. “Did he take the pills?”

“No,” Tess settled back into her seat. “He set them aside while he wrote the letter. Was there anything in the letters to indicate he was dying?”

He shook his head. “His death certificate wasn’t specific, but there’s a photo of him taken shortly before his death. I still have to check with the medical examiner about my suspicions about arsenic use.”

Tess’s neck cracked as her head swung toward him. “The suicide by poison theory?”

Crock sighed as he reached to start the truck. “Or someone doctored his meds.”

Chapter Twenty-Six

No amount of ibuprofen could stop the rhythmic pounding in his head or the gripping pain in his back. Even though Laz didn't want to complain, his entire body ached like a bitch. Thanks to Gram's potions, the family rarely got sick. But when someone did, Gram turned to her natural medicines and cooked up vile concoctions which emerged from every possible orifice.

If you lived, you made damn sure you didn't get sick again.

After the meetings with his students—which were disastrous—he'd looked forward to spending quality time with Tila. He could take her to the park, sit on a shady bench while she played, then take her for ice cream. None of those activities threatened his coexistence with life or required significant movement or thought on his part.

Then he got a text from Tess which altered his entire plan for the afternoon.

After a quick conference with the dean over the issues with the dissertations, he'd trudged to his car, only to find some little twerp had been busy vandalizing his SUV. The tires were slashed, his headlights were sparling little rubies and diamonds on the ground, and—rather than protecting the inside from the elements—the smashed windows littered the floorboards and seats.

That was one phone call he didn't want to make. He hated asking Tess for favors. And now a favor was owed to Crock, and that was even worse. By the time they reached him, the tow truck had taken his car away, and the headache had risen to DefCon twelve. Pain meds weren't going to cut it. Amputation of his head might.

They met him in his office as he was locking up. "What happened?" Tess demanded.

Laz rubbed his head and neck as he related the events.

Crock turned on his investigator mode. "Did they take anything?"

"A gym bag," Laz reported, shifting his backpack to his left shoulder. The pain in his neck and back protested. "They didn't get anything but some sweaty gym socks."

"That'll serve 'em right," was Tess's only comment.

"What did campus police say?" Crock wanted to know.

Laz shook his head, immediately regretting it as the pain made his head swim. "There's a gang running around. They shop the cars for any signs of gear they can sell for drugs. Today was my lucky day."

He led them toward the stairs. The combined thumping of their feet pulsed through his head. Nausea churned his gut. He forced himself to keep going, hoping that Tess's twin-dar wouldn't notice.

Tess stopped at the top step before whirling on him. "What's wrong?"

Laz didn't expect the sudden movement and barreled into his sister. His foot slipped off the step he'd been aiming for, leaving him grasping for the railing. He missed.

Time slowed as he teetered on the edge of steps until gravity took over. Tess grabbed for his arm, snagging the strap to his backpack instead. The pack slipped from his shoulder and joined gravity as Laz tumbled down the steps, landing hard on the basement floor.

"Laz!" His sister's shout reverberated through the stairwell and his head.

Before he could get his wits together, a body landed on top of him. All air left his lungs in a hurry when what felt like a knee landed in his gut. Breathing was not an option for several minutes.

"Ow! Fuck!" he rasped when he was finally able to exhale. He fought to keep from throwing up.

"Oh, God! I'm sorry," Tess patted him over, checking for broken bones.

"Give him room," another voice commanded. Tess disappeared from Laz's chest, and he could look up and see Crock leaning over him. One arm held Tess back, but the glare in her eyes said she wasn't happy with the Ranger.

"I…I'm okay." Laz wheezed, assuring himself as much as his companions. Nothing felt broken. Well, maybe his pride, but that was expendable.

He pushed up from the floor and flipped over to his hands and knees. It felt easier to breathe in that position, so he didn't rush to stand up. His head and back wouldn't allow it. After a minute, he climbed to his feet.

Tess was there to help. "Are you all right?"

"I will be." He wasn't certain about that, but it was

what a Corona was expected to say. "Give me a minute."

Laz felt, rather than saw, the look exchanged between Tess and Crock. He fought the surfacing irritation. "Tell me what you found out." He needed something other than their worry to focus on. "What did the letter say?"

Crock pulled a folded paper from his inside jacket pocket. "Dr. Green wrote several letters. They were verified as being in his handwriting, while other items were not. This one is addressed to you."

Laz took the offered paper and tried to read his name on the envelope, but the image swam around, making his stomach and head lurch. He handed it back, then braced his hands on his knees for support. "I don't think I can read it right now. What does it say?"

Tess took the document from the Ranger and opened it. "Dr. Green was proud of you, Laz," she paraphrased. "He thought you had the skills to help bring him and Esme peace."

His throat tightened.

"He blames himself for her death and trusts you to find the answers." Tess glanced up. "He ends with 'Don't overlook the truth.'"

Trust. Truth. Laz swallowed hard. Did he even know what that was anymore? He hadn't recognized what was happening with his ex, Miranda. Tess hadn't trusted him with her secrets. He didn't see the problems with Tila's daycare.

Trust. Truth. How could anyone trust him to find the truth?

Dan did it. He killed his wife.

He didn't know how—or why—but he was certain

of that fact. It should have bothered him, but for some reason—it didn't.

Tess's voice broke through the disturbing thoughts rushing through his head. "There's a bit more. Some things he wanted you to do. Do you want me to read it to you?"

Slowly, he pushed upright. He shook off his sister's help as he began the slow ascent back up the stairs. "Not right now," he grunted. "I'll look at it when we get home."

Boots and tennis shoes followed him more closely and more loudly than he wanted. At the moment, he needed to get home, avoid Gram and her potions, and take a bucket of pain meds—and maybe go to sleep. Permanently.

Where in the hell did that come from?

The light bounced off the windows, blinding him. He stumbled. Two sets of hands grabbed him by his arms to keep him from falling on his face.

"Laz?"

"Are you okay?"

He didn't answer. His balance recovered—his head not so much. One set of hands released him, but the other set—Tess's—kept hold.

Laz refused to show his appreciation for her help. Not that he needed it—but he needed it. The path to the truck didn't look right, and he was more than a bit queasy. He was a grown-assed man, stumbling toward a car in broad daylight without a drop of alcohol to blame. Could he be a bigger moron?

Yes. Yes, he could. Falling down the stairs in front of the world was a bone-headed move. His sister landing on top of him because she had tried to catch him topped that spectacular cake. He wondered how many students witnessed his glorious athleticism—or lack thereof. What the hell would Dean Johnson say?

They don't want you here, anyway.

Laz shook his head. He didn't know where that thought came from. He'd just talked with Dr. Johnson. They discussed the possibility of a full-time contract. That wouldn't happen if they didn't want him.

What in the hell is wrong with me? "Yeah," he lied in answer to Crock's question, taking care to not let the soul-sucking thoughts escape. "I'm okay. Although, sailing down the stairs and Tess landing on my liver wasn't exactly my idea of a good time." *Okay, maybe I can't keep a lid on some things.*

"Did I break anything?" Tess said anxiously. "Maybe we should get you checked out."

"Nah, I'll live." At least, he thought so—until he tried to climb into Crock's truck. Every muscle, bone, and tendon protested hauling his ass into the cab. Even his fingernails threatened revenge. His pride demanded he not ask the Ranger or Tess for help. Somehow, he made it. Barely.

The ride home was almost more than he could handle. Laz gritted his teeth on every pothole they hit. The first time a car cut them off, a surge of anger swept through him. He didn't know why. After all, he wasn't the one driving, and Crock was more than capable of dealing with maniac drivers.

Still, every turn, every stop light, every pebble in the road made him want to grab the wheel and haul ass into a concrete wall, taking the other cars on the road with him. *No! I don't want to hurt people!*

By the time they reached their exit, Laz was barely

hanging on to reality. His back was cramping, and his focus was shot. It was all he could do to keep from opening the door and throwing himself out of the truck. Into oncoming traffic.

Do it!

No! Dammit! Laz buried his head in his hands. *God, my head hurts.*

"Laz?"

He jumped when a hand settled on his shoulder. "Don't!" he shouted. His head throbbed at the sound of his own voice.

Tess yanked her hand away. Both she and Crock eyed him with suspicion.

"I didn't mean to scare you," Tess began, "but you didn't answer my question."

His heart thumped heavily in his chest, and his gut threatened to remove all its remaining contents. "Uh…I didn't hear you."

Tess stared at him as if she was trying to read his mind. "I asked if you wanted to pick up some BBQ. We haven't had that in a while."

His stomach revolted at the idea. "Pull over!"

The door flew open, and he lurched from the cab before Crock brought the truck to a full stop. He crashed to his hands and knees; the gravel burned as it cut into his flesh. The little bit of water he'd drunk spewed onto the mix of weeds and rock. He couldn't identify the putrid and garish mix of the other shit which emerged from his gut, but it wasn't anything he'd eaten. Tremors racked his body until nothing else came up. It was only then that Laz became aware of Tess's panicked shouting. "Get me that bottle!"

A second later, a water bottle was shoved…. "Ow,

fuck!"

"What?" Tess demanded.

"That was my nose, dammit!"

"Well, if you'd sit up a bit, I could see where your mouth is." Tess had learned sympathy and empathy from Gram. Laz was certain the Army shoved any remaining sentiment into a black hole.

That's not right. Tess is a good person. She's just trying to help.

Something wet and warm doused the back of his neck and head. His eyes stung as water and sweat dripped into his face. He tried to shake the water from his eyes, but his stomach protested the move.

"We're almost to your house. Let's get him out of the road."

Hands that couldn't belong to his sister hauled him from the road. It was only then that he noticed the sharp bite of the gravel embedded in his hands and knees. Laz glanced down. Warm blood streaked down his hands, and his good chinos now possessed a shredded hole where his knee skid on the pavement.

"Sit here." Crock man-handled his stunned body to sit on the floorboard of the passenger seat. "Don't move."

Not a problem. With his legs feeling like little more than spaghetti noodles, Laz didn't argue. He heard the Ranger digging around in the back, so he looked up to find Tess's face nearby. She was pale and chewing her lip—a sure sign she was worried.

"I'm okay, Tessie."

"Are you sure?" She didn't believe him. He didn't believe him either.

"Yeah."

Crock slammed a case behind the seat. "I've got some antiseptic for your scrapes."

Tess grabbed them from his hands. "I'll do it."

His sister's nursing skills were lacking on a good day, but Laz figured she needed to do something for him. He bit back a string of curses as she dug boulders out of his kneecap and wiped the wounds down with an alcohol wipe. Fortunately, Crock simply handed him another one for his hands.

Laz tried to make a joke. "What? You're not going to doctor my boo-boos and wipe my tears?"

Crock only lifted an eyebrow. "I *could*—but then I'd have to give you a boo-boo to cry about."

"No thanks."

Tess shoved a dirty wipe into a plastic bag. "While I'm thrilled y'all are able to laugh about this, I really want to know what's going on. You don't usually get sick."

"I don't know." Laz rubbed one hand over his face. His headache had eased somewhat, but he could barely remember the last few hours. Everything was hazy. "Maybe it was a bad burrito or something."

"You don't eat burritos."

"Or something!" he growled, shooting an irritated look at her.

Tess glared at him back. "So, what did you eat? 'Cause I sure as hell don't want to eat there. Ever."

Laz thought back. "Uhm…well, hell."

"Well, hell what?" she demanded.

"I don't remember."

Her eyes grew wide. The look she exchanged with Crock didn't bode well. Especially when Crock pulled out his phone.

"Who're you calling?" Laz demanded, knowing the answer.

"Paramedics."

"What!" he shouted, making his temple give a reminder of intense pain. "I don't need a stinkin' ambulance."

Tess stepped in. "Laz, you fell down the stairs, and I landed on you. You've got nausea and vomiting. That can't be good."

"No." He watched the duo exchange glances. Crock slowly tucked the phone back into his pocket.

Tess turned back to him, her face grim. "Fine. Then, you get to deal with Gram."

"Well, shit." *I'd rather deal with the paramedics*

.

Chapter Twenty-Seven

"I'm fine, dammit! Leave me…oh, hell no! I'm not…fuck…."

Crock waited in the relative safety of the living room, listening to a shaman torture her victim with some vile-smelling concoction. He was concerned about Laz's health and still thought a visit to the ER was in order. Tess had fallen pretty hard on the professor's right side. It was highly likely his liver was squashed, or ruptured, or whatever happened to livers when another body landed on them.

On the other hand, it was damned funny to hear a grown man get some weird herbal tonic shoved down his throat.

"Are you off duty?"

He glanced up to find Tess standing in the kitchen doorway, holding two bottles of beer, complete with lime wedges tucked in the rim.

"I can be." He reached over and accepted his due, with a mental note to limit today's consumption. One hangover a year was a hard maximum. His responsibilities didn't permit drinking to excess any more than that. As Tess settled into the sofa across from him, curiosity took over. "Exactly *what* is she doing to him?"

She popped the lime through the neck of her bottle with her thumb. "When it comes to Gram, I live by a simple rule—don't ask."

Crock snorted as he gave his drink the same treatment. "I guess you've had your fair share of your grandmother's remedies over the years."

"You could say that."

"Do they work?"

Her wary brown eyes shifted over to meet his. "Usually."

There was nothing to say to that answer. They sat, quietly listening to the argument in the other room.

Laz was losing. "Gram! I don't need…" Whatever Laz didn't need got lost behind choking and sputtered curses. "Fuck! That shit's nasty!"

Crock offered a silent prayer that he would never be on the receiving end of one of the older woman's remedies. Ever.

"Where'd Tila go?" Crock realized he hadn't seen the child since they'd arrived.

With a grunt, Tess set down her beer and hauled her body up from her comfortable position to lean over the arm of the sofa, presenting him with a view of her fine, toned ass. She landed back in her original position with a small addition in her lap. A squeal accompanied the loss of his spectacular view.

Crock thought he'd seen enough weirdness in the Corona household, but he hadn't yet seen a miniature ewok, wearing a sparkly, purple tutu and holding one stuffed alien.

The ewok ballerina wasn't happy. "I wanna hear Grammy give Daddy the goop!"

"Then hush so we can all listen," Tess hissed.

But apparently the torment was over, and all that remained was the retching. At least Laz hadn't puked in his truck. Thank God for small favors.

He had seemed relatively normal for the remainder of the trip home. Crock had almost decided the whole episode was a fluke—until Laz tried to get out of the truck and flattened himself on the driveway.

He *claimed* he slipped. *Slipped, my Aunt Fanny.* The man had all but slithered out of the cab, only to do a face-plant in the dirt. It was the strangest thing he'd ever seen. Considering the lack of alcohol involved.

Tess hit the front door, hollering for her grandmother, leaving Crock to haul the brother inside. He might or might not have dropped Laz in the dirt a couple of times before he got a good hold on the man's waistband thanks to Laz's failed attempts to remain upright.

Needless to say—it wasn't pretty.

The older woman had emerged from the kitchen with Tila in tow as Crock hauled Laz over the threshold. Her first words had been what Crock had come to expect of the Corona household.

"What in the hell are you yelling for?" she griped. "I'm senile, not deaf."

One look at Tess's face, then at Laz's limp arm strung over Crock's shoulder, and the witch doctor took over. "Haul him into the kitchen."

Crock used his improvised wedgie-hold to drag the stumbling professor through the living room and into the messy kitchen. Every surface was covered with pots, mixing bowls, and a thick layer of what appeared to be flour. He tried not to think of all the cleaning Tess had done a few days earlier as he dumped Laz into a chair.

"Now, get out."

When a shaman tells you to get out, Crock knew better than to argue. If he were honest, he didn't want to bear witness to whatever was about to happen.

It was bad enough to hear it through the closed door.

He really tried not to ask any questions, but… "What's with the smoke?"

Tess leveled an irritated glance in his direction. "She's either summoned her minions from the depths of Hell, or we won't have any brownies for dessert."

"Ah." Crock sure hoped it wasn't the brownies. They were well worth the paperwork for any demons running amok in Fort Worth. "Where's the fire extinguisher?"

"Gram's got everything under control."

He wasn't reassured. Then another thought struck. "Is there a fire alarm?"

"Uhm…yeah." Tess sounded embarrassed.

"It doesn't have batteries, does it?"

"Well, it kept going off every time Gram turned on the oven."

Crock visualized his neighbor's reaction. Jake Hellier would have the mother of all holy conniption fits.

As he contemplated a run to the nearest Wal-Mart for dessert and safety equipment, the elder Corona emerged from the kitchen.

Tila scrambled off Tess's lap and ran toward her grandmother. "Did Daddy take his medicine?"

"He did. And he didn't like it any better than you do, missy." She lifted the child into her arms—fur, alien, and all—before settling into the comfortable, tie-died recliner. "Anyone want to tell me what happened?"

Crock let Tess do the honors. He'd just been the muscle. "He complained about his head and wasn't focused on anything we said," Tess began, before explaining about Laz's fall down the stairs, and her own graceful descent onto his carcass. "Then he was throwing himself out of the truck and puking up his guts."

"What color was the puke?" Gram wanted to know. "Was it chunky? What did it smell like?"

"I don't know" Tess grimaced but looked to Crock for confirmation. "Slimy, smelly, green?"

"Dark green. Lots of bile. Like rotten garbage." Crock decided it was best to agree since he hadn't looked too closely after seeing the color. "Mrs. Corona…"

"Don't start that old geezer shit with me." She turned her sharp gaze on him. "It's just Doma or Gram. Take your pick."

"Uh…yes, ma'am." Crock decided Texas would freeze in August before he called this woman 'Gram.' "Do we need to take Laz to the ER?"

She shrugged. "He's not dying at the moment. If he continues to throw up, I can take him to the clinic in the morning. His liver isn't what concerns me."

Tess turned white. "Then what's…?"

Whatever question Tess intended to ask died on her lips at the appearance of her twin in the doorway.

Crock now knew what the phrase *death warmed over* meant. And he'd seen a lot of death and those close to it. Lazaro Corona looked like he'd been run over by wild hogs, brought back from the land of the dead, and run over again. Several times.

"What in the fucking hell was in that shit?" the man croaked. He sounded like any dead zombie Crock had ever seen at the movies.

"Bad words, Daddy!"

Crock glanced at the little girl. It was hard to remember there was a child in the room when he was dealing with the Coronas. That was when he remembered this was no ordinary family and no ordinary child.

Laz shook off his daze enough to realize his daughter was present. "Sorry, Punkin." He looked like he could still decorate the rug, but he managed a clumsy pat on the stuffed alien's head. "Why don't you take Mr. Snotbubble to your room?"

Tila put up a fuss but gave in under the pressure of bribery. She disappeared up the stairs with a promise of going to see the latest animated film as soon as humanly possible.

Crock hadn't realized a film had been released. He made a mental note to take Gemma Rae the following weekend if his mother hadn't taken her already. He hoped not because he needed something amusing and mindless to take his mind off this week's events. Until then, he needed to focus and close this damned case.

"Gram?" Tess shifted over, allowing her brother to collapse next to her on the sofa. "What do you think is wrong with Laz?"

The older woman's eyes narrowed as they studied Laz. Instead of answering, she said, "I think it's time y'all fill me in on this case you're working."

Crock leaned forward. "What would his illness have to do with the investigation? We know he went down some stairs. Head injuries…."

“This isn’t caused by any head injury,” Doma stated.

“Then what’s going on?” Crock couldn’t come up with any other explanation for what he’d witnessed.

“That’s why I need to know about this case.”

Tess quickly filled her in on the details, including the information they’d uncovered with the document examiner.

Doma sat silently, rubbing her finger across her lips as she contemplated the information. Her dark gaze shifted to Laz, who protested. “I’m fine, now! I don’t need any more tonic, or potion, or whatever the hell you gave me.”

“You’ll drink it if I say so, Junior,” Doma ordered.

Before Laz could argue, Tess broke in, “Have you seen this before, Gram?”

“I’ll need more information before I can be sure,” she answered, “but, yeah, I remember my granny telling me about this type of ‘bug’.”

Crock watched the twins’ responses. Tess was prepared to hold her brother down for another dose of medicine, while Laz looked like he would immediately relocate to Chernobyl if anyone came at him with anything other than a cold beer.

“I’m not sick.” Laz insisted for the thousandth time since entering the house. No one had believed him yet. And that wasn’t changing any time in the near future.

Tess arched a brow. “If you’re not sick,” she drawled, “then why did you have a splitting headache, lose your balance, fall down the stairs, toss your cookies in a cop’s truck, and…”

A cop’s truck? Smothering a snort of laughter, Crock said, “I doubt that’s going to help, Tess.”

Her mouth snapped shut. If her eyes were any indication, she was cursing him twelve ways to Sunday. He wasn't worried. Much. He focused his attention on the grandmother. "How would this investigation make Laz sick?"

Doma studied him before answering, "I'll need to do research before I make any sort of diagnosis. In the meantime, I'd stay away from that hotel if I were you."

"I can't promise that." He needed to keep his options open on the investigation front. "I have a couple of leads to investigate. Unless Laz and Tess need to do something, I'm not planning to return to Joshua."

Tess piped up, "But if something does take us back, what should we look for?"

The older woman shrugged. "The usual: varmints, STDs, poltergeists. Oh, and I'd stay away from anything that might get you killed."

Crock shook his head in disbelief but noticed that Tess paled at her grandmother's words while her brother turned a sickly shade of green. For all the claims of dementia, the Corona twins seemed to take the woman's words as gospel.

A twinge of pain above his left knee reminded him of why he was here. "So," he added slowly, firmly rubbing his injury site, "are you suggesting that this *bug,* or whatever Laz has, might kill one of us?"

"I'm saying that you should pay attention and learn from your mistakes," Doma said, glaring at each of them, "before one of you idiots winds up on the wrong side of the grass."

Chapter Twenty-Eight

Tess scrubbed the Dutch oven within an inch of its life, cursing Gram's penchant for setting the pots and pans on fire. Okay, that was an exaggeration, but still—clean-up was a bitch when Gram cooked.

"Where do you want the leftovers?"

She turned to find Crock holding the remains of dinner. It had taken a little arm-twisting—and assurances that no chickens were being served—to get him to stay for dinner. His look of relief at learning dinner was pot roast was comical.

"You can put it on the table. I'll find a container for it." She set the lid to the Dutch oven on a towel to dry. "Unless you want to take it with you?"

"No, thanks." He set the dishes on the table, then grabbed another hand towel to dry the pots.

"You don't have to do that!" Tess protested, but was secretly glad to have him pitch in. Laz hadn't eaten much and was holed up in his office after dinner, while Gram convinced Tila to take a bath before bed.

"My mother would tack my hide to a wall if she found out y'all fed me a fantastic meal and I didn't help clean up." Crock answered as he reached for the sparkling clean Dutch oven. "Besides, I wanted to hear your thoughts on Laz's situation."

Tess turned off the water before giving the sink a final wipe-down. "I'm not sure…"

Crock handed her the now-dried pot lid. “Not sure as in you don’t know, or not sure as in you have suspicions and don’t want to tell me what I might be dealing with.”

Tess sighed, “I know you think we’re holding back on you, but we’re not. It’s hard.”

“Because of your abilities?”

“Partly.” She fiddled with the pot lid, tightening the screw knob. “Laz is afraid I’m going to freak and run again, but I don’t want to run from this anymore. According to Gram, I kept a lid on these skills for too long, and now I need to catch up. But,” she added reluctantly, “there’s a butt-load that I don’t know.”

Crock set his towel aside and leaned against the cabinet with his arms crossed. “So, talk to me. What do you think we’re dealing with?”

“I think it falls into the category I just mentioned.”

“The butt-load of stuff you don’t know about?”

Tess wandered to the table and sat down. “Yeah, that one.”

Crock followed and took the seat closest to her. He straddled the chair backward, resting his arms on the back. “Okay, then—why don’t you walk me through what you do know.”

She heaved a frustrated sigh. “Honestly, not much. I know Laz felt something in the stairwell the morning after the investigation, then he acted weird when we went back on Sunday.”

“What kind of weird?”

“Yeah,” Tess huffed, “you’re right. Weird is his normal.”

“That’s not what I meant.” Crock swiped his hand across his mouth, probably to erase the hint of a grin she saw. He seemed to get his humor under control before continuing. "You've got a psychology degree. What do you think was going on with him?"

She snickered. "One of the first things my professors taught was to not analyze myself or my loved ones. If I look hard enough, I'll find all sorts of stuff."

Crock didn't blink.

Tess folded. "All right. Dammit, can you stop with the staring and shit!"

Nothing.

She blew out a gust of air. "Fine," she grumbled. "I…uhm…he's been under a lot of stress. He's a single dad, trying to make ends meet on an adjunct's salary. His mentor set him up for his dream job, but his research and writings aren't mainstream enough for the university to take him seriously. He lives with his grandmother and his sister, both of whom give him enough reason for a daily mental breakdown." She took a deep breath, let it out, then continued, "And he's doing his damnedest to impress a Texas Ranger so that maybe he'd improve his credibility and exposure."

Crock remained silent for a moment. "And?"

Tess eyed him. "Isn't that enough?"

"No."

Well, shit. "Okay," she tried again, "Gram doesn't pull out the cleansing equipment very often, so I think that might be a clue."

That detail seemed to intrigue him. "How so?"

The more she thought about her grandmother's actions over the past few days, the more worried Tess got. "The sulphur, the tobacco. She'd been smudging. She didn't seem surprised when we dragged him in the door today. I think she was expecting it."

"Why do you say that?"

He was asking more questions than Tila. "She had some of the medicines already brewing. She usually makes a tea or whatever after she knows what the symptoms are. That way it targets the virus. But," she said, "some of her herbals take hours, or even days, to prepare."

Crock rubbed his chin. "What would those medicines be for?"

"Nothing good," Tess tried to laugh it off, but it sounded fake to her ears. "She pulls out the recipe book when the illness is out of the ordinary. The harder to treat, the more time she puts into the brew."

"Recipe book." His eyes wandered to the overflowing bookshelf of cookbooks under the window.

"You won't find any over there," Tess informed him. "She keeps *those* books under lock and key—and maybe a hex or two. The only way we'll ever see them is if Laz or I start studying her ways."

That drew his attention back to her. "And why don't you?"

Tess avoided his searching gaze. "I… I don't know what Laz has told you about our family…"

"I know you came to live with her at a young age and that Laz came later." He leaned back in his chair. "Other than that, I know nothing."

"That's about enough." Tess tried to come up with an answer for him that wouldn't rip her to shreds. "I wasn't ready to learn. Gram tried to teach me, but I wasn't the easiest kid to work with for a while. I settled down after Laz came up, but it took everything I had to focus on school. You know about the ghost-hunting.

Then the Army came along and—well, the rest is history." Damn, if telling that much didn't make her throat hurt.

Crock said nothing for a moment. "I'm sorry."

"Yeah, well." She swallowed hard to ease the pain. "I can't exactly go back and change anything."

"If you could change something, what would it be?" he asked quietly.

The pain returned, accompanied by a suspicious burning in her eyes. Tess blinked several times. She would *not* cry in front of this man. Only Teddy was allowed to see her tears, and he wasn't talking.

"Uhm…." Her voice cracked, forcing her to clear her throat. "Well, shit went to Hell in a handbasket when my dad died, so I guess that's what I'd change. But—" she tried to laugh, but it sounded more like a strangled cat. "—that's not going to happen."

His mouth quirked in what she thought might be a smile. "No, but that doesn't mean we can't make up for lost time."

She managed to match his smirk. "Yeah, well, I seem to be having trouble finding the starting point."

"Why not continue what you did in the military? You can work with any law enforcement agency, or even independently as a profiler or an investigator."

Her smile disappeared. "No. I've closed that door."

His head tilted as if he was questioning her decision, but fortunately he didn't ask the question outright. Instead, he asked, "So—what *do* you want to do when you grow up?"

"Who says I want to grow up?" she demanded, relieved of some of the tension, although some remained. "I can't seem to find a fit."

His lips curved into a definite, albeit miniscule smirk. “Maybe you’re looking too hard.”

Tess had only thought the man was sexy. Until now. He understood. She didn’t know how, but he did. And that made him downright irresistible. Now it was all she could do to remember what they had been talking about. *Laz. Right.*

She cleared her throat. Before she could say more, the old Seth Thomas mantle clock in the living room chimed nine o’clock. Tess didn’t realize how late it had gotten.

“I have to be at the office early in the morning. I’d better get going.” Crock pushed away from the table to stand. Tess hesitated a moment before following him to the living room. As he retrieved his hat from the coat rack by the door, he turned back to her. “I think you already know where you need to start. Good night.”

“Night.”

Tess watched him walk out the door and into the warmth of the evening. He was right—she did know where she needed to start. She just wasn’t sure she wanted to go down that path—again.

Chapter Twenty-Nine

Laz had no intention of telling Gram or Tess that he still felt lousy. The drum beat in his head was softer but still present. At least he was vertical enough to get out the front door and into an Uber while Gram was occupied with Tila's breakfast and before Tess returned from her morning run.

He managed—somehow—to get to his office door without being seen by anyone import….

"You are late, Dr. Corona."

Laz winced. The dean's nasal twang sent needles into his brain. It was too damn early to be judged and convicted for whatever infraction he had supposedly committed this time. He didn't have a meeting until ten, and it was only a quarter to eight.

"Dr. Johnson." Laz turned to find the older man close enough to count his nose hairs. Rearing back, he gave his best effort to appear civil to the man who held his future tenure in his pasty-white hands. "Good morning. I wasn't aware of any appointments this early. Did I miss something?"

The man's eyes narrowed. He shook his head. "No, but please recall that I expect you to maintain office hours beginning at seven-thirty throughout the duration of your contract."

It took everything Laz possessed to tamp down the blinding red fury at his boss's words. A quick glance down the hall revealed no line of waiting students in dire need of his advice. Considering his adjunct contract didn't specify hours outside his scheduled classes and posted office hours—he was technically here on his own time. He couldn't remind Dr. Johnson of that fact without jeopardizing his position.

Instead, he took a deep breath, nearly choking on the man's heavy aftershave, before saying, "Why don't you come into the office for a moment?"

"Thank you." No sooner than the door was unlocked, Dr. Johnson stepped inside and turned, his bulk barring Laz from entering his own closet-sized office. He wasn't sure if he could get any more uncomfortable around his boss.

"Uhm—what can I do for you, sir?"

The manner in which the dean looked him over made Laz wonder if he'd remembered to take a shower. Then he remembered Gram's remedies. Some of those made a person reek for days no matter how much their skin was scrubbed.

Dr. Johnson seemed satisfied with whatever he was looking for and gave a minute nod. "I've often wondered why Dan Green thought you deserved this position. While I trust my predecessor's decisions," his tone indicated the opposite, "Dan was my friend and long-time colleague and never mentioned your work to me."

The man straightened, attempting to make himself taller than Laz—which wasn't going to happen by about four inches—and continued, "I was cleaning the closet in my office and came across some boxes that were sealed and labeled with your name. A note from Dan to Dr. Gentry was attached with instructions to give the boxes to you after his death. Do you know anything about this, Dr. Corona?"

Laz was completely lost. Dr. Gentry had retired the previous year but made no mention of storing anything for him. "No, sir, I don't."

"I see."

The simple comment informed Laz that his boss did not see. Sealed boxes meant secrets. Staff with secrets were an abomination to a nosy dean.

"Please make arrangements to remove them from my office today. You may contact Mrs. Hudgens to do so."

"I will, sir." He could only imagine how thrilled Mrs. Hudgens would be to babysit a couple of boxes. He hated to ask, but it was a necessity. "Is there anything else, sir?"

"Have you considered our discussion from yesterday?"

Ah, hell!

"I…yes, sir," Laz truly had thought nothing about the veiled threat to publish a substantial academic work or lose any hope of a tenured position. "I have several potential ideas in the works, and I…."

"Good," Dr. Johnson snapped. "I expect to have a synopsis of a marketable work on my desk by next Wednesday, along with a syllabus for the classes you have requested for the fall semester. Now, if you'll excuse me, I have important matters which demand my attention."

Laz flattened himself against the wall so that nothing kept the dean from leaving his air space as fast as possible. The man didn't bother to look back. Laz waited until he heard the footsteps trail away down the silent hallway before he allowed himself to relax.

"Prick," he muttered under his breath, before leaning his head back against the wall.

The man who had hired him two years before had been a good, intelligent historian who valued his instructors' time and efforts. Upon Dean Gentry's retirement, Dr. Johnson was named his successor. The man had an agenda to enforce, much to everyone's dismay.

So far, the staff hadn't been impressed with his management skills. Johnson was a pompous ass who kissed up to the President and Dean of Instruction while micro-managing his staff and acknowledging no boundaries. The tenured professors either held or bit their tongues while the adjuncts tried to stay out of the dean's way or pounced on other positions.

Laz hadn't decided on his course of action yet. His dream job didn't exist in many places, especially in the Dallas-Fort Worth area. If he went to Austin, he'd have to depend on his mother to help with Tila, and that would give the woman an open invitation to get up in his business.

That wasn't going to happen. His cell phone buzzed, interrupting his pity party. Muttered curses filled the tiny office as he dug it out of his pocket. He shut the door, answering without glancing at the ID, "What?"

"I take it you still feel like shit," Tess grunted on the other end.

Laz dumped his backpack next to the rickety office chair before collapsing into said chair. "What do you want?"

"To make sure you're alive, for one thing."

"I'm okay."

"Yeah, right. Remember who you're talking to."

Laz sighed. "Yeah, I know. You feel it, too."

"Damn straight." It was a statement of fact. "Gram wants me to hunt you down for another dose."

"Oh, hell no!"

"Don't worry about it. Tila woke up with a snotty nose this morning, so your little breakdown has taken a backseat."

Laz let his head roll back. "Thank God! I mean…ah, shit! Is Tila okay?"

His sister's cackle on the other end reminded him of his priorities. Not that they were ever far from his mind. "She'll be fine. It's May. 'Tis the season for allergies and sinus infections. If it's not growin', it's blowin'," Tess assured him. "By the way, you escaped the *hacienda* before I could tell you about your car."

Except for getting a ride to school, he'd totally forgotten about his car. "What about it?"

"Marcos called," Marcos was their dad's cousin who owned a repair shop, "and said he'd have it ready by tomorrow afternoon."

"Did he say how much?"

"Something about the family discount."

Laz groaned. That usually meant cleaning out a grease pit or some other equally disgusting chore. If he wasn't so broke, he'd rather pay the going rate.

"Anyway," Tess kept going, "I'll pick you up around lunchtime, unless you need me to come by sooner. We can grab some lunch before going over to negotiate Marcos's terms."

"Sounds like a plan." Laz rubbed his head, willing the pounding to go away.

"You're still hurting."

It would do no good to deny it. "Yeah, but at least I can see straight." He remembered Dr. Johnson's visit. "Oh, Tess?"

"Yeah?"

"I've got some boxes in the admin office that I need to pick up. I'm not sure how many, but Mrs. Hudgens is holding them for me."

"One plate of bribery brownies to go?"

"Please."

"Gotcha. See you then. And, Laz?" she hesitated, "if you feel like you're getting worse again…."

He'd be damned if he'd call, but he reassured her anyway, "I'll let you know, but right now, I'm good."

"Okay. *Hasta luego*."

"Later." Laz hung up the phone and leaned back. He felt like crap, and it wasn't entirely from whatever bug he was dealing with.

Sighing heavily, he pulled a notebook out of his backpack and attempted to pull an academic miracle out of his ass.

****

"She declined our offer."

Crock glanced up from his paperwork. "Who? Mrs. Hudgens? Yeah, she told me she wasn't going to take the job."

Childs grimaced. "What'd you do to her?"

"Me?" Crock laughed at his boss's frustration. "I didn't do anything."

"What'd she say when you saw her?"

"Not much," Crock shrugged. "She thanked me for recommending her for the position, but said she was settled at TCU."

"Gee golly whiz! She was interested until I brought her over here." His boss glanced around the office, attempting to identify anything offensive.

Crock followed the man's gaze. The only thing he could see was what he saw every day—pictures of the most-wanted criminals in Texas and the United States. One picture snagged his attention.

"Wait." He pulled the notebook from his shirt pocket and flipped through the pages.

"What?" Childs leaned over the desk, resting his massive hands on the surface.

Crock found the page he was looking for and sat back to study the picture on the wall again. The mug shot was old and showed a man in his mid- to late twenties. With hard, drawn features, and multiple tattoos and piercings, it would be difficult to say for certain that there was a family resemblance to the middle-aged woman he'd met. "Collins."

Childs studied the wall of known criminals. "Robert Collins? What about him?"

He tossed his notebook on the table so his boss could see his notation. "I think she might be a relative. Her maiden name was Collins."

Childs lifted up from the table and ran a meaty hand over his bald head. "He's been laying low for over ten years. It's a stretch, but worth checking out. I'll have the file pulled. You see if you can dig up any connection."

"Yes, sir." If there was a link, it'd be a breakthrough along the lines of finding Al Capone or Clyde Barrow.

He hoped like hell there was no connection between Claudette Collins Hudgens and Robert Collins.

****

"Morning, Mrs. Hudgens."

Other professors called the administrative assistant by her first name while the dean called her 'Claude'. On more than one occasion, Laz'd witnessed a subtle cringe at the nickname, so he continued to use her married name out of respect. She seemed to appreciate his consideration. As an added bonus, Laz arrived at the departmental office two seconds before Tess walked in, plate of goodies in hand.

The woman behind the desk glanced up. "Good morning, Dr. Corona. Tess, it's good to see you again."

"Hello, Mrs. Hudgens."

Tess rarely said much when she was in the office. Laz had always thought the academic walls reminded her too much of their mother's demands, but that didn't fly knowing that Tess had at least two degrees and some post-graduate studies under her belt. She silently handed Laz the plate, which he placed on the corner of the immaculate desk.

"That wasn't necessary, Dr. Corona," Mrs. Hudgens offered them a semblance of a smile. "But thank you. I have a few interns which will appreciate the offering. I believe you are here to collect the boxes that Dean Johnson found."

"Yes, ma'am," Laz answered. "I had no idea Dr. Green left them for me. I don't want them in your way."

Mrs. Hudgens gave him a nod and spun her seat away from the desk. Walking quickly, she led them into the side storage closet and pointed to a stack of three, medium-sized cardboard boxes, each labeled in what Laz recognized as his mentor's precise handwriting. It was how they were labeled that made him stop.

"What is it?" He stopped mid-stride, and Tess ran into him. Pain shot through his little toe when her foot landed on it. He bit back a grunt of pain, yanking his foot out from under her shoe.

Both women looked at him like he was a loon. Laz gave a sheepish shrug. "It's labeled with my title."

"So?" Tess didn't seem to care.

"So," Laz cleared his strangely tight throat, "Dr. Green always called me 'Mr. Corona' even after I received my doctorate."

Mrs. Hudgens spoke up, "That wasn't unusual for Dr. Green. His students often remained in the student role until such time that he felt they had achieved a level of academia that he deemed equal to his own. Very few of them met his standards."

Laz had known, or at least suspected, that Dr. Green was waiting for him to push his own boundaries, but to see that seemingly insignificant detail meant the world to him.

His head gave a painful throb.

You don't deserve it.

Tess shot him a concerned glance which he ignored. He picked up the first box and handed it to his sister. As he bent to pick up the other two, he felt lightning strike his lower back. The boxes landed on the top of his foot. The one Tess hadn't stepped on.

"Ow!"

"What happened?" Tess demanded.

"Oh, my! Dr. Corona, are you okay?"

He levelled a glare in his sister's direction, before turning to the admin. "I'm fine, Mrs. Hudgens. I didn't have a good grip."

"You will need to complete an incident report." Mrs. Hudgens moved to her desk and pulled a form from a file. "Do you need to have your foot examined?"

"No!" The thought of filling out paperwork for his own stupidity was terrifying. "I'm fine. It's not a work injury or anything."

The top box had tipped over, revealing binders and file folders. He quickly reassembled the contents and picked up the boxes, ignoring the sharp pain in his back. His foot was another challenge, but he somehow managed to grit his teeth and not limp toward the door.

As an added bonus, Mrs. Hudgens couldn't hand him the form because his hands were full.

"Take this with you." The ever-efficient admin slapped the paperwork on the top box before he could move. Somehow, in the millisecond it took for him to pick up the boxes, she'd added a bit of tape on the form to secure it to the box. "You may email it to me by three today."

Kill me now.

Do it.

No! Laz shook his head to clear the destructive thoughts. He didn't understand what was happening in his head, but he sure didn't like it.

"Yes, ma'am." Defeated, he tried to keep the whining to a minimum. He quickly edged out the door and, giving into the pain, limped his way down the hall as fast as he could.

"Wait up!"

He didn't. If he stopped, the pain in his foot, back, and head would give his twin a clue that something wasn't right. He couldn't tell Tess. She would tell Gram. And he sure as hell wasn't going through that shit again.

"Damn you, Laz! Stop," Tess complained. "The box broke. You're dumping crap all over the place."

Laz stopped at the door to the outside and turned. The outside doors had been propped open for the air to circulate. The breeze coming into the hall was brisk and scattered loose papers everywhere. He looked down and saw the top box had a gaping hole on one side. "Aw, hell!"

Tess set her box down to catch the escapees. He tried to juggle the boxes, but his back protested, forcing him to drop them. A few papers landed outside the doors as he went to shut them. Fortunately, the wind trapped the papers against the windows.

Laz reached outside to grab the papers. He turned back and closed the door which blew a few documents back into a flurry. One slapped his face. He caught it as he headed toward Tess to help. His sore foot landed on a paper and slipped out from under him.

"Fuck!" he yelled as he went down. Hard.

Pain shot through every body part he owned. Spots darkened his vision to mix with the stars that he'd always thought was a clichéd description for a head injury. Now, he knew they were real.

"Laz!" He heard Tess scramble to his side. For some reason, her movements were accompanied by someone groaning.

Oh, hell! That's me.

"Don't move." Tess's hands ran over his head.

"Ow!" Sharp pain sliced through the back of his head. Laz raised his hand to touch the spot she'd hit. As he did, his shoulder announced itself. It was feeling neglected. "Ah, shit!"

"I'm calling an ambulance."

"No!" Laz gasped. The last thing he wanted was attention drawn to his clumsiness. Nor did he want more paperwork to fill out. "Just give me a minute. I'll be fine."

The Army had obviously taught his twin more than how to jump out of an airplane. Their mother would not approve of the names Tess called him. In fact, Mom would strip a tree for a switch and tan his sister's hide if she heard some of the things that came out of Tess's mouth. Gram would take notes.

Maniacal laughter filled his ears. Laz cracked an eye, but Tess wasn't laughing. She was worried. She was cursing. No one was laughing.

God, I hate it when she worries.

Laz rolled to his side—the relatively uninjured side—and struggled into a sitting position. Hands helped him up and steadied him until he gave Tess a nod. "I'm good."

She didn't believe him. She never did, because it was the same lie she'd give him if the tables were turned.

"Really, I'm okay," he assured her.

Tess shoved a handful of papers at him. "Move and I'll shoot you. I'll get your stuff."

Getting shot might improve his day, but he knew better than to argue with her, even if he thought he could get off the ground without her help. While his sister picked up the errant papers, Laz pulled the damaged box to him and tried to fix the hole. The cardboard was torn, but he could shift some of the intact binders over to block the opening.

He picked up a dark blue binder which had split

open. The top paper caught his attention. It was a copy of the article he'd written on paranormal criminal investigation. Dr. Green's handwriting marked the sides.

Laz shifted to another page, then another. Dr. Green's notes showed he had studied the same references as Laz and had reached the same conclusion: that the paranormal could play a role in discovering the truth of criminal acts, and that the paranormal element had the potential to contribute to the criminal activity.

Reaching the last page, Laz found the reason for Dr. Green's obsession: Esme. Dan had outlined the hotel's violent history of murder-suicides as well as the events leading to the day of their anniversary and his wife's death. There were too many similarities to ignore.

There was one glaring difference: Dan didn't commit suicide.

At least not at the time he killed his wife.

"I think I've got everything."

Tess's voice drew him away from the research and his startling realizations. "Take a look at this."

She knelt by his side and exchanged the loose papers in her hand for the binder. "What's all this?"

His neck pulled sharply as he glanced at her. "I'm not sure, but I think these boxes are Dan's way of having me investigate Esme's murder."

And admitting the truth.

Tess met his eyes. "Crock and I wondered about this yesterday."

"What?" Laz didn't remember that conversation.

She set the binder on top of the items in the box. "You were so sick yesterday that we didn't get to share much. It seems I can tell if his writings are forgeries or not. I had a vision of him writing a letter to you. I think he was telling you to continue his investigation so he could join his wife."

Laz swung his head toward her, ignoring the pain between his ears. "Meaning?"

"Meaning," Tess began, "he had a bottle of pills and said something about joining her."

Laz closed his eyes. "Suicide?"

The laughter returned. *I told you so.*

He felt his sister plop next to him on the cold marble.

"Maybe. We can't be sure since his death was never considered suspicious. There was no autopsy. Crock seemed to think there was arsenic involved somehow."

The malicious laughter sounded in his head again. Laz's eyes popped open, and he glanced around. He and Tess were alone, and she wasn't laughing. Again.

I'm losing my mind. "Tess?"

"Yeah?"

"I'm losing my mind."

She snorted, "What else is new?"

He rolled his head toward her.

Tess stopped laughing. "Why're you losing your mind, Lazzie?"

Footsteps interrupted their conversation. Laz didn't want to be caught by students, his boss, or—worse—Mrs. Hudgens. "Come on. Let's get out of here."

Tess glanced around before helping him up. "We can talk in the car. Crock will want to know about those binders."

Laz groaned as he stood, but he accepted one box

from his sister. “Then take them to him. If there’s anything that might help him, then have at it.”

She gave him a nod but said nothing. It annoyed him that she grabbed the last two containers without effort.

Damn, I need to get back to the gym.

Chapter Thirty

The events of the past week had added to Tess's restlessness and sleepless nights. On the plus side, her nightmares were always a problem, but they took a backseat to her concern for Laz. Crock's perceptive comments regarding her life didn't help either.

Her morning run helped to clear her mind and gave her time to reflect on the previous day's situation. She had gotten Laz to the Jeep without any further dismemberment. Thanks to the heat and humidity, both she and Laz had been soaked in sweat by the time they got to the Jeep. The trip to Corona Auto and Salvage was accompanied by Laz's whimpers. The pain in his back, head, and foot didn't help his cause in negotiating the family discount with Marcos.

With his vehicle out of commission, Tess dropped Laz off at the university and—because she was a good sister—spent the morning working at the garage to help pay off Laz's repairs. She hoped she would get home in time to get a quick shower before Crock arrived.

The gorgeous weather that had accompanied Tess's morning run—not too warm, blue skies, and a lovely breeze—had deteriorated to the type of weather Texas was known for. Ominous, low-hanging thunderclouds were building to the west. Tess prayed she could spend a quiet afternoon flirting with a badass Ranger without smelling like sweat and grease and listening to a weather radio.

Tess pulled the Jeep onto her street and was greeted by a now familiar sight—a deep red truck which hid one sexy ass. A week ago, she hadn't known what she was missing. Now, other than the view of Crock's backside, she was sure there were things she'd be happy to miss.

Like rats, cockroaches, and her twin turning into a deranged asshole.

Oh, and Gram baking brownies on a daily basis just in case the Ranger showed up. Tess would have to double her workouts if Gram kept up her baking spree. Those calories did *not* look good on her butt.

Although she was becoming accustomed to the chivalry, it was still a shock when the car door opened before she could reach for her purse.

"Uh, hi." Tess tried to hide her surprise. She hoped she'd have an opportunity to get used to the gentlemanly behavior.

"Hi." Typical Crock greeted her, except this one held a canvas backpack in one hand.

Tess tried to gauge his mood but decided to plunge forward. "Look, I'm sorry about the other day."

His hand raised to stop her. "There's nothing to be sorry for."

Tess closed her eyes, grateful that the man understood. "It's just…Laz has too much going on and needs me to figure this out so he can get the position he deserves."

"And you are struggling with your own problems, as well," he added, leaning against her fender. "Helping him is how you deal with your own insecurities."

Tess stiffened. She didn't realize she was that

transparent. “Maybe. That doesn’t mean I need to dump them on you.”

Crock shrugged. “If I remember correctly, I was the one digging for answers. And I stand by what I said—you know what you need to do.”

Her shoulders relaxed as she released some of her built-up tension. “Okay. So…come on in. I think Gram made more brownies or something.”

“I’m not sure how many more brownies I can eat before I turn into one,” he groaned before his large frame straightened. “I read through Dr. Green’s letters and his original will. There are some things I thought you could get a reading on and a few details that Laz needs to know about.”

“What kind of details?” Tess narrowed her eyes at the Ranger. Laz didn’t need anything else on his plate. He refused admit it, but her twin still felt lousy.

“Nothing bad,” he assured her. “I think the paperwork clears up some of our confusion. It doesn’t answer all the questions, but Dr. Green apparently left some things to Laz in his will.”

“Hmm,” Tess pushed past Crock and headed to the back of her Jeep. “If it was his research, then we picked up three boxes of binders from the school today.”

Crock waited for her to open the tailgate, slinging the backpack over his shoulder. “What boxes?”

She pulled the gate open and pulled the boxes toward her. Her companion reached over and took possession of two, leaving the damaged container for her. “Apparently, Dr. Green left these with the old dean. Dr. Johnson told Laz to come and get them.”

The Ranger looked thoughtful. “These may be part of what he referred to. The will mentioned reference books as well."

Tess groaned. "Like Laz needs more books."

Crock made a noise that sounded suspiciously like a suppressed chuckle. "Isn't that what academics do? Surround themselves with the work of other academics?"

"It's more like geeks coveting other geeks resources," she grumbled. "If Laz pulled his nose out of a book, he might get a life."

"Hey, now," A smirk flashed across his handsome face. "Some of us like to read."

That was a tiny bit of information that Tess tucked away for further evaluation. "Some of us read *and* get a date once in a while." She might as well bait that hook and see what she could catch.

Before she got an answer, the door swung open, revealing a strange sight. A gremlin disguised as a three-year-old, wearing an unfamiliar—but blinding—black and white checked, one-piece, hooded playsuit, stood before her. Ropes of beaded jewelry draped around Tila's skinny neck. The kid had apparently raided both Tess's and Gram's makeup stash. Blue and purple cream shadow adorned her eyelids and mascara made interesting patterns all over Tila's face. Tess wasn't sure what made the lips, nose, and ears the color of sparkly green slime, but she was fairly certain she didn't own anything that obnoxious. And if she did, it was going into the trash.

"Are you kissing?" Tila demanded.

The question—combined with the child's appearance—caught Tess completely off guard. "What?"

Even as she asked the question, embarrassment

flooded her face. She was certain her face was the equivalent of a fire engine—one that was on fire. The man behind her stifled something that might have been a snort. Or a sneeze. She wasn't certain. Unless the man was a masochist, she was *so* not getting a date anytime soon.

"Uhm…" Tess stuttered, "you've got something on your…uh…face."

Big brown eyes fluttered at her, making the odd sweeps of black mascara wiggle. "I look just like you. Did you kiss him yet?"

"I don't look like that!" She felt Crock retreat a step or twelve, but not before she heard a restrained wheeze. The jackass was trying not to laugh in the face of absurdity.

I can never face this man again.

Tess straightened with as much dignity as she could muster. Waving her fingers to shoo her niece inside, she bustled the trio into the living room where she discovered an equally horrifying sight.

Gram sat in her swivel rocker, studying her appearance in a handheld mirror. Her lip color was at least in the general color scheme that lips should be, but they were a shocking neon pink that escaped well-beyond the boundaries of normal lip lines. Shiny green globs coated the older woman's eyes and appeared to melt into a burnt orange cheek color. What wasn't covered by cakey make-up had wisps of black mascara that matched some of the markings on Tila's face.

She was glad her grandmother was ignoring them because if Gram said anything, Tess would bust a gut.

Leaving the clowns in the living room, Tess silently led Crock into the kitchen. The man dropped his boxes on a chair but didn't stop. He proceeded to exit out the back door. Sounds of choking and gasps could be heard coming from the deck. Obviously, Crock needed a moment to contain his shock or hysteria. Tess certainly did.

When he returned, red-eyed and only occasionally choking on his own spit, Tess was back in control of the situation and calmly waited for a pot of coffee to finish brewing. She plunked two large mugs on the table and motioned for Crock to park himself.

Nothing was said for several minutes while they avoided eye contact and sipped their drinks. An occasional glance toward the living room or a smothered grin was the only indication of what he was thinking. She was glad he was enjoying himself. She wasn't. He could escape—she had to live in this madhouse filled with psychotic lunatics.

A throat clearing was her first warning that he'd gotten ahold of himself. "I guess we need to look in those boxes," he rasped. "When will Laz be here?"

Tess shrugged. "He'll be awhile but said to go ahead without him. We didn't have a chance to go through anything." She paused before admitting, "Laz wasn't feeling well and threw out his back at the same time he dropped a box on his foot. When the box broke, we got a glimpse of some of the papers that flew out."

"And?"

Tess pulled the broken box off of the others and lifted the lid. The pages Laz had shown her sat on top, and she handed them to Crock.

All laughter was gone as Crock sat, musing over the information. "So, he made the same connection to the ghosts that we did. Was there anything about arsenic? Or his meds?"

"Not that I saw, but we only glanced at these few pages. I seriously doubt he'd put that information in his research notes. There was information about the other incidents at the hotel which seemed to tie everything together. There might be more in there. Let's wait for Laz to figure out what's relevant," Tess suggested. "You found something in the letters?"

"Yeah," Crock reached over to his backpack and removed a plastic file folder. "These are the originals."

As her hand touched the sheet, the kitchen disappeared. In its place, she saw a familiar, bald head seated behind a desk.

"What do you want it to say?"

A large man in his fifties placed his pudgy hands on the desk. "That the entire estate goes to me and my sister."

Tess gasped as she returned to the kitchen. Crock's comforting hand sat on her shoulder. She could get used to his steady support. The visions—not so much.

"You okay?" His deep baritone was filled with concern.

"Yeah." Her voice sounded weak even to her own ears. "Give me a minute."

The hand disappeared. She heard the fridge open and close before a cold bottle pressed into her hand. Beer or water—Tess didn't much care as she chugged the cool wetness down her dry throat. When she finished, she buried her head. After a few minutes, she managed to lift her head from her hands. Crock hovered nearby.

"It was the same guy," she croaked. "The one that I saw at Karlyn's. The rings are wolves with ruby or garnet eyes."

"What was he doing?"

Tess rubbed her head. "He…uh…there was another guy. The forger was asking what the guy wanted the letter to say."

Crock moved back to his seat. "What did this other man look like?"

"Big," Tess reached for the water bottle. "Middle-age, overweight."

"That sounds like the nephew," Crock grunted.

She nodded, "He mentioned a sister."

"That'd be our guy."

Before Crock could say more, Tila strutted into the kitchen. If Tess had any delusions that the freak show in her living room was a figment of her imagination, reality slapped her on the head.

"Uh, Tila?" she began, glad for the diversion, "whatcha doing?"

"Getting juice."

"Okay…uhm…what's with the outfit, Miss T?"

Tila shrugged, continuing her quest to open the fridge and get a juice box. Prize in hand, the girl held it out to Tess. "Grammy says bad things are in the air and I need potekshun."

Tess glanced up from the tiny straw she was trying to spear through an even tinier hole. "Protection? From what?" Something around Tila's neck caught her attention. "Are those my fetishes?"

Her favorite fetish necklace hung among the tangle of beads around Tila's neck. The stones of turquoise, coral, and lapis had been a Christmas present from her father. It was the last gift he'd given her before he died. She remembered him telling the old legends of the carved animals. He had said to wear it for luck and protection.

"Uh huh." Tila grabbed the juice box from Tess's hand. Not bothering with the straw, the little heathen began sucking juice through the small hole in the top.

Tess tried to remain calm and hopefully teach Tila a lesson about borrowing personal belongings. "Did you ask permission before getting into my jewelry box?"

Tila shrugged and turned away. "Grammy said I could wear them." With those parting words, the demon child was gone.

Tess sat with her mouth open for several minutes before turning back to the man who was trying not to bust a gut. "Can you arrest a three-year-old?"

Crock lost it.

Chapter Thirty-One

Much to Tess's displeasure, Crock took *way* too long to stop snickering. Before he could respond, a shout came from the front room. "What in the freaking hell have you done to my daughter?"

Tess jumped from her seat and made it through the door before Laz's last, angry words finished. She didn't need to hear him to know Crock was right behind her.

In the living room, a livid Laz stood in the front doorway, taking in the sight which had previously melted Tess's and Crock's composure. Beyond her brother, Tess noted that the sky had grown darker, and the light had turned greenish—never a good sign in Texas weather. The big tree in the front yard swayed back and forth with increasing violence. By the look of Laz's sweaty armpits, the humidity had kicked up to intolerable levels. Either that or Marcos had disagreed with what Laz was willing to pay for the tires and had disconnected the AC in his car. Although their cousin had a devious mind, Tess put her money on the changing weather and Laz's disposition being the culprits.

"How could you do this to her, you crazy, old bitch?"

Cold terror settled in Tess's gut. One did not call Gram a *crazy, old bitch* to her face and live to tell the tale. Personally, she wouldn't even think the words because Gram could read minds.

The old woman's reaction to the insult was only one of many concerns. A man wearing grimy mechanic's coveralls emerged from behind Laz. The whites of his dark eyes nearly eclipsed the dark centers as he slowly backed away from the man he'd brought home.

"Hey, Marcos." Tess greeted her older cousin as Crock's hand landed on her shoulder. The Ranger couldn't know that Marcos was smart enough to not stick around when there was going to be fireworks.

"Uh…hey, Tess. *Hola*, Tia Doma. Gotta run. Bye!"

The man's boot heels thumped on the porch as he ran for his tow truck. The squeal of tires let the entire neighborhood know that Marcos had made his escape.

With sweat streaming down his red-face, Laz didn't notice that his ride had vamoosed. Instead, he stood in the middle of the front room, his fists clenched, with a look in his eye that Tess had never seen before. She had dealt with some evil bastards in the Army, but this is what she would call a murderous look if she was prone to romanticizing her brother's actions. Which she wasn't.

"Uhm, Laz?" Tess moved forward, shaking off Crock's restraining hand. "It's just a little makeup. No harm, no foul."

She hadn't thought it was possible for her brother to get even redder, but Laz turned almost purple. His jugular vein was visible, pumping blood in pounding glubs. Tess shot a look at Crock, whose eyes narrowed in warning. He stayed at the kitchen door, ready for anything. A quick glance toward the recliner showed her grandmother sitting, calm but intent.

In that instant, Tess understood: the bizarre sight of her family and their adornments took on new meaning. Images flooded through the barriers she'd built years before. Memories of sitting at Gram's oak table, finger-painting arrows and circles while learning their ancient and traditional meanings. Tila and Gram weren't wearing makeup.

It was war paint.

The markings were loose interpretations of Native American and Christian symbols. Even the fabric of Tila's new outfit was the closest Gram could find to crosses, and, with the hoodie in place, covered Tila from head to foot. The long sleeves probably hid more protective symbols painted on her arms. Even the fetish necklace now made sense.

The sight of the tiny, scared girl, clutching a clay cross and partially hidden by Gram's recliner, sent Tess between the threat and his targets. "Laz," she began, "I think you need to take a breather here."

"You stay out of this," he roared. "It's all your fault. If you'd been doing your job, Tila wouldn't be covered in whatever that shit is!"

Tess had no idea what she was dealing with. The only thing she was certain of was that this wasn't her twin. The knowledge didn't keep the pain from punching her in the gut. It was her responsibility to watch Tila until they resolved the day care issue. Instead, this week she'd fallen easily into her old role as an investigator and abandoned the child to a woman in her seventies.

She would have to deal with the guilt later. Over her shoulder, Tess hissed, "You don't happen to have any more of that paint, do you, Gram?"

"Might have if you hadn't been wasting your time sexing up a man on the front porch."

Tess wasn't sure why she expected a different, slightly more helpful answer. In Gram-speak, she was on her own to deal with whatever held Laz captive. Gram was responsible for protecting Tila. It was Tess's job to ensure Gram didn't have to curse her own grandson to Hell—not that she hadn't threatened to do so a hundred times before.

"Tess?"

A quick glance over to the kitchen door showed Crock in a ready stance, his left hand loose at his side, but the right was tucked behind his hip and close to his holster.

God, I hope no one needs to get shot tonight.

"Laz," she began as she spread her hands in a non-threatening manner but prepared her feet to move. "I think there's been a big misunderstanding. Let's sit down and…."

"Fuck you!" Laz's dark eyes narrowed as they followed her movements. He grabbed the brass poker from the fireplace set and took a step toward her, his stance widening into an all-too-familiar aggressive position. An unnatural growl sounded from his chest.

A match was struck, and the scent of sage filled Tess's nose. Gram had dug up more smudge materials from somewhere. Tess wanted to believe it would work, but the extra smudging Gram'd done in the past week hadn't prevented this showdown. The old woman must have seen this coming in time to prepare for extra materials, as well as make a protective cover for Tila.

Crock tried his hand at peacekeeping. "Hey, Laz, why don't you put that down, and we'll come into the kitchen to discuss this over a cup of coffee?"

Tess appreciated his effort but instinctively knew it was too late. Whatever held onto Laz had no interest in discussion. Probably never had.

"Come here, Tila," Laz demanded, his tone harsh and unyielding.

"No." Tess heard the fearful resolve in the child's voice. Gram had been preparing Tila for this kind of situation. Tess was aware of Crock moving closer. There were three people for Laz to get through before he could even think of reaching his daughter. Maybe only two, because Crock would probably shoot him first. That meant Tess would have to stop Laz before he became a lead magnet.

Behind her, Gram began a chant. In the recesses of Tess's mind, she remembered that chanting was important. With their feet planted in three different cultures, Tess and Laz grew up speaking some Spanish and German. She didn't retain much of Gram's native language, which wasn't surprising since the native speakers were dying out, but Tess did remember Gram's go-to chant.

Our Father,

Who art in Heaven,

Hallowed be thy name.

The familiarity of the Lord's Prayer drifted through Tess's mind and created a rhythm. Other verses and prayers emerged in a combination of Spanish, German, English, and a few Arabic prayers she'd picked up in the Middle East.

Outside, thunder rumbled as the wind picked up and it started to rain. It was only a matter of time before a full-fledged Texas thunderstorm hit. A tornado had nothing on the storm brewing inside the house.

Laz took another step. "Tila, get over here."

"No!" Tila began to cry but remained behind her grandmother's chair.

Raising the poker, her father lunged.

"Run, Tila!" Tess shouted as she blocked Laz, grabbing the poker with both hands.

Tess was accustomed to sparring with men who were taller and bulkier than her. In the Army, she had taken down men intent on killing others, usually with a weapon, but occasionally in hand-to-hand combat. However, she didn't know and love those other guys. They were criminals with violent histories. She did what was necessary to keep herself and others safe.

But this was her brother, and while she often threatened to strangle him, she didn't want to hurt him. But she sure as Hell wasn't going to let him injure her or her niece. Laz wrenched the poker from her hands and swung at her head. Tess dodged his attack while searching for an opening. Despite his career choice and busy schedule, her twin had kept up with his belt-training and was in great shape. But whatever possessed him had eliminated all the vulnerable spots that Laz was prone to have.

Behind her, Gram shouted warnings which weren't all that helpful, while Crock attempted to direct Gram and Tila to safety. Out of the corner of her eye, Tila appeared behind the sofa, near the front door. Her escape route was cut off by a madman.

"Daddy!" The little girl's sobbing scream brought Tess's attention to her. For half a heartbeat, no one moved—then all Hell broke loose.

Gram moved just as Laz lunged for Tila. Tess

grabbed the poker and shoved it into his chest to get her twin away from the door. Crock blocked the front door after the oldest and youngest Coronas disappeared through it. With his target escaping, Laz threw off Tess and started toward the Ranger.

"No!" Tess whacked Laz on the head with the poker, drawing his attention back to her.

"Tess!" Crock yelled. "Watch out!"

Laz lunged at her. She ducked under his outstretched arms, shoving his off-balanced weight to the ground. She would have tackled him if his hand hadn't hooked her arm, forcing her down under his heavy body.

They landed with a *thud* and a grunt. Pain shot through Tess's head as it bounced off the hardwood floor. Laz landed on top with one long leg across her knees, the other knee plowed into her gut. She couldn't breathe, but she didn't have time to give in.

She heard Crock shouting for Laz to stand down. She heard Gram yelling curses. Over the commotion, she heard Tila screaming for her daddy to stop hurting Aunt Tessie.

It was up to Tess to stop the madness before someone—namely her—got killed.

She blocked another punch that she felt more than saw. It didn't deter him. Instead, he shifted to a choke hold. Shifting her body with a strangled battle cry, Tess managed to throw Laz's bigger body off balance enough to pull her knee up and into his chest. As black spots filled her vision, she grabbed his left forearm arm with her left hand and jabbed her right palm into the back of his elbow.

Crack!

Tess felt the joint give under her hand but didn't have time to think about the injury to her brother's arm. The crazed entity possessing Laz wouldn't slow down because of a dislocated elbow. But it did give her a precious second to push him off and haul herself up. She had another half a second to gasp for air before Laz came after her again.

Tess did the only thing she could do—she bolted.

Through the kitchen. Into the backyard. With Laz on her heels.

****

"Ah, fuck! Tess!"

Crock raced after the twins. He'd witnessed many domestic disputes, but this was the first time he'd seen someone behave like a demon. Family members often didn't press charges against abusers because the abuse was out of character. He'd never believed it until now.

Now, he was faced with a man—a coworker who was fast becoming a friend—doing his damnedest to kill his sister while shouting what sounded like obscenities in an unfamiliar language. That sister was chanting what sounded like Bible verses in English and a mix of languages that Crock wasn't sure he recognized either. He added his own prayers, thinking it couldn't hurt.

Crock thought of his father and wondered how he would have handled the situation. His dad probably hadn't dealt with ghosts and whatever the hell was going on with Laz. Crock recalled Hell's tale of the side of the road.

Maybe…?

"Dad," Crock muttered, "help me if you can."

The twins circled each other in the middle of the

backyard. The storm wasn't cooperating, with the rain coming down in sheets, pinging against the metal roof of an old toolshed. The *pings* became *thunks* as Mother Nature decided to add hail into the mix. Tiny beads of ice landed in the yard. Within seconds, the pea-sized pellets amped to the size of golf balls. And to top it all off, a piercing siren rent the air.

Crock barely registered the threat of the rapidly worsening weather thanks to an enraged bull of a possessed man, who howled as he charged his sister. Blinded by the rain and the sharp bruising pelts of hail on his skin, Crock looked for an opening as Tess spun to face Laz, slipping on the ice chunks on the ground.

Her foot slid from beneath her, and she landed hard on her hip. Laz's foot caught her side, and he tripped, flying across the yard to land with a pained grunt.

Crock ran toward the duo, tackling Laz to the ground as he rose up. Cursing and howling like a maniac, the other man struggled to buck him off. The rain and mud added to the challenge of keeping a hold on Laz.

He sensed Tess coming to help. "Get inside!" he shouted over the wail of the warning siren.

In typical Corona fashion, she ignored him. Tess threw herself over her brother's kicking legs, but one foot caught her in the shoulder, throwing her back.

At the same time, Laz managed to dislodge Crock's hold and flipped him over his head. He'd only seen that type of strength a few times, mainly while arresting someone manic on drugs, but that didn't describe what was happening with Laz. This was something completely out of Crock's experience.

Crock somehow landed on his feet, but his boots

couldn't get traction on the grass saturated with mud, hail and rain. He went down, landing hard on his ass. A lightning shock shot through his spine, which coincided with an actual lightning strike that was entirely too close for comfort.

He needed to get this shit under control. Crock hauled himself out of the mud, turning to find Laz charging Tess again. In a move worthy of a pro-baseball player, she sprinted toward Laz and transitioned into a base-stealing slide. Her aim put her going directly between her brother's legs. Without room to change course, Laz hurdled over her. Tess caught one of his ankles as it passed over her and jerked hard. Laz landed face first into a puddle of muddy water.

Crock moved to attempt another tackle but was distracted by the sight of Doma and Tila on the back porch. They took precedence in his book, so he changed direction and ran toward them. Doma raced toward the melee, a fierce look on her clown-like face, leaving the little girl on the deck.

"Storm shelter!" Doma shouted as she raced by. Her finger pointed to the corner of the yard to a concrete-covered mound he hadn't noticed before. "Get Tila in there!"

Tila met him with eyes and arms wide open, and Mr. Snotbubble clutched in one hand. Grabbing her into his arms, Crock used his body to protect the small girl from the pelting rain and hail as he ran for the shelter. Fortunately, the steel trunk hasp latch wasn't secured with a lock. With one hand, he flipped the catch and yanked the heavy door open. A narrow, dark hallway with a stairway leading to a pitch-black nether region greeted him.

"Have you been in here before?" he asked, hesitant to let the child go alone.

She gave him a nod, wiggling out of his arms and into the safety of the shelter. Crock turned away in time to see Doma smear something on Laz's head as he tried to rise from the muddy pool. Once done, she headed toward the shelter.

"What…?" he began.

"No time," Doma panted. "Get them in here. There's a funnel cloud heading this way."

With that fabulous news, she disappeared into the black hole to find Tila.

Well, shit! A quick glance at the ominous sky confirmed the news. The wall cloud had lowered, but he couldn't see much past the other houses and trees. It didn't matter. No day was a good day for a funnel cloud. And he had enough problems going on without having to dodge a tornado.

He turned his attention back to the fight. Laz had shoved himself out of the mud but his left elbow hung at an odd angle. If Crock needed any other proof that Laz wasn't in control, then there was his evidence. A dislocated elbow wasn't slowing the man down. Laz either had an incredibly high pain threshold, or he was feeling no pain thanks to whatever was making him act like a demon.

He also noted that Tess wasn't the aggressor. She fought defensively to avoid doing any permanent damage to her twin. With brother and sister faced off in the middle of the yard, Crock could only think of one thing that might end the fight without the pair killing each other or the tornado carrying them both off. He unholstered his gun.

"Tess!" A clap of thunder nearly drowned out his shout.

Her head turned toward him as a bright flash of lightning illuminated the backyard. Crock saw her eyes widen at the sight of his gun. "No!" She threw her body between Laz and Crock.

"Damn it, Tess! Move!"

"No!" she yelled. "I have to do this!"

Laz released what could only be described as a war whoop before lunging, catching her arm. Tess swung around and landed a fist into his jaw. The possession must have solidified his bones because she let out a pained yelp. Laz didn't stop as his left arm moved toward her throat. She shoved her knee into his crotch.

Even at a distance, Crock cringed at the sight. His gut rolled over in sympathy for the other man's balls.

Despite the hit, Laz didn't go down as a normal man would—no scream of pain, no covering himself. He released Tess as he stumbled back several steps. A bolt of lightning struck the power line in front of the house. The electrified air singed Crock's eyebrows, and the gun dropped out of his numbed hand into the mud. Anything was better than holding onto a lightning rod.

He slogged his way toward the fight. Tess slipped and fell as he got to the pair. Laz landed on top of her, his hands at her throat.

Crock hooked his arm into Laz's left armpit and yanked the injured arm away. "No, you don't."

Tess managed to dislodge her brother's other hand and get a foot positioned into his gut. With Crock's pull and her shove, Laz landed a few feet away.

Laz scrambled to his feet as Crock put himself in

front of a choking and gasping Tess. He'd be damned if he let Laz have another go at her.

Before Laz could move, the world lit up, accompanied by a deafening crash.

Crock's arm flew up to cover his eyes. When the flash faded, he lowered his arm to find Laz lying prone in a muddy puddle.

Tess appeared at his side. "What happened?" she shouted over the wind and rain.

"I don't know." Crock glanced around. The corner of the metal shed was missing, and the wood frame underneath smoked despite the steady downpour. "I think the shed was hit by lightning."

"Again?" Tess didn't seem fazed by her proximity to the strike. "How about Laz?"

"I think the strike knocked him out."

A chill spread through his spine. The hair and skin on his arms prickled as he realized the pouring rain and wind had died down. He wasn't sure if his hearing was gone thanks to the lightning or if something more threatening was approaching. He straightened and glanced over the top of the smoldering shed.

The sight definitely wasn't on his agenda for today.

He shoved Tess toward the shelter. "Move!"

Tess dug in her heels. Her eyes widened as she recognized the danger. "We can't leave Laz out here in a tornado!"

Crock had no intention of leaving Laz to be swept away and was already at the unconscious man's side. He tried to haul him up by the uninjured arm, but Laz was dead weight. With Tess's help, they managed to raise him off the ground enough for Crock to get under and into a firefighter's lift.

His back and left leg protested and almost didn't allow him to rise from the kneeling position. Tess grabbed around his waist, helping to lift and steady him. His eyes found his target, and he forced his legs toward the shelter as the sound of an approaching freight train told him he was running out of time.

Doma waited for them, fighting to keep the door open against the swirling winds. Crock felt pricks and stabs across his back and arms but ignored the sharp pains. Tess held on to his belt as he stumbled his way to safety. Nothing else mattered.

The door was more than a foot away when Crock felt rotation and lift around his legs. Lightning crashed somewhere behind him. His back seized.

He had no intention of going anywhere. Pain wasn't going to keep him from getting to safety.

"No!" he yelled as he lunged forward.

An invisible hand shoved him forward, and by some miracle, his hand latched onto the door frame. He let his burden fall off his shoulder. Doma grabbed Laz's jeans and arm and hauled him into the shelter. She then reached out again. Crock twisted around, grabbed hold of Tess's sport bra and shirt and threw her toward her grandmother as his left leg gave way from the strain.

The cold and pain in his spine intensified. Hands grabbed for him. His right shoulder separated from its socket as his body rose into the air. A second, intense flash of light blanked his vision and hearing. The agonizing burn at the base of his spine disappeared as quickly as it began, leaving him unresisting to the forces at work. But, instead of swirling away from the shelter, he found himself stumbling forward, landing on his knees.

"The door!" someone shouted near his ear.

Crock somehow turned back and caught the door with the arm that wasn't numb. The last thing he saw before pulling the door closed was the metal roof flying off the remains of the shed.

Chapter Thirty-Two

While Crock threw the inner latch to secure the storm door, Tess's legs melted as the burst of adrenaline faded. She landed hard on the edge of a concrete step before sliding down three more steps. She came to a stop two steps from her brother's limp body and offered a prayer of thanks for her great-grandfather's foresight.

Underground basements and storm shelters weren't common in Texas because of the clay soil. Before he'd been shipped off to prison for a robbery he didn't commit, Grandpa Manuel had built the house and shelter for his wife and family. She couldn't imagine how difficult it had been to dig enough gumbo out to make the shelter functional, but, somehow, he had done it without heavy equipment.

Gram kept the shelter stocked with bottled water, non-perishable snacks, and emergency supplies, including some of her remedies and a first-aid kit. Tess glanced around to find Tila standing in the corner of the twenty-by-twenty room, holding a battery-operated lantern.

They were safe from lightning, tornadoes, and—fingers crossed—a demon or two.

"Ow!" The groan came from behind her. Tess turned to find Gram prodding Crock's shoulder.

"It went back in place on its own," Gram

pronounced. "We can slap some ice on it when we get above ground."

Crock rolled his shoulder, trying to hide a grimace of pain. "It'll be all right. I've had worse."

"Sure you have. Like you've almost had your ass carried off to Timbuktu before," Gram said. "I've got some medicine for that shoulder. You can put it on that leg too, if'n you want it." She turned her attention to Tess. "Anything I need to work on?"

Tess did a quick inventory. "No, ma'am."

Gram nodded. "Good. Help me with this nitwit." She pointed at the unconscious lump at the base of the stairs.

Laz lay face down, his left arm at an odd angle. His head was bleeding, but all other body bits seemed to be intact.

"You probably shouldn't move him," Crock muttered as he stumbled down the steps.

Gram ignored him, indicating Tess should do what she was told.

Tess hauled her exhausted body over and shoved her brother's carcass. His big body rolled to his backside without too much trouble. He didn't wake up but released a soft moan. He was still breathing. She counted that as a plus.

"That's my girl." The faint whisper accompanied by a cool wisp of air, shrouding her in a phantom hug. Tess stilled at the memories that came with the presence—ones she never wanted to forget. *Thanks, Dad. I miss you.*

A second pressure settled over the ghostly one on her shoulder and drew her back to reality. The physical grip was her first indication that Crock had moved. She didn't realize how chilled she was until he knelt behind her. Fortunately, the man smelled like leather and spice instead of the scorched rat stench that wafted from her brother.

She put her hand over Crock's to keep it in place and received a light squeeze in return. The bite of a bruise told her she might not be as uninjured as she'd first thought, but she bit her lip to keep that information to herself. Gram had enough to worry about without dealing with minor cuts and bruises.

"Is Daddy okay?"

Tess turned to find Tila peering at Laz from her corner. Fortunately, the child didn't appear afraid, but more concerned about her daddy's condition.

"He's going to be fine, Miss T." Tess gave the girl as much reassurance as she could. "Grammy needs to check your daddy over."

Quietly, she and Crock stood by and watched Gram examine Laz in the dim light of the shelter. "Hold that lantern closer."

Tess reluctantly released Crock's hand and reached for the lantern that Tila held just out of reach. "I wanna hold it."

Tess rolled her eyes. "Fine. But if your daddy wakes up in a bad mood, get out of the way. Pronto. Deal?"

"Deal."

Tila scooted closer to her father's head and held the light high. Gram gave the child an approving nod before lifting Laz's eyelids. From her position, Tess couldn't tell if his pupils were reactive or not.

"Crock," Gram ordered, "come hold his arm so I can put the elbow back in place."

"Shouldn't we…?" Crock started.

Tess cut him off with a wild shake of her head. No one questioned Gram's expertise. No one.

Heaving a sigh, Crock did as he was told and held Laz's shoulder and arm steady. Everyone held their breath while Gram manipulated the joint.

Thunk!

Tess exhaled as the sickening sound told her that Gram was successful.

"Hand me something to splint his arm." Gram pointed to the corner where her emergency supplies were kept. "Keep his arm just like this," she instructed a pale, but stoic Crock.

Tess grabbed the necessary items. Before she turned back, she noticed a cross on the table. Thinking it might be helpful, she picked it up and returned to Gram's side. While Gram splinted and wrapped the arm, Tess centered the cross on Laz's chest. She glanced up to find Crock watching her with one eyebrow cocked.

"Do you think that'll help?" he muttered.

Gram answered for her, "It certainly won't hurt."

Laz moaned as she put the final touches on the splint. Tess grabbed for the lantern and shooed Tila across the room. Thankfully, the child went without protest.

"Laz?" Tess asked, keeping a close eye on her brother.

"Uh?" He sounded normal. For Laz.

"Are you still possessed?" She might as well get that all-important question answered right up front.

"What?" Laz tried to move but wound up gasping in pain. "Who the fuck ran over me?"

"Oh, good," Gram retorted. "You're normal."

"Gram!" Tess was up to her limit with smart remarks. "Laz, open your eyes."

"Uh uh."

Tess exchanged looks with Gram and Crock. "Why not?" she asked.

Laz tried to swirl the index finger of his left arm. "Ow! Fuck!"

More cursing commenced as he threw himself to his left side, rolling onto his splinted arm, and retched. The vile green chunks reminded Tess of the previous vomit-fest. If that was an indication of whatever was attached to Laz, then they still had a major problem.

Gram scrambled to her feet, moving more like a twenty-year-old than a septuagenarian as she headed for her supply cabinet. "Hold him down."

Crock and Tess each took a side and moved Laz to his back. Crock was closer to the icky side than Tess. "Ah, shit!"

"Sorry." Tess couldn't help but apologize to the Ranger. "You'll probably need a new wardrobe after a few close encounters of the Corona kind."

Crock didn't look amused.

Well, I tried.

Gram returned with a putrid-smelling concoction. "Move!"

Tess lurched out of the way as Gram smeared some of the goop on Laz's face. Instructing Crock to rip open the downed man's shirt, she continued to coat Laz's throat and chest. With a small amount remaining, Gram grabbed the sides of her grandson's jaw and shoved some of the gunk into his mouth. Tess lost control over Laz's good arm as he ripped it from her hands.

Lurching upward, he threw up more green, smelly slime onto Crock's lap.

Horrified, Tess watched the Ranger's jaw clench. She wasn't sure if he was angry or ready to puke himself. The smell was enough to make her gag, and she wasn't wearing it.

Giggles came from the corner of the room.

At least Tila thinks this is funny.

"Hush, missy." Gram pulled the still-heaving Laz over to his back and ran her hand a few inches above his body. "That's it," she muttered.

"Gram?" Tess couldn't resist.

"Hush."

When her grandmother said *hush*, people hushed.

Unfortunately, Crock never got the memo. "What are you…?"

"I said hush, dammit!" the woman hissed.

Tess sent Crock a wide-eyed look and shook her head. One eyebrow lifted. She held his gaze, waiting breathlessly for Gram to finish her examination. The only sounds came from their breathing, Laz's moaning, and a strange, metallic bang coming from outside.

Finally, Gram sat back. "I think it's gone."

"Gone?"

"What's gone?"

Both Tess and Crock spoke at the same time.

Gram ignored their question and ordered, "Check the radar. I don't hear sirens anymore. We should be clear for the moment."

Crock pulled his phone from his belt. Tess eyed it. She hoped it was inside a waterproof case. Otherwise, the electronics would be toast.

"The cell seems to be breaking up," Crock

announced, climbing to his feet. "I'll check outside."

The man seemed to be in a bit of hurry to get to the top of the steps. Of course, the chunks of green bile dripping from his pants probably incentivized him. When Crock threw the latch and opened the door, the sound of heavy rain hit her ears.

Breaking up, my ass.

Horrible weather didn't stop Crock from plunging into the deluge. Not that Tess blamed him. He'd had as bad a day—if not a little worse—as hers. No one's day had been as horrible as Laz's.

Mother Nature's shower would probably remove much of the slime, but she doubted his pants and shirt would be salvageable. His tooled leather belt and attachments wouldn't fare well, either.

Tila edged closer to her side but said nothing. After a quick glance to see how the child was doing, Tess turned her attention to the man responsible for the chaos. He had quieted down, but Tess didn't think Laz was going to hurl again.

He stirred, the movement of his good arm and legs accompanied groans and whimpers of pain and effort. Carefully, she supported him as he struggled to sit up.

Once Laz was propped against the workbench, Tess got out of his way—just in case. He rested there, eyes closed, supported by his right hand and still looking a lovely shade of green,

"Lazzie?"

"Uh?" he moaned.

"Are you going to live?"

One brown eye opened and narrowed into a glare before he croaked, "You can't have my office."

Tess almost smiled at the running argument. Over

the years, many battles had been fought over the largest spare bedroom. Laz had claimed the room when she joined the military. When she returned, she'd teased him about kicking him out of the room to turn it into a craft room—or a crap room as Laz liked to call it.

"Unless you intend to become one with the concrete, you might want to get up off the floor," she said.

Both eyes were open now. Laz looked around the shelter in amazement. "How'd we get down here?"

"Well, there was kind of a tornado, and…"

"A what?" Laz's neck gave a loud crack as his head spun in her direction.

"Daddy!" Tila's tiny body—accompanied by her stuffed alien—was a blur as it passed by Tess.

Laz yelped as his daughter slammed into him, her arms wrapping around his neck and her leg kicking his splint. Mr. Snotbubble's foot landed in Laz's open mouth and stifled his screech of pain.

****

Frantically swiping an alien leg out of his face and wondering why it tasted like minty tar, Laz's reply came from behind gritted teeth, "Hey, Punkin. Can you please let me breathe?"

The little girl released her stranglehold and plopped down hard on his groin, kicking his injured arm a second time. Laz swayed as his eyes rolled and his mouth opened in a silent scream.

Panting as he struggled through the pain, Laz adjusted his daughter's position in his lap. Wicked laughter came from his sister's direction. He shot her a glare.

Tess sat back and smirked. "You deserved that."

Fortunately, Laz's left arm wasn't so damaged that he couldn't flip her off.

Before she could respond, Crock reappeared in the doorway. A familiar object in his hands.

"Is that your gun?" Tess asked.

"Yeah," Crock answered, wiping the mud from the weapon. "I think it'll be okay if I can get it cleaned up." He glanced up and noticed Laz. "You gonna live?"

Laz huffed, "I guess. If I have to."

"Good. But," Crock added, "next time you want to pull shit like that, tell Tess to let me shoot you."

Laz's eyes widened as he swung his gaze toward Tess. "Sure. I'll do that." He shook his head and mouthed *no* at her.

Tess rolled her eyes, then stood, offering a hand to Laz. With a pained grunt to shift Tila off his lap, he was grateful for the help to haul his ass off the floor.

"Daddy?" a tiny voice piped up. "You sounded like a piggie."

Laz gave his little girl a pained grin. "Yeah, Punkin, I probably did."

"Auntie Tessie beat you up."

"She did not."

"She did, too!"

He glanced at his splinted arm before turning his attention to their surroundings and his companions. The war paint on Gram and Tila's face shut off any further arguments.

Tess smirked at him, but she looked like a drowned cat that had been in a fight. Crock had obviously been rolling around in the mud, and despite his impassive face, frustration and irritation rolled off him in waves.

Since he didn't want to get shot, Laz gave in. "It

seems that I've missed a few things. Anyone care to fill me in on the details?"

Chapter Thirty-Three

Explanations had to wait.

Although the power was out, Gram sat each person down—each under protest—at the kitchen table and doctored all war wounds by lantern and candlelight.

Fortunately, aside from Laz's dislocated elbow and Crock's separated shoulder, there was nothing more serious than cuts and bruises. Tila was mostly unscathed but demanded equal attention to a tiny tear on Mr. Snotbubble's foot.

Mr. Snotbubble needed stitches.

While Gram and Crock got Laz situated and doped up on painkillers, Tess surveyed the house and yard for damages and discovered one hell of a mess. The shed roof was neatly wrapped around a huge shade tree that pre-dated her grandad. The vehicles all had minor hail damage, but the only other major victim of the storm was her Jeep. A large limb from the neighbor's magnolia tree relocated itself to be comfortably wedged into the hood and windshield.

All in all, Tess counted the Corona household lucky against Mother Nature.

Crock left shortly after getting patched up, refusing an offer of dry clothing and an adult beverage. With the supercell moving in the direction of his home, he said he needed to ensure his family's safety.

The following morning, when he returned, Tess

was attempting to haul the heavy limb from the hood of her car. “Everything okay at home?” she called as he emerged from his truck.

She braced one foot against her front grill while grasping a good-sized branch. With a tremendous shove, Tess found herself on her backside with a three-foot stick of wood in hand. The remaining twenty feet of tree limb remained stubbornly in place.

“Yeah.” A hand appeared before her. She threw the stick onto a nearby pile of debris and allowed herself to be hauled off the ground.

Crock seemed to be holding back a chuckle as he continued, “The storm went over the north side of the lake. There was some wind damage, but no other tornados were reported.”

“That’s good to hear,” Tess decided to argue with the tree limb another time and headed to the front porch.

“How’s Laz?”

“Grumpy.”

Crock stopped her with a hand on her arm. “Do we need to take him to a doctor? I know your grandmother is a healer, but…”

Tess met his concerned gaze. “One thing about Gram that we might have forgotten to mention—she’s not *just* a medicine woman. She’s *also* a semi-retired osteopathic doctor. She knows what she’s doing.”

“Okay.” Crock’s expression didn’t change. “I can understand that, but doesn’t he need x-rays or something?”

Tess shrugged and resumed walking. “If it’s not getting better by the time she goes back to the clinic next week, she’ll order an x-ray and refer him to a specialist if necessary."

"He won't need any specialist," Gram announced, meeting them at the door.

"Oh, good," Tess smirked, "then he can help me clean up this mess."

"I didn't say that," Gram groused. "I just said he doesn't need a specialist."

"So, when can he…?"

"When I say so," Gram growled.

"Yes, ma'am."

Tess led Crock into the kitchen, where Tila sat on top of the table to assist Laz with his breakfast. Her brother didn't look thrilled to be spoon-fed by a three-year-old but offered no complaint even when cold milk and soggy corn flakes landed in his lap.

Tess considered—briefly—putting a plastic trash bag over his lap for protection, but then decided against it. Several of the bruises she inherited from their fight were achy and tender. He could suffer.

Gram busily cut into her applesauce cake. She gave Crock a generous slice of fresh, spicy cake drizzled with a warm caramel sauce. Everyone else got not-so-generous slices. The power had come back on overnight, and the household had woken to the smells of Gram's baking, but she had refused to serve the goods until after the Ranger arrived.

Said Ranger's eyes grew glassy as he took a deep breath, inhaling the spices and the sugary sweetness that was placed before him.

Tess choked. "Addict."

Laz followed with his own cough, "Suck up."

Crock didn't seem to notice as he tucked into the huge slice of cake. Nor did he bat an eyelash when

Gram brought a wooden spoon down on each of their heads.

"Ow!" Laz tried to cover his head, but the splint bounced off his ear instead.

"What was that for?" Tess bitched, rubbing her head.

"That's for making fun of our guest," Gram stated firmly.

Glancing at Crock, Tess thought he might be smirking, but it was difficult to tell for sure with his mouth full.

Crock resumed the conversation after a few bites, "Why all the secrecy about being a doctor?"

The temperature in the room suddenly dropped about twenty degrees at Crock's innocent question.

Tess placed herself between her grandmother, who tried to reclaim her baked goods, and the Ranger who realized that he might have put his foot in his mouth.

"I wasn't trying to insult your skills," Crock tried to appease Gram while protecting his cake from being confiscated. "I thought your splint job was fantastic, but he took some hard falls. Shouldn't he get some scans to check for what we can't see?"

Laz took over the explanation because Gram was growling. "In some cases, yes. Gram's good at what she does and will keep an eye on me for a couple of days." He pushed his bowl away and gave Tila a weak smile. "Other than the fact that I'm still not clear on what happened, I feel better than I've felt all week."

"That's a plus, I guess," Crock paused, keeping a close eye on Gram's response. His plate slowly made its way back to the table. "But, why was being a doctor a big secret?"

"It's no secret." Tess glanced over to her grandmother. Gram seemed a bit calmer. "She's experienced a lot of prejudice over the years."

"I thought shamans were respected. And female doctors have been around over a hundred years," Crock protested.

"We aren't shamans, we are spiritual healers and medicine men or women. Yes, we are respected within our communities." Gram appeared back in control of her temper. "Doctors of Native American descent aren't. Especially those of us combined western medicines with traditional 'heathen' remedies 'off the reservation' if you will."

She used air quotes to emphasize the criticisms she'd been subjected to throughout her career. Her bitterness edged back into her tone, "*And then* I went and married a Mexican. It didn't matter that that Mexican's family was here long before Texas was even a republic and fought for its independence."

Tess watched Crock consider that information. It didn't seem to bother him. Hell, the man was an investigator exploring the use of a paranormal team to find a killer. Crock was more open-minded than most people the family had run across.

"Okay," he said. "I can work with that."

Gram narrowed her eyes at the man, trying to determine if he had an underlying prejudice. "That's it? *Okay*?"

The man tucked into his cake, his eyes rolling to the back of his head as he savored the sweet caramel and warm, spiced apples. Chewing and swallowing took *hours*, but finally he answered, "Why would I have a problem with you practicing your beliefs in a manner that you have researched and studied? I assume you have the necessary education, certification, and licensure, and nothing has been revoked by a regulating body. As long as it's all legal, life is good."

Nothing was heard for a moment except the *chink* of Crock's fork on the plate.

Gram moved to a cabinet on the far end of the kitchen where she kept her brews. Selecting a small brown bottle, she moved to the table. Setting the bottle next to Crock, she said, "Rub this into the muscles on your shoulder and leg. It'll take some of the soreness out, especially when you overdo it."

With that, she picked up two plates and left the kitchen with Tila in tow.

****

Laz forced his jealousy into submission, especially when Crock uncapped the bottle and the pleasant scent of mint and lemongrass filled the air. Gram was never that nice when treating one of *his* injuries. She simply grabbed hold of the most painful and disgusting remedies she could find to shove down his throat. Or she'd manipulate his neck until he was looking down his backside. Never once had she handed over a bottle of ointment and said, "Here. Use this. It'll help with the pain."

No, when it came to her family, Gram didn't trust them as far as she could toss them. Plus, she liked torture.

Laz decided he'd better change the subject before he stole Crock's remedy just for the hell of it. "So, what exactly *did* happen last night?"

Tess was also eyeing the little bottle with a fair amount of lust. Or she might have been eyeing Crock with a fair amount of lust. Laz couldn't be sure which was the case. Since she wasn't paying attention to him, he chunked a soggy corn flake at her.

"Uh," she said, "what do you remember?"

Laz had to think. "You dropped me off at work. Marcos called and said my car was patched up enough to drive it, so I called a ride. When I got in my car and made it down the street, the clutch went out." That, on top of Marcos's idea of paybacks—which included scrubbing some kind of slimy shit off the walls of his restroom—hadn't set the tone for a good evening. "I got it back to Marcos, and he offered to bring me home." Bribery had been required—brownies—but not delivered. "I don't remember much after that. Did he get the brownies I promised?"

"Nope, he hightailed it out of here when you lost your shit."

Tess gleefully launched into the tale. It took a few minutes, but he learned that he had broken a number of Corona sins and hard no-no's in the span of ten minutes. He was shocked that he wasn't a greasy spot in the mud for calling Gram a crazy old bitch. Hell, he knew to not even think those words, much less say them out loud.

"So, I got pissed over some makeup?" Laz couldn't believe everything he heard. It had all the makings of a bad action movie scene. Just the fact that he even *considered* taking on both Tess and Crock in the middle of a supercell thunderstorm was unbelievable.

He *hated* thunderstorms. They ranked right up there with Tess's phobia of shadow people. Laz wondered if Gram had done some sort of rain dance for the thunderstorm which knocked him out for almost half an hour.

Of course, he also hated handcuffs. He was grateful that Crock didn't slap him in a pair. With his elbow throbbing like a bitch, being handcuffed would really suck.

"You weren't pissed," Tess stated. She brushed crumbs from the table onto her empty plate. "You were possessed."

"And I was going to hurt Tila?" He couldn't imagine going after his daughter under any circumstance.

Crock answered, "She was smart enough to stay back, but you wouldn't have gotten close enough to do anything."

Laz knew he would have been stopped—one way or another. By every bone in his body broken, some sort of hex, or a bullet, the manner of being stopped didn't matter. The thought of lead poisoning made him lose his appetite, but he would rather be dead than hurt Tila.

"I'm glad y'all did what you had to do," he said. There wasn't much else he could say.

Crock got up and took his plate to the sink, gathering Tess's and Laz's plates on the way. "I'm still not clear on what exactly was going on."

"He was possessed." Gram confirmed what Tess had told him as she came back in, followed by Tila. The little girl carried their empty dishes and handing them to Crock while Gram sat at the head of the table. "He probably feels a hell of a lot better now that his little freeloader is gone."

Three pair of expectant—yet cautious—eyes turned toward him. Laz quickly swallowed and did a quick inventory of his status. The pounding headache and back pain was gone, replaced by the pain in his elbow. "Yeah," he said quickly, "I think I'll live."

Crock placed the dishes in the sink and washed his hands. When he turned back, he asked, "Let me see if I understand correctly—a ghost possessed you and turned you into some kind of puppet?"

Laz shook his head. "A ghost can't take over like that. They can jump a person, but not make them think or do things they wouldn't normally do. This was something a little stronger."

"Like what?"

Embarrassed to admit it, Laz glanced around the room before answering, "I don't know. I haven't run across one of these before." He thought for a moment, before adding, "Probably the closest thing I can think of would be a Skinwalker or a Wendigo, but those aren't typical Texas legends. I'll have to do some research."

"So, what happened to it?" Crock asked again. "Is it gone to another realm?"

Tess took over. "We can't be certain. The lightning strike dislodged it from Laz and probably stunned it into some dormant state, but it's probably still around. There's no telling where it might be, or what it'll do next."

"Great." Crock didn't sound thrilled as he settled back into his seat. "Do I need to put a BOLO out for people acting like zombies or a mass of murder-suicides?"

Tess grinned. "Nothing like that. Whatever this is got about a billion-volt electrical shock. It'll need time to get its particles back together. Then, it will need an invitation or someone receptive enough for it to take over. Which means," she shot a glance at her grandmother, "we might need to reinforce our barriers."

"Meaning?" Crock pushed for more answers.

"Meaning," Laz forced himself to admit a new reality, "since I've already hosted this thing once, and I brought it to the house, we need to do a cleansing and make this place less homey so it can't return here."

Crock glanced around the room as if trying to decide what to ask next. He finally focused his attention on Laz. "What were you feeling? The other day you had the most drunk hangover I've ever seen, but what was going on inside? And you were talking in some language. Any idea what that was about?"

Laz thought for a moment. Strange words and sounds floated through his brain. He wasn't an expert in native languages, but he was certain he knew what he'd said and the meanings. "Most native languages are all but extinct, but what I remember was probably Comanche or something along that line." He rubbed his head, remembering the urges he'd suppressed. "There was a lot of negative talk. You know…things like *it's all your fault, they're better off….*"

He stopped. There were things a father probably shouldn't say in front of his daughter—suicidal-type things.

Tess must have understood. "You know that none of that is true, right?"

Laz shrugged. "I don't know what I could have done differently. I've never had a problem with possession before."

"You've been playing with fire," Gram snorted. "This time you got burned. If you'd've listened to me, you would've stopped this nonsense when Tess got spooked. But no! You kept digging."

Laz tried to interrupt, but Gram stood up, slamming her hands onto the oak table. Her eyes shot fire and were fiercer than he'd ever seen, even when she and Mom got into a fight. "You wanted to find answers and solve crimes. Guess what? You found them, and you got a taste of what those ghosties can do to make your life miserable. You're just lucky that lightning bolt knocked the shit out of you and ousted your little hijacker before it killed one of you idiots."

The room was quiet for several minutes.

"May I go to my room?" Tila's small voice broke the spell on the room.

"Huh?" Laz started. "Uh…yeah. Why don't you…uhm…take Mr. Snotbubble and…."

"Okay." Tila didn't wait for a suggestion. She had enough ideas of her own, many of which were probably illegal in most states. She ran from the room with her stuffed alien in tow.

Laz glanced around. He cleared his throat and tried to come up with an intelligent response. "Gram, I'm sorry. I didn't…"

"You didn't think I knew what was going on," she finished. "You thought all that fancy study and expertise would save your ass. Well, you forgot to ask a few important questions of the ones who might have a tiny bit more experience with the paranormal than you."

It was true—he had learned much from his grandmother, listening to her stories and the legends of her people. One vital detail he hadn't given credit to was that those stories and legends had basis in fact, and Native Americans used those truths to protect themselves against evil. His blatant disregard for his own culture had put him and his family at risk. "I'll do better," he promised.

"See that you do." Gram knocked on the table and sat back down.

It seemed that the uncomfortable discussion was over, but Laz knew it was anything but finished. It was Crock who turned the conversation back to the investigation.

"Well, I'm not sure what all this has to do with the Green murder, but I don't like thinking I've put all of y'all in danger to solve my case."

Laz turned toward the Ranger. "It explains a lot about the case."

Crock cocked his head to the side. "What do you mean?"

"The voice in my head told me some things," Laz took a deep breath and leaned forward to rest on the table. The splint on his left arm made him curse the action, forcing him to balance his weight on the right side.

Tess spoke up, "What'd it say?"

"That Dan killed Esme." Laz still had difficulty believing that his mentor would do anything to harm his wife, but he also never would have thought that he would try to hurt Tila. He swallowed hard. "That thing was probably responsible for the other incidents at the hotel as well. I think if that lightning hadn't struck, then I might have done something to hurt you or Tila or…."

"Don't think that!" Tess protested. "You're forgetting who you are dealing with. There's no way in hell we would have let you or that thing hurt any of us."

"You don't know…"

"No," Crock stepped in, "we do know. You weren't in control, and we knew that. And we were prepared to stop you from doing any damage to anyone—including you."

Tess snorted, "You were going to shoot him!"

Crock shot her a look. "Yes. And I would have kept him from endangering others. Which reminds me—what the hell were you doing putting your ass in front of a gun? Didn't the Army teach you better than that?"

"Actually, my daddy and grandaddy taught me that, but your training taught you to shoot to kill. The Army taught me to run *toward* the bullets," Tess insisted. "Laz is *my* brother. If anyone's going to shoot him, it'll be me."

Laz didn't feel much better about that scenario either. "Thanks, sis."

"She's right." Gram interrupted with a glare at the Ranger. "The Coronas take care of their own."

Crock was nearly pouting at lack of appreciation for his efforts. "I'm the one who hauled his heavy ass into the shelter to get him out of a freaking tornado."

"For which we are grateful," Gram gave him a nod. "Now, if y'all will excuse me," she said as she pushed away from the table, "I've got some prayer bags to assemble for each of you. Y'all're going to need them."

Ashamed, Laz turned his attention back to the crumbled cake on his plate. Forgetting about his arm, he reached with his left hand for one of the glasses of milk that Gram had passed out. Pain shot through his arm at the added stress to his elbow. "Ow! Damn! That hurt!"

Tess turned to him. "Oh, hush, you big baby!"

Chapter Thirty-Four

Crock heard them arguing before they got out of the car. Although he'd only known the family seven days—which felt like decades—he'd come to expect chaos from anyone with the last name of Corona.

This time it was the vehicle that made his jaw drop.

When he left the house to head to the Parker County Courthouse, Laz and Tess agreed to bring the boxes to his office that afternoon so that anything important could be processed immediately. With Laz's car still in the shop and a large tree limb embedded in the hood of Tess's Jeep, he didn't think to ask how they would get from Fort Worth to Garland.

Now he knew.

"What in the hell is that?"

"Is that paint job street-legal?"

"That thing still works?"

The comments coming from the fellow Rangers gathered at the office doors told Crock that either BJ Childs was a gossip, or all hands were on deck to watch this train wreck happen.

A land yacht was docked in the visitors parking lot. A car that was bigger than most cabin cruisers, but definitely had more glitter than most jazzed-up fishing boats. The sun was out, so the custom silver Lincoln Continental sparkled and blinded anyone for a mile around.

God help me if Gemma ever sees that bling!

Crock took a deep breath and stepped away from his truck. He re-donned his mirrored sunglasses as he ambled toward what he could only think of as the Corona Boat. His approach was met by the expulsion of *three*—not two—cranky adults.

"I do not drive like a grandma! I oughta bust your ass for even thinking that."

"Gram, you were going thirty on the freeway!" Tess protested.

"Why should I care?" Doma smacked her hand on the horn. *La Cucaracha* blasted through the parking lot. "I'd have driven faster if they hadn't been such buttheads. Served them right! Next time I'll change lanes in front of anyone being a prick."

Laz looked a little carsick as he stumbled out of the back seat. "There won't be a next time if you keep doing that. Some dumbass will run you off the road!"

Crock nearly backtracked when he got a glimpse of the rhinestone-covered steering wheel and fuzzy, pink, leopard-print seats. He *really* didn't want Gemma to see this car.

As the trio argued about who was *not* going to drive the monstrosity home, he did the only thing he could think of to get their attention—he stood there, arms crossed, silent and waiting.

An eternity later, Tess finally noticed his presence. Her eyes drifted behind him and grew wide. If Crock had to guess, there were ten or fifteen Rangers stood behind him in various versions of his no-nonsense pose.

Tess slapped at Laz's splinted arm, causing him to yelp.

"Fuck! Why'd you do that?" His protest drifted off

as he followed Tess's stare. "Oh…uhm…hey, y'all!"

Crock nearly lost his composure at the look on Laz's face when he realized he wouldn't get a response.

Tess took over. Grinning, she announced, "We brought brownies!"

That broke the universal silence.

"Yes, ma'am!"

"Captain said those were the greatest!"

"Do you need help?"

Crock shook his head as the bunch of suck-ups that he had the good fortune to work with converged on the car. Two large boxes of chocolatey goodness were quickly removed from the backseat and given an escort of honor into the inner domain of Company B. He just hoped there'd be one or two left when he got inside.

"Don't worry." Tess appeared by his side. "You've got your own plate."

His neck popped as it jerked around. He saw no evidence of more brownies. "Where?"

She laughed. "They're safe in the trunk with the boxes."

Doma wandered to the back of the car and inserted her key. A mental warning went off. Crock wasn't sure what he would find on the inside of that trunk, even as he hightailed it over to get his prize. Fortunately, the trunk was bare of any bling, dead bodies, or illegal contraband; however, an almost visible cloud of sulphur emerged from within.

Praying that his goodies wouldn't taste like rotten eggs, he found a large, plastic-wrapped plate of brownies nestled in the remains of one cardboard box with its contents scattered into the depths of the cavernous trunk. Two other—intact—boxes sat side-by-side. The farthest container caught his attention.

"Where did that come from?" he asked, knowing he probably wouldn't like the answer.

"What?" Tess rounded the back of the car, stopping to curse, "Ah, hell!"

"What?" Laz came up beside him. "Ah, man. Tess! Your duct tape job didn't work!"

He grabbed handfuls of papers and tucked them into the sides of his splint and purple tie-dyed sling, which Crock suspected had once been a TCU T-shirt. Tess brought a purple tote from the car to hold the debris.

Crock closed his eyes and counted to ten. He wasn't much more in control of the situation when he finished. "Not the papers. Where'd *that* box come from?"

The twins exchanged glances and gave identical shrugs.

"The school?" Tess answered. "Why? What's the matter?"

"You don't see what that is?" He pointed at the box in question. The woman had been in an investigative unit. Crock was surprised that she hadn't recognized the container.

She reached over and pulled it up. Turning it around, her eyes grew big. "Oh, shit! I didn't even pay attention to it."

"What?" Laz squawked. "What is it?"

Crock took the well-worn box from Tess and looked it over. Marked on the side was the appropriate identification for his case. With his suspicions confirmed, he answered, "This is the missing evidence box. How in the hell did Dr. Green get ahold of it?" He didn't expect an answer. At least not a good answer.

"Hell if I know." Laz sounded pissed. "I didn't even know about the boxes until Wednesday. And if you recall, I wasn't exactly in great shape yesterday."

Crock began counting again as he tucked the evidence box under one arm and set the second, intact container on top. It was going to be a long afternoon, and he would need every single one of those brownies to survive.

He waited as patiently as he could for the twins to stuff the loose papers and remains of the deceased box into the plastic tote. Tess took possession of the tote with a glare at her brother. Crock bit the inside of his cheek and guided them into the office. Sounds coming from the breakroom proved that he was glad to have his own personal supply of chocolate currently in the safe hands of the chief baker.

Leading them to a conference room where they could work in separate corners, Crock pointed with his elbow. "In here. We can spread out."

Before he could shut them in, his captain stomped in to investigate. "What's this I hear about brownies?" Childs had his priorities.

"In the…" Crock tried to divert his boss, but it was too late. Childs noticed the plate in Doma's hands and sidled up to shmooze the older woman.

"Hello, my lovely lady," he crooned, "and how are you this fine day? And where is my little friend and her alien?"

Laz interjected, "We dropped Tila off to harass her teacher for a few hours."

His comment earned him a searing look from his grandmother. "And I'd be a helluva lot better if my two idiot grandkids didn't pester me about driving."

Childs' hand crept toward Crock's plate. "And what are they complaining about? Your excellent driving?"

"Hell, no!" Doma turned her flashing eyes to the man who towered over her. "They know I'm a lousy driver—being senile and all—it's the car itself they object to." She shifted the plate into her left hand and smacked the captain's fingers away with her right.

Crock dumped his boxes on the table with a *thump*. It was all he could do to contain a snort of laughter. He wasn't sure which was funnier—the comment or the punishment.

Shaking his hand, Childs' eyebrows shot into outer space. "Uh…what's wrong with the car?"

Tess answered for her grandmother, "Nothing is wrong with it. Except that its blinding to all other drivers."

"It's got an obnoxious horn," Laz added.

"It's old."

"It stinks."

"It…"

Childs cut off Tess's last complaint. "I think I'll have to see this in order to believe it. What kind of car is it?"

Doma took over before the younger set could say anything, "It's a 1979 mint-condition, customized, Lincoln Continental Mark VI. My husband bought it for me when I finished my residency. Marcos, his nephew, has kept it in good, working order for me since he took over the family garage." She paused to glare at her grandchildren again. "One of these two idiots will inherit it one day. And if they even think about getting rid of it, I'll come back and haunt them every day of their miserable lives."

Crock heard grumbling from the other side of the room, which sounded something like, "She already makes our life hell. How would that be any different?"

Childs turned and glanced at him. Crock arranged his face into an impassive mask. His boss quickly changed the subject, "I heard from the Johnson County Sheriff. That evidence box was checked out before they went digital. It was never returned."

"Yeah," Crock drawled, "I figured as much."

"How so?"

Crock tapped the box in question. "Because it's sitting right here."

The captain's attention drifted to the box Crock was leaning on. "You're sure?"

"It matches the case number," Crock answered, "but I haven't checked the contents yet."

"Well, let's fix that."

"Yes, sir."

Crock moved the top box over and opened the evidence box. He removed a yellowed piece of paper that he'd only seen in textbooks. Before digitization, all chain of custody paperwork was in written form and this one was dated 1998, releasing the box to Dr. Daniel Green, and signed by a G. H. Green.

"What do you want to bet that G. H. Green is a relative to Dan?" he muttered.

Laz had set up his laptop on the table and, after a few one-handed clicks, answered, "Gerald Henry Green was Dan's older brother. He apparently worked for the Johnson County Sheriff's Office until 1999. He died in 2006."

“So,” Tess spoke up, “Dan was all alone?”

Laz made a few more clicks before confirming their finding, “The brother had two kids—a son and daughter—but no other family that I could find.”

Crock and Childs exchanged looks. Crock nodded. “We know about the niece and nephew. They’re more interested in Uncle Dan’s estate than finding answers. But how’d you get that information so fast?”

Laz smirked as pink crept up from the collar of his T-shirt. “Genealogy is a hobby and helps me dig into the legends and myths that I research. When you first contacted me, I created a family tree for Dan. I took him and Esme back several generations.”

Crock was impressed, as was the captain. “I can see where that’d be helpful.”

“It can be.” Laz’s face and neck turned even darker. “It’s another way of bringing our ancestors to life. To tell their stories.”

“Their truth.”

All eyes turned toward Tess.

“Yeah,” Laz finally answered, giving her a nod. “It’s what Dan would have wanted.”

Childs stepped toward the door. “I’ll leave you to it, then.”

“Wait a minute.” Doma halted the big man with a hand on his arm. “Don’t you want your brownies?”

The captain’s eyes widened before his mouth broke into a blinding white grin. “You brought me some?”

Doma dragged the last unopened box to her and proceeded to remove a large plate of goodies covered in plastic. Taped to the top, a small child’s drawing depicted a man’s round head with spikes sprouting from the top. Crossed marks formed what Crock loosely interpreted as dandelions. He was willing to bet that Tila's drawing would be framed and placed with pride on Child's desk by Monday morning.

Childs admired the artwork, "Aw! That looks just like me!"

He unwrapped his gift, being careful to not tear the picture, and selected a brownie from the large pile, popping it into his mouth without delay. With his eyes rolling to the back of his head, he moaned, "Fank ooo!"

Crock tried not to watch a grown man talk and eat at the same time. Fortunately, the captain left them to their work while scarfing down another treat.

Laz returned his attention to the screen before him. "Let's get back to the family tree. Dan's family came to Texas after 1900, but Esme's family was in the Waco area as early as 1820. Her great-grandfather, Jacob Smith, settled north of Cleburne around 1850. In 1863, there was some dispute between the settlers and the native tribes—probably either Wichita or Comanche—that left several warriors dead on the Smith land."

Tess broke in. "The hotel's historical plaque mentioned a massacre."

Laz nodded. "On both sides. Jacob Smith and three of his sons were killed. Esme's great-grandmother and her grandfather were in Waco when it happened. According to the report I found, Jacob sent his wife and younger children to visit family when the hostilities worsened. They were the only surviving members of the family."

"Let me guess," Crock rested his hands on the table, supporting his weight, "that hotel sits on the disputed land."

"Looks like it." Doma rose from her perch to read

over Laz's shoulder. "Great grandma opened a boarding house to make ends meet. Esme's grandpappy turned it into a hotel and saloon. Whatcha wanna bet he ran a bordello?"

"I'm not touching that one with a ten-foot pole," Crock said. "So, what does that mean for us?"

"It means," Tess took over, sharing a glance with her brother. "Laz's little hijacker was probably a pissed-off, Comanche warrior trying to exact revenge. Either that, or Jacob Smith is still protecting his property. My money is on a warrior-demon continuing his attack on the family."

"It makes sense," Laz said. "Most of the other deaths were associated in some way with Esme's family. She was the last of her line. Her grandad died in a shoot-out at his saloon, and her dad was gored by a bull on the family farm. I'd say that spirit didn't want the Smith line to continue, considering what happened to any children born on the property."

"Is that what happened to Dan and Esme's children?" Crock eased back into his seat. "They died within days of each other."

Laz nodded. "They were playing by the creek. A water moccasin bit Francine. Michael fell and hit his head while trying to get her out of the creek bed. He drowned. Francine lasted a couple of days before the venom and infection got her."

Images of a brother trying to protect and help his sister pierced Crock's mind. He could only image that little boy pulling his sister to safety only to fall to his death. That anyone—dead or alive—would harm small children to serve some century-old vendetta made him sick.

Swallowing his disgust, he voiced an immediate concern, "Does that warrior-ghost have a chance of coming back? Or what?"

The twins exchanged looks, shrugged, and turned to their grandmother.

"Hopefully, the tornado gave that demon a good ride, and he'll stay away," Doma replied.

With her hands on her hips and a fierce expression, Crock had no doubt that the medicine woman was ready to take on any threat to her family—corporeal or not. He turned his attention back to the evidence box. "We have a few answers; now we need the proof. Let's hope it's in here." Digging in, he issued his orders, "Laz, why don't you and Tess sort those two boxes while I go through this one."

They got to work, but the amicable silence lasted less than three seconds.

From the intact box, Tess lifted a tattered gray cloth-bound book. "*The Lusty Texans of Dallas.* I'm not sure I want to know what that's about."

Laz grabbed it out of his sister's hands. "It's a history of Dallas from the 1950s. Kinda dry reading, but it has some interesting bits. I never knew that two women wearing the same dress to a party could kick up such a fuss."

"How did you not see Missy Stevens and Becca Carter get into a pissing match on prom night over their dresses?" Tess asked. "Same design, different color. Neither wore it well."

"I think I was busy." To Crock, Laz appeared to be getting excited about his so-called inheritance but looked a little uncomfortable with his answer.

"Yeah, busy getting into Lanna's dress," Tess

snorted as she pulled a few more ratty, old books from the box and handed them to her brother, who handed them to Gram to stack in a neat pile.

"Okay, you two, stay focused." Crock wanted to wait patiently for the twins to stop arguing, but the odds of wasting another day as a result were too high for his comfort.

Laz changed the subject. "I can sort most of this stuff later. Just make a pile for any books or notebooks that don't look relevant."

It took little time to verify the contents of the evidence box. As Crock suspected, there was no new information to shed light on the case, however he did find the full investigation report that had been missing from his working file. He pulled the purple tote closer to sift through the contents. He lifted out the first few papers and glanced through them.

"These are the ones you mentioned yesterday," he said, handing over the notes and the broken binder. "The papers that made you think he wanted you to investigate Esme's death."

Laz didn't spare a glance at the papers. "Dan had the history of the hotel and Esme's family, my research on paranormal investigations, and an outline of the events around Esme's death. I think he knew he was responsible but didn't know how."

Crock raised his eyebrow. "You mean he didn't know what happened just like you didn't remember the fight in the yard?"

"Right," Laz nodded, "but he'd done enough research to know the possibilities."

Tess had continued to sort through the loose papers in the box. "The stuff in this box seems to be based on that hypothesis."

Crock barely suppressed the sigh that fought to escape. "Then let's weed through this mess and see what we've got."

****

"Where's the sex?"

Gram's voice broke the silence, causing Tess to straighten up so fast, her back popped. She turned to find Gram flipping through the ancient copy of *Lusty Texans of Dallas*. "Laz said it's a history book, Gram. Not erotica."

"Well, it's a dud." The older woman tossed the text onto the stack she'd stolen it from—a plume of dust rising from the pile—and grumbled about false advertising.

A quick glance around showed Laz and Crock burying their head into whatever paper or book was closest. The idiots couldn't hide their snorts of laughter.

Ignoring the juveniles, Tess glanced back at the next paper in her pile. She figured that if she hovered her hand over an item before touching it, she might sense if it was safe from visions. So far, it had worked. At least that's what she told herself. Time would tell if her theory was valid or not.

She didn't need her senses to know this page was important. "Uh…Laz?"

"Yeah?"

"It's another letter."

Both men glanced up.

A chair scraped on the vinyl flooring as Crock moved around the table. He braced his arms on either side of her to read over her shoulder. If it'd been Laz, the temptation to put her elbow in his gut would be difficult to resist. With Crock, Tess had other ideas, and it took all her willpower to keep her hands to herself.

"What's it say?" Laz asked, not moving from his spot.

"Basically, what we were thinking." As Tess scanned the document, she recited the salient points, "He admits that the evidence points to him killing Esme, but he has no memory of what happened. He believes something possessed him, and that same entity caused all the other events at that hotel. He exhausted his efforts and decided it was time to pass his research on. Dan wanted you to learn the truth and thought you might have the expertise to eradicate the danger so no one else dies."

She stopped and shot a concerned glance to her brother before continuing. "Dan had mixed his heart and Parkinsons medicines with arsenic. He planned to take double doses so that he could die on their anniversary and finally dance with her in the hotel where they began their life together."

The room was silent for several minutes.

Laz spoke first, "He really loved her. I'm surprised he didn't go sooner."

To hide her envy of one man's all-encompassing love for one woman, Tess shuffled through the next few pages. "He included a copy of his will."

Crock held his hand out. Tess passed the documents to him. "This one is dated a few weeks before he died. The attorney mentioned a newer will but hadn't found it. This might be it."

"Yeah," Tess confirmed, "Dan knew the niece and nephew would be a problem. In fact, this one states if they try to circumvent the will, they get nothing."

Turning around to prop his hip on the table, Crock grimaced, "Oh, they'll get something, all right."

Tess snorted. "Yeah, jail time."

Crock pulled his notebook over and made a notation. "Let's hope they decide to cooperate with a fraud and forgery investigation."

Laz piped up, "So, if the family screwed the pooch on their inheritance, where does the money go?"

Tess looked up from her study of the documents. "Apparently, Dan bought the hotel through his attorney when it was going under, then willed it to the manager, Mary Dunham, who was a good friend and like family to him. The attorney has been approving any of expenditures until he could locate this will and turn it over to her. She also gets a chunk of change to help with repairs. Laz gets his research, books, and rights to his prior and current publications. TCU's history department also gets grant money for—get this—'Dr. Lazaro Corona to continue his innovative and invaluable research into paranormal studies and the effects on historical and contemporary cultural and criminal activities.'"

Laz's eyes widened with shock. The opening and closing of his mouth reminded Tess of a fish gulping for air, but she figured this wasn't the time to make fun of her twin. Not when one of his biggest dreams was on the cusp of reality.

"I…uhm…" Laz sputtered. A nervous hand wiped his face. "I can't believe this. He…I…."

"He believed enough in your work to support it," Gram spoke up from the corner which she had settled in, pretending to take a nap. "He believed in you. You need to do the same."

Tess heard the pride in her grandmother's voice and fought the tears that threatened. For all the woman's sarcasm, Gram loved them and would do anything in her power to support them, whether that meant taking in a homeless, grieving teenager and her runaway brother, shoving vile potions down their throat, or providing a swift kick in the ass whenever needed.

"Congratulations, Laz," Crock offered his two cents, "but don't get too excited, yet. This will needs to go to the estate attorneys for authentication and probate. It may take some time to get this settled." He pushed away from the table and headed for the door, grabbing a brownie on the way. "In the meantime, I need to close a murder investigation."

Tess nodded her head. She thought about the gravesite and the restlessness and guilt she'd felt from Dan's spirit. "I want to go back to the cemetery and make sure the Greens are at peace."

She glanced around the room. Each face nodded their approval. Gram even looked pleased with her decision. Holding her hand out for the keys, she said, "I'll drive."

Chapter Thirty-Five

"Holy tamales, I needed that!"

By the time Crock finished giving his report, concluding with the argument over who would drive the Corona Boat through rush hour traffic, Childs was wiping away tears of laughter. The captain struggled to maintain a serious face but failed miserably. The fact that the case was solved—and no one got shot—gave his boss a much-needed stress relief.

"Glad you enjoyed it." Crock didn't think it was all that funny, but the man was entitled to some entertainment. From what he could see, his captain had at least found time to shave his head.

The Coronas had finally left the building amid accolades for Doma's brownies. Crock had managed to pull an overwhelmed Laz aside to ask, "Do you know anything about Mrs. Hudgens or her family?"

Laz seemed confused by the question. "Not really. She's got some solid boundaries. I only knew of a husband, but I've never met him."

Crock found it frustrating that, while one case was solved by the written confession of an old man, two other cases had surfaced. The similarities between the forgeries presented by the Green siblings and the fake documents which stole a daycare meant there was possibly a forgery ring active in the area. With the involvement of government and corporate dollars, the investigation would require assistance from the FBI or the Secret Service. He doubted that either entity would give a shit about Tess's visions and the valuable intel she'd stumbled upon.

Mrs. Hudgens presented a potential link to the Robert Collins case. The trail of the organized crime boss and escaped convict had been cold for over ten years. If there was any connection, Crock needed to find it.

"What happened to the professor?"

His boss's question pulled Crock back to the situation at hand. "There's no way to be certain without exhuming the body, and even then, there might not be enough answers. But from what we've gathered from the documents he left behind and Tess's visions, we're fairly certain he took arsenic as a form of slow suicide. The description of his body is consistent with taking an excessive dose."

Childs leaned back in his chair. "And Doma Corona was able to confirm that from the picture and the manager's report?"

"Yes." Crock nodded as he shifted his weight to lean against his boss's doorframe. "Without studying the body or the situation, and considering she doesn't specialize in forensics, she agreed that arsenic was involved, and most likely self-inflicted with small doses over a period of time and a final, fatal dose at the hotel. His letter confirmed his intent."

He didn't mention the phone call he'd received from the irate hotel manager, demanding to know what had happened to her ghosts. He wondered how Mary would market the hotel when she discovered she now owned the property. Was *formerly haunted* a selling point?

The no-longer missing evidence box waited for him on his desk. The will, Dan's letter and research were placed in a plastic folder for safekeeping. The estate attorney had already been notified that the will had been found, but Crock still needed to update the box's inventory, establish a new chain of custody, and finish his report, but otherwise the case was considered closed.

After picking up yet another brownie to stuff in his mouth, Childs eyed him. "I asked you to get this closed by Friday. You're only a week late."

"You didn't specify *which* Friday."

Childs gave a grunt, followed by a moan as the brownie disappeared. When his eyes quit rolling back in his head, he cleared his throat and changed the subject. "Tell me about these visions."

That wasn't what Crock expected to explain, but he managed to put his rudimentary understanding into words. "Sometimes, when Tess touches an object, something happens. She was able to sense the forgeries, even from a copy. The gravestone, the bedside table, even my gun have given her details of what happened."

Childs moved the tempting brownie plate behind his computer monitor. "What about your gun?"

Crock hesitated. "It wasn't an accident." At his boss's raised eyebrow, Crock quickly clarified his statement, "She said it was a shadow person, and it intended to kill me."

"A shadow person?"

"Some kind of evil ghost, I guess."

Childs was quiet for a moment. "It's a good thing it didn't succeed. I haven't lost a Ranger yet, and I don't intend to start now."

"No, sir." Crock didn't know what else to add.

"And Tess's reaction?"

"Varies," Crock admitted. "Since she's not expecting to see *anything*, it's disturbing."

"Do you think it's dangerous for her?"

Now Crock was confused—and curious. "Why do you ask?"

Childs leaned forward, placing his massive arms on the table. "This information doesn't leave this office."

Crock didn't consider himself stupid enough to break the man's trust. He gave a curt nod.

"I have a small *concern*," the captain said and paused. "Someone with that kind of skill might be helpful. I don't want to ask for her assistance if it will hurt her."

Crock hesitated. "I can't speak for Tess. It would have to be her decision."

"I'm asking for your opinion."

There was only one answer to give. "She's accustomed to ghosts. Touching items—it isn't fun to watch, much less for her to experience. Is it dangerous? Not physically, although the visions have given her panic attacks. Mentally or emotionally? Only time will tell if she can handle that kind of stress."

Childs stared at him for a moment. "That's what I thought. I'll try a couple of other options first." That said, the captain reached for a pile of case files. "In the meantime, once you get the Green case finalized, we have a fine selection of old cases that need to be reviewed, including—" Childs waved the top file at him "—the Collins case."

Crock had anticipated the case would come his

way, but he hadn't expected seven or eight other cold cases to be shoved in his direction. "Gee, thanks, boss."

"You're welcome." Childs shot a grin in his direction. "Just think, someday maybe you'll sit in the captain's seat."

"And put up with the bullshit from guys like me? No, thanks."

With a cocky grin and case files tucked under his arm, Crock left his boss's office and headed for his desk. The evidence box sat on top with its inventory spread out on the desk's surface, waiting for him to do his paperwork. Amidst the papers on the blotter, lay the little bag Doma had thrust in his hands before she left.

"Keep this prayer bag handy. You never know when you might need it."

The pouch was handmade of white fleece with a yellow, orange, and turquoise southwestern design covering it. A piece of abalone worked as a fastener for the flap. Inside, Crock found a bundle of wrapped sage, a palm-sized abalone shell, and three plastic bags. One contained sand and a stub of charcoal, another held what looked like loose tobacco, and the third was filled with cedar fronds.

He didn't know how he was supposed to use the items, or what they meant, but he was sure of one thing: he hoped he would never need it. However, having the Coronas around meant the need was a given.

"Some of us read and get a date once in a while."

Tess's throwaway statement was almost forgotten in the face of a tornado and a demon-possessed brother. Did he want to go out with a sexy, former military, psychic? Hell yes. Did he want to create a conflict of interest and contaminate a valuable resource? No. No, he did not.

After carefully tucking the little bag into his backpack for safekeeping, he began repacking the evidence box, paying careful attention to organize the paperwork. A black-and-white photo drifted to the desktop.

It had first surfaced in the conference room when Tess did a final search in the research-filled container, and its appearance had brought all banter to a hard stop. Tucked between two panes of cardboard, the photo showed a happy, newlywed couple dancing in their wedding finery.

A simple reminder that despite the hopes and dreams of youth, the ravages of time and adversity would be met with love and determination.

Crock placed the picture on top of Dan's confession. Tess had promised she would visit the cemetery. Having been there and witnessing some of the disturbance at the grave, Crock hoped that what they had discovered was enough to put the couple to rest. He resolved to visit the Green's grave site one last time with the hope that they were finally able to dance and be at peace.

Placing the lid on the box, Crock recalled Tess's words about death. While he knew his dad and grandad were at peace, their memories would die with him if he didn't do something about it. Gemma might enjoy the stories but would never understand their sacrifices. Those tales were too valuable to be lost.

He settled behind his desk to finish his report. As he opened his laptop, an idea formed in his head. And Crock knew the right man—and woman—to help make it happen.

A word about the author...

Tiffany was born and raised in Texas where she continues to live with her husband. She has two amazing adult daughters, a gorgeous granddaughter, and she's owned by a rescue dog who is often referred to as a rare black pygmy hippo. Tiffany works as an occupational therapist. In her spare time, she crochets, writes, haunts antique stores and old cemeteries in search of family history.

In 2013, Tiffany took her love of reading books and began writing them. Her favorite genres are romance and mystery, preferably with a touch of the paranormal or supernatural.

Thank you for purchasing
this publication of The Wild Rose Press, Inc.

For questions or more information
contact us at
info@thewildrosepress.com.

The Wild Rose Press, Inc.
www.thewildrosepress.com